our stolen child

BOOKS BY MELISSA WIESNER

our stolen child

Melissa Wiesner

bookouture

Published by Bookouture in 2022

An imprint of Storyfire Ltd.
Carmelite House
50 Victoria Embankment
London EC4Y 0DZ

www.bookouture.com

ISBN: 978-1-80314-418-4
eBook ISBN: 978-1-80314-417-7

For the LOTBs
Thank you for still being here, more than ten years later.

PROLOGUE

NORA

I sat on the cold, hard marble at the edge of the bathtub, clutching the white plastic stick in my hand. It had only been a minute, maybe two, and the box said to wait at least five minutes before checking for results. Still, I couldn't help staring at the little plastic window, squinting in the hopes that the result that I desperately wanted would appear there. One line for *not* pregnant, the instructions read.

Two lines for pregnant.

My breath hitched at the idea of it. I'd never seen two lines, I couldn't even imagine them. Two lines were a unicorn. They were hitting all six numbers in the Powerball. They were something that happened to other women. Women who'd been lucky enough to meet the right partner when they were still young. Women who hadn't wasted their childbearing years with a man who never intended to marry them. Women whose ovaries weren't sad, and tired, and all dried up.

I squeezed the pregnancy test tighter, well aware that this would be my last chance to have a baby. At age forty, it was growing harder and harder to justify the procedures: the daily shots to stimulate my ovaries, the time off from work to make the long drive back and forth to the clinic. Not to mention the cost. At close to $15,000 per round of IVF, I was burning through the money I'd spent my twenties and thirties saving.

Plus, there was the crushing disappointment every time a cycle failed. When I'd started trying to get pregnant over five years ago, I'd picked out a sperm donor and undergone a couple of rounds of intrauterine insemination, or the *turkey-baster method*, as some people like to jokingly call it. When that didn't work, I'd been disappointed but still confident that I had plenty of time and options, and I'd moved on to in-vitro fertilization. *The big guns*, where my egg and the donor's sperm were combined in a lab and implanted in my uterus. I'd been in my mid-thirties when I'd started IVF, and had read stories about celebrities who'd gotten pregnant well into their forties. Gwen Stefani was forty-four. Halle Berry, *forty-seven*. It was definitely going to happen for me.

Except it hadn't happened. Over and over, the pregnancy tests cruelly showed a single line when I would have given *anything* for two. When I'd turned thirty-eight, my friends had started questioning why I didn't just adopt. As if adoption were simple, as if you could just sign up and bring home a baby the next week. At forty, they'd started asking when I was going to give up.

I lunged to my feet and paced across the bathroom and back again.

This is it.

If I didn't get pregnant with this cycle, it was time to give up. Time to move on and somehow come to terms with the fact that I'd never be pregnant, never hold my baby in my arms. Never be a mother.

I squeezed my eyes shut tightly, sending a prayer out into the universe. Prayers had never worked before, but they were all

I had left. *Please God, please let there be two lines. Please let me be a mother.*

I opened my eyes and looked down at the plastic stick in my hands. And then I fell to the floor in a heap of laughter and tears and hope and wonder, still clutching the pregnancy test.

Two lines for pregnant.

1

QUINN

Four and a half years later

Quinn Marcello folded the worn copy of *People* magazine she'd been pretending to read and tossed it onto the table next to her. She didn't even care about celebrity gossip on a normal day, and this was *not* a normal day. She shifted in her chair, crossed and uncrossed her legs, and then shifted again. It wasn't that the chair was uncomfortable. Patients paid big money for the privilege of sitting in that waiting room, and the clinic staff went out of their way to make it feel more spa-like than medical. But all the scented candles, gourmet teas, and cushy chairs in the world couldn't calm her nerves on a day like today.

Quinn clicked on her phone, glanced at the time, and then fidgeted again. *Where is James?* He hadn't taken the day off work today because he wanted to save his vacation time. Quinn knew he was hoping to use it for an extended leave in... oh... *about nine months from now.* But of course, saying it out loud could jinx it, so James had simply told her he'd meet her at the clinic. He'd promised to be on time, though, and already he was ten minutes late.

In the beginning, James wouldn't have even considered sending her to the clinic on her own. The first few times they'd been through this, he'd sat with her in the waiting room, made her a cup of that fancy tea, and wrapped her in the warm shawl she'd packed in case the exam room was chilly. But that was almost five years ago, back when they were still excited and hopeful, still convinced everything would go smoothly for them.

Lately, James had left it up to Quinn to navigate the procedures, showing up only when strictly necessary. Quinn knew it was becoming harder and harder for him to get away from work. There were only so many excuses he could use for disappearing in the middle of a meeting or sneaking out before the end of the day. Quinn didn't completely understand it, but James had insisted that telling his boss and co-workers the real reason he had to leave wasn't an option for a guy working in a field dominated by men. The last guy who'd announced his wife was pregnant had apparently stood up in an all-hands meeting and declared that his "boys could swim." If those guys knew how many doctors had examined James's sperm though a microscope, he'd never hear the end of it.

The irony was that James's boys could swim, too. It was Quinn's eggs that were the problem.

Quinn checked the time on her phone again. Today's appointment wasn't anything close to ordinary, and it would've been nice if James had gone out of his way to try to get there. This was their very last embryo transfer. Their very last chance to have a baby. They'd agreed that it had become too expensive —both financially *and* emotionally—to continue. If this round of IVF didn't work out, it would be time to stop trying. Time to accept a future where they were childless.

Quinn shoved that thought from her mind—*Don't jinx it*— and then she nearly laughed. If prayers, or spells, or superstitions really worked when it came to fertility, she would have gotten pregnant a dozen times over.

"Quinn?" A nurse named Susannah stood in the doorway that led back into the clinic. In the early days, Susannah used to address Quinn as *Mrs. Marcello*, but they'd done away with formalities years ago. "Can you come with me, please?"

Quinn checked her phone one last time, anxiety building in her chest. It wasn't that the doctor needed James to be there for the procedure. In this round of IVF, they were using an embryo that had been created in the lab years ago and then frozen. The transfer would be a fairly simple procedure, one she'd been through half a dozen times before. But Quinn needed James here, holding her hand, hoping against hope that this last embryo would finally be the one to stick.

Where is he?

Just as Quinn stood to follow Susannah, the front door of the waiting room swung open and James hurried in. "Quinn!" he panted, rushing over to her side. "I'm so sorry I'm late. The traffic at the Squirrel Hill tunnel was ridiculous. If I'd known, I would have taken—"

"James," Quinn interrupted. "It's fine." There was no sense in making a scene and raising her blood pressure. "It's... time." She nodded in Susannah's direction.

James took a deep, shaky breath and then let it out slowly, and something about that gesture tugged at Quinn's heart. He didn't always show it, but James was nervous too. "Okay," he said. "Let me carry that." James took the bag from Quinn's shoulder with one hand, and with the other, he weaved his fingers through hers. She flashed him a grateful smile, and together they headed into the clinic.

"Here we go again," Quinn said to Susannah with a nervous laugh.

Quinn had noticed that Susannah never speculated about whether a patient's procedure would be successful, but she always had an encouraging word for them. *I'm rooting for you.* Or, *Don't worry, you're in great hands with Dr. Baxter.* This time, though, she simply said, "Come this way," and then turned to lead them through the door.

The procedure rooms were all the way at the end of the hall, so Quinn hurried to keep up, tugging James along by the hand. About halfway there, Susannah stopped so abruptly that Quinn nearly crashed into her.

"Dr. Baxter asked that you wait in here," Susannah said, swinging the nearest door open.

"Oh," Quinn said, peering in at the large mahogany desk and the diplomas on the walls. They'd only met the doctor in her office once before, and that was almost five years ago, when they'd first come in to discuss their problems with getting pregnant. Dr. Baxter had gone over their options and then called in the woman from billing to discuss the cost of the various procedures with them.

"Is there a problem?" Quinn asked Susannah, her heart stuttering in her chest. On previous embryo transfer day, they'd headed directly for the procedure rooms.

Susannah pressed her lips together as if she were debating what to say. Finally, she shook her head. "I think Dr. Baxter just wants to go over some things with you." She waved them into the office and then quickly disappeared.

Quinn watched the door swing shut behind them and then sank into one of the two chairs across from Dr. Baxter's desk. Was it a problem with their latest bill? They'd always paid on time, but you never knew with medical procedures. Maybe they still had a balance for an extra blood test or an ultrasound. If that were the case, Quinn wished they'd mentioned it when they'd called to confirm her appointment. She could've given them a credit card number over the phone and saved her this additional stress.

All of her fertility books had advised her to remain as calm as possible on transfer day to ensure the best possible conditions for an embryo to implant. Stress could cause in influx of cortisol, a hormone which might interfere with the carefully controlled doses of estrogen and progesterone she'd been taking in daily shots to prepare her uterine lining. Just to be on the safe side, she'd gone for a massage earlier in the week, seen her acupuncturist yesterday, and had avoided caffeine and alcohol for the months leading into this cycle, opting for green juices and raspberry leaf tea instead. The last thing she needed was a minor issue over an unpaid bill to undo all her careful preparation.

"What do you think is going on?" Quinn glanced over at James, who'd pulled out his phone and was scrolling through his emails.

"Hmmm?" he asked, brow furrowed at his screen.

"Do you think everything is okay?"

James finally looked up. "Of course." He reached over and squeezed her hand. "Dr. Baxter knows this is our last embryo. I'm sure she just wants to say something encouraging before we start the procedure."

Quinn released a breath. "You're probably right." They'd spent the past five years working with Dr. Baxter. She'd seen the doctor almost every single month during that time, and when they were in the midst of an IVF cycle, Quinn had seen her every single *day*. Dr. Baxter had cheered with Quinn when her egg retrievals went well, held her hand when she cried over negative pregnancy tests, and helped her to pick herself up and keep going. Lately, Quinn felt closer to Dr. Baxter than her own friends, many of whom had drifted as they began having their own kids or making the conscious decision to remain childless. Nobody could quite relate to Quinn's obsession to get pregnant.

But Dr. Baxter had understood. They'd been in this together. So, it made sense that she'd want to take a moment to share some words of encouragement on their very last cycle.

The office door swung open, and Dr. Baxter entered the

room. "Hello, Quinn. James," she said, with a nod in their direction as she slid into the chair behind the desk.

"Last embryo transfer," Quinn said with a nervous smile. "I really think this is going to be the one." She held up her hands with her fingers crossed.

"Yes. Your last embryo." Dr. Baxter hesitated, and the fine lines around her eyes deepened. "I need to talk to you about that." She looked down at the papers on her desk. "As you know, the embryo that we'd planned to use for this cycle was created during your first IVF cycle about five years ago, and then frozen. Given your age and the fact that you'd hoped to have more than one child, I advised you to hold on to your frozen embryo until the very end in the hopes that you'd achieve a successful pregnancy with a fresh cycle, and then could try again for baby number two with the frozen embryo."

Quinn nodded. It was almost laughable that in the early days, she and James had actually thought they might have *two* children. When those fresh cycles never produced baby number one, they'd finally made the decision to move on and use the frozen embryo for one last shot. Ideally, they would have had more than one frozen embryo to transfer during this cycle, but in the end, this single embryo was all they ended up with.

Quinn shifted in her seat. She already knew everything Dr. Baxter was saying, and something about it had her heart pitching. Did the doctor say they'd *planned* to use the frozen embryo for this cycle? As in—past tense? "Yes, I remember all of this," Quinn said, her voice shaking. "Is there a problem?"

Dr. Baxter continued to stare down at her desk, and Quinn reached over and grabbed James's hand. Finally, Dr. Baxter looked up, and the regret in her eyes nearly knocked Quinn over. "I—I don't know how to tell you this."

"Please just say it," Quinn whispered. "Is the embryo damaged? It didn't survive the thaw?" Her gaze swung to James who was sitting up in his chair now, phone tucked into his pocket. He looked back at her, wide-eyed. Surely Dr. Baxter had delivered the news to other couples that their embryos hadn't made it before? So, why did the doctor look like she was alarmingly close to throwing up?

Dr. Baxter shook her head. "No... it's not that."

James cleared his throat. "What is it, Doctor?"

Dr. Baxter pressed her hands to her temples. "In my twenty years of working as a reproductive endocrinologist, nothing like this has ever happened before. It's not that the embryo is damaged. It's that—" She finally met Quinn's eyes. "It's that the embryo is missing."

2

"Missing!" Quinn paced across her living room floor. "*Missing.* How can it be missing?" She spun on her heel and paced back again. "How did this happen?"

James's gaze followed her from one side of the room to the other. They'd headed home after it had become clear that Dr. Baxter didn't have any more answers for them at the moment, and Quinn had been wearing a groove from the couch to the TV ever since.

"Well, the doctor explained it," James said.

Quinn shook her head. Sure, Dr. Baxter had explained how they'd managed to trace the embryo from the clinic to the storage facility. She'd said the embryo had been logged into the system and supposedly placed in a sealed liquid nitrogen freezer for long-term storage. But when the facility had gone in all these years later to retrieve the embryo and send it back to the clinic for the transfer scheduled today, it wasn't where they expected. So, while the doctor's description of how this happened accounted for a vague timeline of events, it didn't actually explain *anything*. Like, who was responsible? When did the breakdown occur? *And where was their embryo now?*

"Quinn, stop pacing and come sit." James patted the couch cushion next to him. "Dr. Baxter is on the phone with the storage facility, and she might call any minute to say they found it."

There was no way Quinn could calmly sit while her embryo—*her last chance for a baby*—was out there somewhere, unaccounted for. She moved to the fireplace and began straightening the frames on the mantel, her hand pausing on the photo of their wedding day. She and James looked so young, so happy, as they gazed into each other's eyes on the steps in front of Heinz Chapel. The breeze had picked up just as the photographer snapped the photo, lifting the delicate fabric of her veil into the air as if it were carried by Cinderella's sparrows. And that was exactly how she'd felt that day. Like a princess in a fairy tale.

Growing up, Quinn had always been shy and introverted, preferring to stay home with a book while her friends went to dances and parties. After college, when it had seemed like everyone around her was getting married, Quinn had remained single. She'd dated some—a few set-ups by friends, a couple of online matches—but nothing had ever really worked out. On her thirty-sixth birthday, it had occurred to her that the right person might not come along, that she'd never marry or have the baby she'd always wanted. The thought had broken her heart, but as a children's librarian, fertility treatments to get pregnant on her own were out of reach financially. And both her parents had passed away when she was in college, so she was wary of entering single motherhood without any help from family.

Quinn had never expected that, a week later, the tall, handsome man in line behind her at the coffee shop would strike up a conversation. James had noticed her skirt—a knee-length A-line printed with a pattern designed to look like books lined up on a shelf—and had rightly assumed that she worked at the library two doors down. He'd asked Quinn to recommend a couple of novels for his aunt's birthday, which had led to an invitation to buy her coffee and share his table by the window.

James had proposed less than a year later. They were both north of thirty-five and both wanted children, so why wait? Quinn had thrown out her birth control pills the month before the wedding, hoping to get pregnant on their honeymoon.

That was six years ago.

She whirled around to look at her husband. "What are we going to do if they don't find the embryo in time to complete this cycle?"

"There's no sense in getting worked up about it until we have more information. I know it's your nature to default to doomsday scenario, but it's not going to do us any good. Dr. Baxter said she'd call as soon as she knows something. Until then, try to relax."

Quinn stared down at her husband who calmly sat on the couch, phone in hand, one leg crossed over the other, and a wave of resentment rolled over her. Was he serious? *Try to relax?*

Maybe she *did* tend to be the more anxious one in their relationship. The one who needed more information, a tighter grip on a situation, while James was easily able to let go of things outside of his control. But in her defense, going through all these years of fertility treatments hadn't exactly been conducive to *going with the flow*. Everything about the procedures she'd undergone—the drugs and shots and tests—had required careful planning and impeccable timing. An embryo transfer demanded a perfect uterine lining, something that took constant monitoring. Forty-eight hours in either direction could tank an entire IVF cycle.

So, it was easy for James to tell her to relax. He hadn't spent the last half-decade of his life being poked and prodded by doctors, sticking needles in his thighs, or staring at a ceiling with his feet up in stirrups. At that very moment, Quinn had a cocktail of estrogen and progesterone pumping through her system, the result of weeks of shots to prepare her for this day. If they didn't find the embryo soon, would it all have been for nothing? Would they have to start over completely?

And that wasn't even the worst of their problems. "What if they don't find the embryo *at all*?"

"Quinn, this isn't doing anyone any good." James sighed, his shoulders sagging beneath his light blue Oxford shirt. "Maybe you should go take a bath, or a walk or something."

Quinn clutched one hand in the other to control their shaking. "I'm serious. What if they don't find it? Are we—finished? Forever?"

James gazed across the living room at her, the silence stretching between them, answering the question louder than if he'd shouted.

"No," Quinn whispered, slowly shaking her head. "This can't be it." They were supposed to have one more try. Maybe it was a long shot, a Hail Mary pass, but it *wasn't supposed to be over yet*. It was unthinkable that *this* could be the end of the road. Unthinkable that they'd wake up tomorrow facing the rest of their life as a childless couple. What would she do with herself? How would she survive it?

And how could James be so calm? His phone buzzed, and he clicked it on, bending his head to read whatever email or text had come through. It was probably about the meeting he'd had that morning. The one he absolutely *couldn't* miss. Quinn's resentment grew, winding around her like the neighbor's vines that climbed up their shared wall, pulling the mortar from the bricks. James might have been increasingly checked-out about their fertility treatments, leaving it up to her to coordinate the details, but never for a second had she thought he wasn't 100 percent invested. Never had she thought he'd approach the end of this long, painful journey with his head buried in an email and a shrug in her direction.

"Can you put the phone away for one damn second?" Quinn snapped. "Does work really matter at a time like this?"

James looked up slowly, as if her outburst didn't warrant a quick response. "I was only emailing to let them know I'll be taking the rest of today and tomorrow off." He spoke calmly, his voice carefully measured. "I didn't want to be fielding work calls while we're waiting to hear from Dr. Baxter."

"Oh." Quinn's eyes flew from the phone in his hand to the frustrated expression on his face. "I'm sorry, I'm just tired. And, you know..." She dropped down onto the couch next to him, waving a hand in the general direction of her lower abdomen. "Hormonal."

James reached over and took her hand. "I know this is stressful for you. But the clinic is going to figure this out. Facilities don't just *lose* embryos. Can you imagine the lawsuits? I'm sure it's something simple, like a number that was entered wrong into their system, and they're sorting it out right now."

Quinn took a deep breath and released it slowly. "Do you really think so?"

"Yes, I really do. In the meantime, why don't I make you some tea and we can see if there are any cheesy romcoms on Netflix?"

Quinn pressed her lips together to hide her smile. The two of them hadn't hung out in the middle of the day in forever. When they were first married, they used to meet for coffee during her breaks at the library, and on weekends, they'd go for hikes in Frick Park or brunch at the Square Café. But then Quinn quit drinking caffeine and started eating an anti-inflammation vegan diet, so coffee and brunch were out. And her acupuncturist had recommended that she cut out vigorous exercise, so she'd replaced hiking and biking with slow walks around the neighborhood listening to fertility podcasts. At the same time, James had gotten busier at work, exceeding his sales numbers three years in a row, traveling more, and often going in on the weekends. She could hardly blame him for hustling to earn more money. The amount they'd poured into fertility treatments should have paid off their house and put their soon-to-be baby through college.

Maybe a Tuesday mental-health day was exactly what they needed to relax and reconnect. In the meantime, Dr. Baxter would find their embryo, they'd reschedule the transfer for tomorrow, and everything would be fine.

"How about instead of tea—" Quinn flashed James a tentative smile. "Maybe you want to make popcorn?"

He grinned in return. "With butter?"

"Oh, why not?" At this point, a little dairy wasn't going to hurt anything. And if it raised her endorphins, maybe that would counteract all the stress of the day. Besides, she was so tired of quinoa and leafy greens.

They'd just settled on the couch with a Meg Ryan classic on the TV and a huge bowl of popcorn in Quinn's lap when the phone rang.

"See?" James took the bowl and set it on the coffee table. He held up the phone to show Quinn the name of the fertility clinic flashing there. "I bet they found it already." James swiped to answer and set the phone to speaker.

Quinn rubbed her suddenly sweaty palms on her yoga pants.

"Hello, Dr. Baxter," James said, and Quinn could hear a slight waver of nerves in his voice. "Any news?"

"Hi, James." The doctor's voice came through the phone. "Is Quinn with you there?"

"I'm right here. Did you find the embryo?" Quinn held her breath.

"Well... yes, we did."

Quinn let her head flop back against the couch cushion as the tension left her body. "Oh, thank God."

"Where was it?" James asked, his voice cheerful now. "Behind the ice cream in the freezer?" He gave Quinn a wink.

Through the phone, Quinn could hear Dr. Baxter suck in a breath. "Well, I wish I could tell you that was the case..." There was an edge to the doctor's voice that had Quinn's shoulders sliding back up toward her ears. Her heart thumped against her sternum.

"Actually..." Dr. Baxter took another breath and exhaled slowly. "Your embryo was found in... Mt. Lebanon." The last part came out a bit choked.

Quinn turned and squinted at James. Mt. Lebanon was an upscale suburb about fifteen minutes from where they lived in Pittsburgh. It seemed like an odd place for a bio-storage facility, but maybe there was another fertility clinic in Mt. Lebanon. It was the kind of town that attracted doctors and lawyers, women who'd put off having kids when they were young to focus on their careers. Either way, the fact that their embryo was there seemed easily solvable. If Dr. Baxter couldn't arrange to have it sent back to her own clinic, they could drive out to Mt. Lebanon for the transfer.

"Okay," Quinn said. "That's no problem. We can be in Mt. Lebanon in half an hour."

"Well, I wish it were that simple. But the fact is... your embryo isn't an embryo anymore."

Quinn glanced at James in confusion. "What do you mean, *it's not an embryo anymore?*"

"Your embryo—" Dr. Baxter hesitated. "It was transferred to someone else by mistake. I don't know how else to tell you this, so I'll just come right out and say it... Your embryo was successfully implanted in another woman. And now... well, now, it's an almost four-year-old girl."

3

Quinn sat frozen on the couch. It felt like there was something wrong with her mouth because it was hanging open and no sound would come out.

Thank God James was there, because he finally managed to pull himself together. "Are you—" James choked. "Are you saying that we have a child? A three-year-old child? Living just five miles from here?"

"Biologically speaking, yes," Dr. Baxter said, her voice measured. "There was a child born from your embryo. But, legally, it's more complicated than that. She was born to another woman who has been raising her for almost four years, believing her to be her own daughter. This child only knows that woman to be her mother."

The word *mother* finally snapped Quinn out of her trance. They had a daughter. All this time, she and James had a little girl out in the world. A child with James's eyes, maybe. Or her hair. His smile. Or her laugh. The thought of it filled her with such longing she could barely breathe.

And then the rest of the doctor's words hit her, and Quinn's hands began to shake. *Four years.* Another woman had given birth to their child without their knowledge, and they'd missed almost four years. Four years was an eternity in a child's life. She was no longer a baby, no longer a toddler even. Another woman had been there, feeding her, caring for her, wiping her tears and putting Band-Aids on her scrapes. While she and James had sat here, hoping and praying for a baby, with absolutely no idea their baby lived only a few miles away.

"How? How did this happen?"

"We're still looking into it," Dr. Baxter said. "I assure you, we're conducting a thorough investigation."

Nothing about that assured Quinn whatsoever. "Who is this woman who ended up with our embryo?" she whispered.

"She's—" Dr. Baxter hesitated. "She was a patient of mine for many years."

"Is she a good person? Do you think she's—" Quinn choked on the words. "Do you think she's taking care of our daughter?" A wave of nausea hit her. Their child could be with anyone. *Anyone.* Quinn's anxious mind grasped onto the worst-case scenario. What if this other woman was mean and abusive? Or neglectful? What if she didn't have enough money to care for the child properly?

"Oh, Quinn, she's absolutely taking good care of the child." Dr. Baxter's voice soothed her through the phone. "She lovely, and I'm sure your—" She hesitated there for a moment. "I'm sure the child is deeply loved."

"And does she have a partner? A co-parent?"

"No, Nora came to us because she'd decided to have a baby on her own. If I remember correctly, she has a close-knit family in the area. I recall a brother who sometimes drove her to treatments. But there is no second parent."

Nora. Quinn's mind seized on the name. Quinn was tempted to grab her laptop and cyberstalk every Nora in Mt. Lebanon. Maybe she'd find her on Facebook with photos of the girl. Would she and James recognize their daughter by a photo?

Would she look like Quinn in her own baby pictures, the ones she'd tucked under the bed in a storage box after her parents had passed?

"What else you can tell us about Nora?" Quinn asked. Any tiny shred of information would do. *Like her last name. Or her address, so I can drive by the house and peer in the window.*

"Oh, I shouldn't have mentioned her name. Please forgive me, I admit I'm a bit flustered," Dr. Baxter stammered. "I'm afraid I can't say any more. She was my patient, so I have to be mindful of HIPAA. But please rest assured that I've known her through years of treatments, and she desperately wanted a baby. I know she's turned out to be a wonderful mother to the child."

There was that word again. *Mother.*

It used to be such a simple concept, and suddenly, it wasn't. That morning, they had nothing but a wish and odds that were stacked against them. And now they had a child. A child being raised by another woman. "Genetically, *I'm* her mother. And James is her father."

"Yes, I understand that," the doctor murmured. "I know this puts you in a very difficult position."

"So, what are our rights here?" James got to the point.

"Again, there are legalities, and I really can't advise you..." Dr. Baxter trailed off.

"Dr. Baxter," James said sharply. "You're an expert in assisted reproductive technology. I understand you're not an attorney, but surely you have some sense of what it might mean if a couple's embryo was given to another woman without their consent."

Quinn's gaze darted to James. His face had gone white and his spine stiff. She was so grateful he was there to demand answers. How could she have thought for one second that he wasn't invested in this with her?

The doctor hesitated before she spoke. "This is a very unprecedented situation. I wish I could tell you more, but unfortunately, I never imagined breaking news like this to one of my patients."

"We'll be allowed to meet her, right? The child." Quinn hugged her knees to her chest to stop them from shaking. "We'll be allowed to be a part of her life?"

"Well." The doctor sighed. "The embryo was yours, and of course, you are the biological parents. But James, Quinn... we're not talking about a group of cells anymore. We're talking about a child. Nora carried her, gave birth to her, and has parented her from infancy. And now, well, quite a bit of time has passed."

"So, what are you saying?" Quinn's words came out as a whisper. "We're just supposed to move on?"

"I'm afraid I can't tell you anything more, other than recommend that you speak with an attorney. To be very honest, our legal counsel advised me not to speak with you at all, to leave it up to the lawyers, but..." Dr. Baxter's sad sigh drifted through the phone. "Quinn. James. I've known you for five years. You can't know how devastated I am over this."

Not nearly as devastated as I am. Quinn bent forward, clutching her rocking stomach, glad she'd only had herbal tea and a small piece of toast for breakfast.

James rested a comforting hand on Quinn's back and shifted the phone in his other hand. "Dr. Baxter, you said you're investigating, but I'd like to know how you think this happened."

Dr. Baxter hesitated. "Again, I really shouldn't discuss it."

In a matter of moments, the burning in Quinn's gut switched from nausea to white-hot anger, and it was a relief. Anger was good. She could handle anger. What she couldn't handle was the feeling of absolute powerlessness, of *injustice* that she had a child out in the world, and she'd had no idea. A baby that she'd been robbed of carrying for nine months, of nurturing and giving birth to. She'd missed out on feeding her, holding her when she cried, watching her take her first steps.

"You shouldn't *discuss* it? This is our biological child your clinic gave away to another woman." Quinn's voice rose with each word. "At the very least, you can tell us what you know."

On the other end of the line, Quinn could hear papers shuffling and a person whispering something she couldn't quite make out. Finally, Dr. Baxter's voice came back through the phone. "Well, as I said, we're still investigating. But what we've managed to uncover is that about four and a half years ago, you and Nora had your egg retrievals on the same morning. We had a new lab tech who we suspect mixed up the embryos, and yours was accidently kept at the clinic and transferred to Nora a few days later. Her embryo was sent to the long-term storage facility."

Quinn stumbled to a stop. "So, this woman—Nora—still has an embryo in storage?"

Dr. Baxter sighed. "Unfortunately, no. That embryo was labeled incorrectly, and there was nobody paying the storage fees. The clinic tried to track down the owners, but eventually, they deemed the embryo abandoned and they... destroyed it."

Quinn's heart rocked at the doctor's words. For a brief moment, she'd considered that she and James could have that embryo. They could still do the transfer, still get pregnant and have a baby. But no, the embryo was gone. And it wouldn't have been *their* baby, anyway. Their baby was out there with another family.

If Quinn had thought her longing to get pregnant was fierce, it was nothing compared to her desperation for the child who was made up of a unique combination of genes belonging to her and James.

The child that should have been theirs.

Quinn was aware that biology wasn't everything. There were millions of adopted children whose parents loved them as much as any biological parent would. She and James had seriously considered adoption over the years as the fertility treatments had failed them. But this wasn't a case of adoption. When children were given up for adoption, the bio-parents were allowed to make the choice. She and James had never been given a choice. Their child had been taken from them.

James leaned into the phone. "Dr. Baxter, is there anything else we need to know before we speak with our attorney?"

"No. Only—" Dr. Baxter cleared her throat. "Only that I'm deeply sorry."

"I assume your clinic's attorneys will cooperate with ours?" James said, all business now. He wasn't the type to wallow over feelings if there was nothing he could do to change the situation. Not like Quinn.

"Of course," Dr. Baxter assured him.

With nothing left to say, they hung up the phone.

Quinn and James sat for a moment, silent on the couch, staring at each other.

"James, we have a biological child." Quinn closed her eyes as an image of a little girl with dark curly hair, just like hers, flitted through her mind. A child on a playground, smiling, laughing, calling for her mother to watch her climb the jungle gym or push her on the swing. Quinn's heart folded in on itself and her eyes filled with tears. "She's out there somewhere, living with another family. How did this happen?"

James stared out across the living room, shaking his head. "I don't know. We picked the most reputable clinic in the area. A mix-up like this is inexcusable." He took a deep breath, but just as he was about to say more, his phone rang with the name of the fertility clinic.

Quinn's heart stuttered as James quickly swiped to answer.

"Hello?" He paused as Quinn leaned in to try to hear the person on the other end of the line. "Oh, hi, Linda. Yes, hold on, let me get a pen." James put the phone on mute. "It's just Dr. Baxter's admin assistant calling to give us the name and phone number of the clinic's attorney." He scribbled down the information for the law firm representing the clinic and then hung up.

Quinn's shoulders slumped. She didn't know what she'd been expecting. That it was the doctor calling back to say that she was wrong, and the clinic had found their embryo after all? But instead, it was just the doctor covering her ass. "All they care about is being sued."

After five years and countless treatments, Quinn had believed that Dr. Baxter was invested in helping them build a family, that she cared about them and not just the thousands of dollars they'd shelled out over the years for treatments. But it looked like Quinn was wrong.

James tossed the pen and paper on the coffee table. "Of course they're worried about being sued. They *should* be. This is a shocking mistake. I'm going to call around for recommendations, because we're going to need a good lawyer."

Quinn blinked at the determination in his tone. "You think we should sue the clinic? What could we possibly hope to get out of that? Money?" The clinic had screwed up—*more* than screwed up—and they'd deprived her and James of years of their daughter's life. Damn right Quinn wanted somebody to pay for that. But suing wasn't going to give them their daughter back. And neither would any amount of money in the world. It would only drag this out, reminding her that another woman was raising her baby and she wasn't.

For years, Quinn had agonized over her body's inability to sustain a pregnancy. She'd had over a half a dozen embryos transferred into her uterus, and not one had stuck. Not one had found a welcoming environment where it continued to grow and thrive. For years, it had been nothing but month after month of going to the bathroom and finding that her period had started. Month after month of negative pregnancy tests. It was hard not to blame herself. Maybe she hadn't taken good enough care of herself. Maybe she'd waited too long to try to get pregnant.

Maybe she wasn't fit to be a mother.

The fact this Nora woman had been able to carry and nurture their embryo, when Quinn hadn't, only made it hurt worse.

James scrubbed a hand across his eyes. "I'm not only talking about suing, although I hope we can at least recoup the money we poured into treatments over the years." He turned and met Quinn's eyes. "I'm talking about the child. The child is biologically ours, and we didn't give her up willingly."

Quinn stared at him. "What are you saying?" Dr. Baxter had implied it was unlikely that they could meet their child and be a part of her life. But now, a tiny ember of hope flickered in her chest.

"I'm saying that we have rights."

Quinn wished it were that easy. "What about the other woman? Nora?" Quinn closed her eyes. Dr. Baxter had said that Nora had desperately wanted a child. That she loved the girl deeply. Was Dr. Baxter calling her right now to break the news? How would Nora feel if a couple she'd never even heard of came along and tried to stake a claim on the child she'd believed to be her own for almost four years? If she was a good person like Dr. Baxter had said, there wasn't any plausible scenario in which that wouldn't completely devastate her.

But what were Quinn and James supposed to do? Walk away from their own child?

"I'm sure Nora isn't going to be happy about this." James shook his head. "We wouldn't be happy if the situation were reversed. But we also wouldn't be happy knowing that another poor couple out there had lost their child."

Quinn's heart seized and her eyes filled with tears. *They'd lost their child.* Thanks to a careless lab error, their daughter had been taken from them. And the girl had lost her biological parents, too. Didn't their child deserve to know where she came from? And *who* she came from? Didn't she deserve to be a part of her own flesh-and-blood family?

"I wish I knew the answer." Quinn sat up straight, wiping her eyes with the back of her hand. "Of course, we should do whatever is in the best interest of the child. But I honestly don't know what that is."

"I think our best option is to call an attorney and see where we go from here."

Quinn nodded, relieved by the idea of an expert helping them to sort this out. When they'd decided to pursue fertility treatments, they'd known there were all sorts of risks. But they'd never, ever imagined that they risked losing their child to another family. Or the agony of having to decide what to do with that information. "We're the child's mother and father, after all."

"I guess we are." James looked at her, amazement drifting across his face. "We're parents. I can't believe it."

Quinn reached out and squeezed his hand, reminded of that day she'd met him in the coffee shop all those years ago. Unlike other men Quinn had dated, whose eyes had glazed over at the slightest hint that she was looking for something serious, James had brought up kids on their very first date. He'd made it clear that he hoped to meet a woman who wanted to start a family right away, and he wasn't interested in wasting time. He'd been married once before, to a woman who'd claimed she wanted kids until it was time to start trying, and then she'd made every excuse to avoid going off her birth control.

Quinn knew his desire to be a dad stemmed from the fact that James's own father had died of a heart attack when James was only seven years old, so he'd missed out on the many father-and-son activities he'd grown up watching other kids experience.

Though it wasn't her fault, sometimes Quinn wondered if

James had begun to resent her because she wasn't able to get pregnant, and that's why he'd been pulling away from accompanying her to IVF treatments. Deep down, did he secretly feel that she'd pulled a bait-and-switch, just like his ex had?

James squeezed her hand back, and the hope in her chest burned brighter. They were in this together, and maybe all that was behind them now.

With a burst of energy, Quinn picked up the bowl of popcorn off the coffee table in one hand and straightened the throw pillows on the couch with the other. There was so much to do. Find the bills and paperwork from their past IVF treatments to hand over to the lawyers. Clean the house. Then she should organize the guest room. In the past couple of years, it had become a dumping ground for all the things they didn't feel like dealing with—clothes for Goodwill and sports equipment and old paperwork. But they'd always intended for it to be a nursery someday.

At that last thought, Quinn froze. *A nursery?* She was completely getting ahead of herself. Legally, the child was the daughter of this woman Nora, and it would be dangerous to start thinking otherwise. But the more she tried *not* to think about it, the more her mind drifted to the image of a pink-canopied bed and matching dresser. To a bucket of toys on the shelf in the living room, and a child's booster seat tucked under the table in the kitchen. To a little girl running through the front door, the sound of her feet pounding on the stairs, her laughter echoing in the halls.

4

"How'd it go, Quinn?" Quinn's boss breezed past her desk in a cloud of perfume, raising both thumbs in a *you got this* motion. "I have a good feeling that this could be the one."

Quinn smiled weakly and held up her crossed fingers. "Hope so." She wished that—like James—she'd had the luxury of keeping quiet about her fertility treatments at work. But after a while, it had become impossible to explain the constant requests for time off, her need to use a private office to administer the shots in her thighs, and the bruises on her arms from all the blood draws.

Sonia, her boss, had been more than understanding, offering Quinn whatever accommodations she needed. But as a go-getter type with an MBA who managed the largest library branch in the city, she wasn't one to sit quietly and let things play out. It was Sonia's acupuncturist Quinn had been using, and every couple of weeks, Quinn arrived at work to find a new book about fertility treatments, a relaxing herbal tea, or a bottle of green juice from the smoothie place down the block on her desk. Quinn was willing to try anything that might help her get pregnant, but her boss's involvement only made things harder when she had to report that her latest treatment hadn't worked.

"Got to keep up the positive attitude." Sonia headed for her office, heels clicking on the linoleum floor. As soon as she was out of sight, Quinn closed her eyes and slumped back against her chair with a heavy sigh.

"She's a little intense."

Quinn's eyes flew open and focused on Elise, one of the reference librarians and Quinn's closest work friend, standing next to her desk. "You could say that."

"I just came by to see how the transfer went, too." Elise held up a hand. "But you don't have to talk about it if you don't want to."

"It's okay." Quinn smiled for real this time. Elise was the opposite of Sonia, quiet and unassuming, exactly how you'd picture a reference librarian. She and Elise had hit it off right away when they'd sat next to each other at lunch after a staff meeting during Quinn's first week on the job. They'd bonded over their favorite novels and then laughed at what a cliché it was for librarians to talk about books in their downtime.

"It went... unexpectedly." Quinn glanced around to make sure no one else was listening. Her desk was situated in the middle of the children's room of the library, but noon was the quietest time of the day. Storytime ended at eleven, and all the moms took their toddlers home for naps. The children's section would get busy again around three o'clock when the older kids began to trickle in after school let out.

Quinn nodded at the opposite chair, inviting Elise to sit. Ever since she and James had discovered they had a child in the world, she'd been holding it all in, waiting to hear from the attorney James had hired to find out what would happen next. When little girls of the approximate age of three or four came into the children's room at the library, Quinn couldn't help imagining her own daughter. What books would she be interested in? What songs would she sing along to? Suddenly, Quinn was grateful to have someone to talk to.

"We got some shocking news on the day of the transfer."

Elise's eyes grew wider as Quinn shared the events that had unfolded, from how they'd found out about the embryo switch to what they knew about Nora and the child.

"Oh, my God. Quinn..." Elise's face softened, and she reached out across the desk to give Quinn's hand a squeeze. "I'm so sorry. This is heartbreaking. What are you thinking of doing?"

"Well, we've hired a lawyer. She's reviewing the information, and our first meeting with her is in a couple of days. But beyond that—I don't really know." Quinn looked down at her desk. "We've been trying to have a baby for years, we've poured everything we have into it—financially, emotionally. We wanted this *so badly*. And, suddenly, there's this child in the world who is biologically ours."

Elise nodded. "It's a lot to wrap your head around."

"But this woman—Nora—has been raising her for all this time. The girl thinks of Nora as her mother. And Nora thinks of her as a daughter. So, do we have any right to barge into her life now?" Quinn lifted a shoulder. "But at the same time, how can we possibly walk away from her?" She met Elise's eyes. "What would *you* do if you were in our situation?"

Quinn had met Elise's elementary-aged daughters dozens of times when they came into the library after school. They were good kids—well behaved, polite—and they loved to help out in the children's room while they waited for their mother to get off work. Quinn had always hoped to be a mother to girls like Elise's.

Elise gazed across the library for a moment, out into the main room. "Honestly... I don't know. On the one hand, I feel for Nora. If she gave birth to the child and has been raising her all this time, she's the girl's mother. Biology doesn't really matter. If someone came along and tried to claim my daughters, I'd fight to the death to keep them."

Quinn's heart ached at Elise's words. But she'd asked for her opinion, and in the end, was only confirming what Quinn already knew.

"But..." Elise swung her gaze back to Quinn. "I do see your side, too. My girls are..." She trailed off, looking for the right words. "Well, they're *my* girls. They're everything to me. If another woman was raising them due to a horrible mix-up, I don't know if I could live with that."

My girls. Quinn's longing was so fierce, she almost doubled over.

"You could argue that I wouldn't have known them like I do now," Elise continued. "That I wouldn't have seen them grow up to be the kids they are now, so I wouldn't have known the difference. But I don't know about that. I think some part of me would feel their absence."

Quinn nodded. That was exactly how she felt. From the moment she'd found out that her child existed, it was like a hole had opened up inside her that nothing would fill. Like she'd lost a limb, and the place where it used to be ached constantly. Maybe, deep down, she'd felt it even before she found out her child existed. Looking back at the past five years of constantly trying and failing to have a baby, she realized she'd been feeling this emptiness for a long time.

"Now that I know she exists, I don't know how I could walk away from her?" Quinn asked. "How could I miss out on seeing her grow up and knowing the person she becomes?"

"I don't know how you could." Elise leaned forward in her chair. "All the time, I'm amazed at the ways my girls resemble me and Dave. Not just in looks, but in personality, too. You've met Lily—you know she's a quiet bookworm, just like me. The two of us are content to sit around all day reading, and now that she's old enough, it's been one of the joys of my life to share the books of my childhood with her." She gestured toward a shelf of books. "We just read the entire Anne of Green Gables series, and now Lily wants to take a trip to Prince Edward Island together."

Quinn smiled, remembering how she'd loved those books when she was Lily's age.

"And Vivian, she's exactly like Dave. Fiery, outgoing, extroverted. They're always signing up to do things together—he coaches her in soccer, they go camping with other families while Lily and I stay home and read."

Quinn's heart pitched. It sounded so familiar. She'd always hoped to be the kind of mother who read books with her child, and James was dying for camping trips and baseball games. Maybe their daughter would have an interest in both, or maybe she'd completely resemble one of her parents. Either way would be okay. Either way would be perfect. But what was heart-breaking and unfathomable was the idea that they might not ever know.

"I've never even met my daughter, but—" Quinn's voice cracked, and she paused, taking a deep breath. "But I feel like I love her already. Like I've always loved her."

Elise gave Quinn's hand another squeeze. "Of course you do."

"Really? You don't think that sounds ridiculous?"

"Absolutely not. She's your child." Elise dropped a hand to her stomach. "I loved my girls from the moment I found out I was pregnant. And I have friends who adopted a child from overseas. The moment they found out he would be theirs they would have done anything for him. Sometimes, you just have that connection. You just know."

That was exactly how Quinn felt. Like she'd do anything for her child. It didn't matter that she'd never met her. Now that she knew the girl was out there in the world, Quinn couldn't imagine pretending that she didn't exist. Couldn't imagine going on with a permanent hole in her heart, a missing limb, while another woman raised her.

Quinn shot Elise a grateful look. "Thanks. This is really helpful."

"Keep me updated, okay?" Elise stood up and took about two steps toward the main part of the library before she swung back around. "I'm here for you, you know."

Guilt stabbed Quinn. She and Elise used to be close— they'd eat lunch together every day and both attended a once-a-month book club where they talked more about their lives than they did about the books. But once the fertility treatment had taken over Quinn's life, she'd started to pull away from every-one, especially her friends who had kids. It wasn't that she wasn't interested anymore. It just hurt too much. "I do know that. You're a good friend."

"You know, book club is tonight. Why don't you come? Everyone misses you—" Elise smiled. "And you know it doesn't matter if you haven't read the book."

For a moment, Quinn was tempted. She missed Elise and the other women, too. But their meeting with the attorney was scheduled for tomorrow, and she and James had a lot to discuss. "Thanks, but I don't think I can tonight."

Elise nodded, as if she'd expected this answer. "Maybe next month."

"That would be great." A shiver ran up Quinn's spine. By next month, her entire life could change. She might have met her daughter and be well on her way to having a relationship with her. Maybe—she sucked in a shaky breath—maybe she'd end up converting the guest room after all.

Quinn didn't know what was going to happen. But she was pretty sure she knew what she had to do.

5

"There really isn't any precedent for this."

The lawyer's words weren't quite what Quinn had been hoping to hear. She sighed and slumped back in her chrome and leather chair in the spacious, glass-walled conference room on the 45th floor of a downtown office building. Out the windows, the view of the city stretched from the incline climbing Mt. Washington to the stadiums on the Northside. In the center of it all, the Allegheny and Monongahela rivers meandered through the city to meet at the Ohio, carrying barges headed for West Virginia.

One of James's work colleagues had recommended this firm, and Helena was reputed to be the best family law attorney in the city. Quinn had been hoping that Helena would be able to tell them what to do. That magically, she'd have all the answers for exactly how to work this out so she and James could raise their child, and Nora would be okay with it. But, not surprisingly, there weren't any experts available in the legal intricacies of fertility clinics accidentally switching embryos. And there was no way that everyone was going to come out of this unscathed.

Quinn and James had stayed up well past midnight the night before to go over and over their options. In the end, they'd decided that they couldn't give up the opportunity to be a part of their child's life or to deny her the chance to know her family. They didn't know anything about Nora. Dr. Baxter said she was a nice person with a loving family, and Quinn hoped with her whole heart that it was true. But their child deserved to know her biological family, too. She deserved to understand where she got her physical features, to learn her medical history, to experience the stories and culture of her ancestors. She wasn't old enough to make the decision for herself, so Quinn and James had a duty to fight for her.

Sitting there in the attorney's office now, Quinn was grateful to have Helena on their side. She had close to twenty-five years of experience in custody cases and adoption law, and if her designer suit and office straight out of a network-TV law drama were any indication, Helena was very good at her job.

Helena looked back and forth between Quinn and James. "My first question is what you're both hoping to get out of this."

Quinn swallowed hard. "Well, I guess we were hoping you could tell us what our options are."

"Legally, what can we hope to get out of it?" James chimed in.

Helena cocked her head. "Well, like I said, there really aren't any cases exactly like yours that we can draw from. We might be setting some precedent here." A gleam in her eye told Quinn the attorney was relishing the thought.

Good. Quinn wanted an attorney who had a stake in this.

"But I suppose the first thing I need to tell you is that I reached out to Nora Robinson's attorney." Helena tapped her pen on her notepad. "And Nora is not interested in resolving this matter through mediation."

Quinn clutched the arms of her chair. "What does that mean?"

"In plain terms, it means she's denying you any access to the child, and she's not willing to work with us. Her attorney stated that as the gestational mother, she is the legal parent, and, well, to sum it up... you're out of luck."

Quinn's mouth dropped open, and next to her James sucked in a breath. "Can she do that?" he asked.

Helena raised an eyebrow. "Nora can do anything she wants right now. She *is* currently the legal parent. If you want access to the child, and the legal parent is unwilling to grant it..." Helena shrugged. "This case is going to have to go to court."

The legal parent. The mother. Quinn ached hearing those words to describe Nora. "But don't we have any rights? Biologically, the girl is ours." Her voice rose with each word. "The embryo was taken from us against our will."

James put a calming hand on Quinn's knee, and she appreciated his solid presence. But, right then, she didn't want to calm down. She shouldn't *have* to calm down. Quinn deserved to be angry, outraged, to scream and cry and throw things. Instead, she was sitting in a lawyer's office wearing a skirt that dug into her stomach because she was still bloated from the hormone injections that had turned out to be useless. She was paying thousands of dollars to some attorney after already pouring her life savings into creating an embryo that had gone to another woman. A woman who was now denying them the rights to their own child.

Helen nodded, seemingly unfazed by Quinn's frustration. She was probably used to emotional outbursts in her office, all those contentious divorces and parents fighting each other for custody. "Well, if you want to pursue this, that will be the basis for our argument. The fact that you didn't give up the embryo willingly—there was no legal agreement or paperwork signed—could constitute duress. In an adoption case, if consent was given fraudulently or under duress, the adoption agreement would be null and void."

Quinn sat up in her chair. "We didn't even know the embryo was given away. We didn't know the child existed."

"Well, keep in mind that this isn't an adoption case, and there are other factors in play." Helen sank back into her ergonomic office chair. "There *are* few cases of embryo mix-ups at fertility clinics." She rolled her eyes and shook her head as if to say *How could a clinic be so incompetent?*

Quinn was encouraged by that gesture. Helena was a powerhouse attorney. She would never mix anything up or make an incompetent mistake.

"What happened in those cases?" James asked.

Helena looked back and forth between them. "In most cases, the biological parents were granted custody."

Quinn took a shaky breath. They hadn't been considering full custody. She'd assumed they'd work with their attorneys to come to some sort of agreement with Nora about visits and shared custody. But Nora was refusing to cooperate with that.

Was Helena suggesting that full custody might be an option?

"Let's not get ahead of ourselves, though." Helena held up a manicured hand. "The reason I mentioned that there is no precedent for this particular situation is because all of the cases we found involved newborn babies or mix-ups that were discovered before birth. In those situations, the judges generally ruled for the biological parents. However, in your case—" Helena picked up her leather-bound notepad and flipped through it. "We're not talking about a newborn who won't know or remember any different. This child is—" She slid on her glasses and peered at the page. "Almost four years old."

Quinn's hands shook. They'd missed four years. She glanced at James, and the agony slashed across his face mirrored the pain she was experiencing. Four years, and now that they knew the truth, this Nora person was trying to keep them from their child even longer. She was trying to keep them from their child forever.

"In your case," Helena continued, seemingly unaware of the emotion radiating from across the table, "the child *will* have bonded with the gestational mother." Helena flipped through her notebook again. "Opposing council will likely cite a 2019 case from the New York Supreme Court where the judge noted that genetics should not be the only factor in deciding parentage." Helena looked at them sideways. "And I can guarantee they'll build their case around a 2016 case that expanded the definition of parenthood to include non-biological parents."

"What does that mean?" Quinn tried to wrap her mind around all this legalese. She imagined Helena would tell her to get used to it.

"The ruling was based on a custody dispute between a same-sex couple, but it's set a precedent in visitation and custody cases for other types of non-genetic caretaker relationships."

"So, what you're saying is—" James rubbed his temples like the whole thing was giving him a headache. "Because Nora has been the child's caretaker for almost four years, the judge won't care that we're the biological parents?"

"That's the worst-case scenario. But it's a possibility. I don't want to candy-coat this."

"And the only option is taking this to court? Nora really won't work with us?"

"I'm afraid not."

Of course, Quinn had known that nothing about this would be simple. But she and James had been open to a scenario where they could all be a part of the child's life. They didn't live far from Nora. It might have been unconventional, but if it was in the best interest of the child, why would Nora want to stand in the way? Quinn shook her head. What kind of person would deny a child access to their own biological parents? Nora hadn't even asked to meet them first. She'd just sent her attorneys to shut them out.

"We want full custody," Quinn blurted out.

Helena looked up, her impassive expression finally cracking. "*Full* custody?"

"Yes."

James's gaze swung to meet Quinn's. "Honey?" he murmured. They hadn't discussed full custody.

Quinn shrugged off their surprise. "Yes. Nora can have visitation rights, but we want to be the sole legal parents."

"Okay..." Helena hesitated, and then finally said, "I should warn you, that's going to be a bigger fight than I was anticipating."

James turned in his chair to face her. "Are you sure about this?"

"I wasn't until now. But if Nora isn't even willing to entertain the thought of allowing us access to our own child, well—" Quinn crossed her arms over her chest. "What kind of judgement does that show?" She swung her gaze to Helena. "What kind of person claims to love their child, and then intentionally keeps them from their own biological family?"

Helena lifted her hands in a *don't ask me* gesture.

Quinn reached over and grabbed James's hand. "If this is how Nora is going to react to our request to be a part of our own daughter's life, what will the next fourteen or so years be like, until she's an adult and can make her own decisions? Even if we got shared custody, how could we share parenting and decision-making with someone who is so selfish and inflexible? And about something as important as a child."

She shuddered. They could be back-and-forth in court until

the child was eighteen, arguing over which daycare to send her to and whether she was allowed to go on high school trips. And what about medical decisions? "For the child's sake, I think we need to get full custody."

James cleared his throat and turned to face the attorney. "I think Quinn makes a good point. No offense, Helena—" James gave the attorney a wry smile. "But I don't want to be back in your office every six months when this Nora woman won't cooperate with us."

"Okay." Helena picked up a heavy gold pen and scribbled in her notepad. "If that's what you want, that's what we'll ask for."

Quinn took a deep breath and blew it out slowly. "So, what's our first step?"

"Well, we'll want to arrange a DNA test. From the clinic's records, there isn't much doubt the child is yours. But we'll want to be crystal-clear so opposing council doesn't try to hold us up later."

"The test won't be a problem for us. But will Nora agree to it?"

Helena shrugged. "To be honest, Nora won't really have a choice. If she doesn't go along with our request, the judge will likely order it, and then Nora will look uncooperative."

Quinn was glad that the DNA test, at least, would be fairly easy. She had a feeling this process would only get harder from there.

"Next, we'll file a petition to the court asking for custody," Helena continued.

"Can we file that today?" Quinn asked. On *The Good Wife*, it seemed that court cases were open-and-shut in under a week, but Quinn had a feeling it wasn't like that in real life. They'd already missed so much time. She couldn't bear it if they had to wait much longer to be a part of their daughter's life.

"Yes, my associate can start working on it right now."

"And what happens once it's filed?"

"It could take eight to ten weeks for the preliminary hearing to get on the schedule." Helena took off her glasses and gazed at them across the conference table. "But I need to warn you that given the nature of this situation, this case could drag on. Opposing council will petition to call additional witnesses, and likely, I will, too. Your fertility doctor, possibly friends and family. The judge may request a home study."

Quinn shoulders tightened. She knew it was standard in adoptions to have a social worker assess your fitness to be a parent. But if they'd given birth to the girl, nobody would have required them to submit to a home study.

James sat up straight in his chair, obviously as annoyed as she was. "A home study? Is it really necessary to have a social worker poke around in our private life?"

Helena's eyebrows shot northward. "It might be. Is there any reason why we should be concerned about that? If so, as your attorney, I suggest you let me know now so I can get ahead of it."

"No." Quinn leaned into the table. They didn't have anything to hide. "It's nothing like that. James means it's the principle of it. We're the biological parents. If I'd been given the chance to give birth to our child, we wouldn't have to prove we're fit to raise her." She turned to James. "Right? That's all you meant?"

"Of course." James nodded, his jaw still tight.

Helena looked back and forth between them for a moment before finally nodding. "I should also warn you that winning this case won't mean it's over. If the judge rules in your favor, I'd bet my membership to the bar that opposing council will file an appeal. But we'll cross that bridge when we come to it. In the meantime, I'm going to request temporary visitation."

Quinn's breath hitched. "Will the judge grant it?"

"I'd say it's likely. You should have the right to meet your biological child."

"And the child. Can you tell us anything about her? What's her name?"

"The child..." Helena slid her glasses back on her nose and peered down at her notepad. "The child's name is Emily."

6

For the past four years, Quinn had been hiding a secret under the bed.

It wasn't a dead body, a box of love letters from an ex, or anything similarly shocking. But James didn't know about it, and for some reason that Quinn couldn't quite articulate, she hadn't told him.

It had started a couple of weeks after their wedding. Quinn had gone to the mall to return some duplicate wedding gifts to the department store, and on her way out had passed by a store window showing off an adorable display of teeny-tiny pastel clothing. Gorgeous knit sweaters and gingham pinafores and miniature socks covered in ducks. *Sugar Babies*, the store's sign declared in soothing charcoal-gray lettering that floated away in a puffy white cloud.

I'll just take a quick look around, she'd told herself.

Inside, the sales associate had welcomed her warmly, inquiring whether she was shopping for her own bundle of joy or for a gift. Before Quinn could stop to think about it, she'd stammered, "My own," and rubbed a hand over her stomach.

The sales associate had lit up like the moon-and-stars light fixture hanging overhead, gushing her congratulations.

Quinn hadn't been lying. Not really. After all, she *had* been shopping for her own baby. Back then, Quinn had been sure the baby would be become a reality in no time. In fact, on that day, about two weeks after the end of her honeymoon, Quinn had been counting days on the calendar and wondering if maybe she should swing by the pharmacy for a pregnancy test. Maybe it was a good omen that she'd passed by this store on this particular day.

She'd wandered into the newborn section, gently stroking a pair of organic cotton footie pajamas and the ruffles on a pink dress with lace trim and matching bloomers. Then her gaze had settled on the softest cream-colored button-up jumper with two tiny bear ears sewn on the hood. It would be absolutely perfect for bringing a baby home for the hospital. Quinn had checked the rack. There were only two left. If she waited until she took a pregnancy test, they might be gone. Besides, driving out to the mall was an inconvenience. It made sense to buy it now.

She'd grabbed the bear suit and headed for the checkout.

When Quinn had arrived home later that day, James was still at work, so she'd carefully folded it up, planning to surprise him with it when she got the positive pregnancy test. Of course, the test hadn't been positive that month, but Quinn hadn't been deterred. It would happen soon.

After that, Quinn had begun noticing baby things everywhere she went. It wasn't that she'd browsed often, just once in a while. When she'd stopped into the cute little gift shop on Butler Street to buy a card for her college friend's birthday, Quinn couldn't help tucking a colorful wooden train and a onesie that declared, *Nobody puts Baby in a corner* into her shopping basket. And then there was the teeny-tiny knitwear a co-worker at the library had been selling in her Etsy shop to make extra money. Quinn had told herself it was important to support a local artist when she'd ordered baby hats in two different colors.

She'd tucked her stash into a couple of special boxes under the bed that also held a favorite stuffed bear from her own childhood.

After that, all they needed was a baby.

———

The day after their visit to the attorney's office, Quinn had the day off from work. She often hosted special events at the library on Saturdays, so it wasn't unusual for her to take a day off in the middle of the week. Usually, she spent those days doing fertility yoga, baking sugar-free granola bars, or listening to a podcast by an expert in Chinese medicine. But there was really no point in doing any of those things anymore. Her last embryo transfer was over, and all the meditation, healthy food, and herbal tinctures in the world wouldn't bring her a baby.

Now, it was all in Helena's hands.

After Quinn had vacuumed the entire house, cleaned both bathrooms, and called to make a dentist appointment, she began to wish she could go to work. Shelving books and planning story-time crafts would at least be a distraction from the lure of her laptop and all the things she wanted to Google about custody cases and switched embryos. So far, she'd held off, but it was just a matter of time.

James had discouraged her from clearing out the guest room until they knew more about what would happen with their case. He didn't want to prepare for Emily to stay until they knew for sure that her presence in their home would be a reality. Just in case it didn't happen.

If that was how he felt about preparing the guest room for Emily, it was probably better that he didn't know about the boxes of baby things under the bed.

Quinn paced down the upstairs hallway and back. They'd bought this three-bedroom, two-bath with the intention of raising their family here. The house wasn't huge, but it was in a good neighborhood near a park and down the street from the best elementary school in the city. In addition to the primary and guest bedrooms, James had an office in the back of the house, and a finished attic upstairs currently held their exercise equipment. They didn't use those rooms very often, and either one would make a good playroom. Quinn was itching to start measuring corners, shopping for rainbow prints for the walls, and selecting stacking bins to hold children's books and stuffed animals.

She was eyeing the far side of the guest room—a perfect spot for a canopied twin bed—when the phone rang. The name of Helena's law firm flashed on the screen and, heart pounding, Quinn pressed the button to answer it.

"Hi, Quinn, I wanted to give you some updates and good news about your case," Helena's no-nonsense voice carried through the phone.

"Yes?" Quinn asked, breathlessly.

"We have a court date set for eight weeks from now."

Quinn's shoulders drooped as she sank down on the guest bed in between a couple of file boxes. She knew better than to expect that a judge had gone ahead and granted her and James custody of Emily, but still. A little part of her had hoped. "That's the good news?" She should be happy about this. Eight weeks wasn't that far away. It was just that she'd waited for almost four years to meet her child. And she'd already missed so much of her life.

"Well, it's always good news when the judge schedules a hearing and doesn't throw a case out. It means we *have* a case." Helena chuckled. "But no, that's not the only news. We were pretty confident from the start that we had a case."

"So, there's something else?"

"Yes, the good news is that the judge has decided to allow you a visit with the child. There will be a hearing to agree on visitation soon, but she felt that you and James have waited long enough, and she granted you one short meeting now."

Quinn sucked in a breath, for a moment, too overwhelmed to react. *My daughter. I'm going to meet my daughter.* Finally, she managed to whisper, "When? When can I meet her?" She'd get in the car right now. Drive wherever she needed to go.

"Opposing council requested that the meeting be brief and supervised. I suggested that we have it here at my office, and they agreed. Just an hour for everyone to get acquainted."

"Okay. So, you'll be there? And—" Quinn's voice grew hoarse. "Nora and her attorney, too?"

"Yes."

Quinn tried to picture all of those people stuffed into one room watching her meet her child for the very first time. "I guess that sounds fine for a first visit. But what about after that? How will we get to know Emily in a cold conference room surrounded by lawyers?" Quinn paused. "No offense, of course."

"None taken," Helena assured her. "As I mentioned, after that meeting, we'll have a hearing where we'll request more informal visits. We'll ask that you be allowed to take the child to the playground or for ice cream or... whatnot." Helena said it as if spending the day in the county jail would be preferable to spending it with a child.

But Quinn didn't care. Helena didn't have to like children. She just had to be good at winning custody of them for her clients.

"When can this first visit take place?"

"If you're amenable, I've set up a meeting for nine o'clock on Monday morning. Does that work for you?"

Literally any day and time would work for her. Quinn

would skip her best friend's wedding to meet her daughter. "Yes, of course."

"And what about James?"

James would fit it into his work schedule. It was only an hour in the morning. And this was his daughter they were talking about. "Yes, I'll let him know. But I'm certain it will be fine."

"Wonderful. I'll have my assistant send you the calendar invite. And I'll plan to see you on Monday."

"Wait!" Quinn said, before Helena could hang up. She chewed on her thumbnail, suddenly humming with excitement and terror. "What should we bring? Who will they tell Emily we are? Can we take photos? Can we ask Nora to bring baby pictures—?"

"Quinn." Helena's much calmer voice interrupted her. "It's a quick visit. Don't overthink it. There's no need to bring anything, and I'd hold off on photos and baby pictures for now. Just say hello to everyone, and spend a few minutes with Emily. The child is not even four. I don't think she'll be overthinking it."

"But—" Quinn's voice shook, and tears welled in her eyes. "What if she doesn't like me?"

Through the phone, Quinn could hear papers flipping. Probably Helena's leather-bound notebook where she wrote everything down. "You're a children's librarian, correct?"

"Yes."

"The child will like you just fine." Helena sighed. "She's not expecting magic tricks and Broadway show tunes. Just say hello and ask her if she likes Big Bird or something."

"All children like Big Bird."

"Well, you're all set, then."

Quinn sniffed and wiped her eyes with her sleeve. "Okay, you're right. I'm just nervous. This is the most important moment of my life."

"I know." Helena's voice was kinder now. "You'll be fine. I've coordinated dozens of supervised visits for all manner of custody cases. And the one thing I can tell you is that children pick up on the adults' energy. So be friendly and calm, and don't put too much pressure on the situation. This meeting isn't the be-all and end-all. It's just a quick visit to say hello."

Quinn nodded, suddenly grateful they'd hired Helena. She might not like children, but she really knew what she was doing with emotional, anxious adults. "Thank you so much, Helena. I can't tell you how much I appreciate this."

"It's my pleasure."

After noting that they'd see each other on Monday, she and Helena hung up the phone. Quinn switched to her texts to send James a message letting him know the details of the call, and asking him to hold the date and time to meet Emily. After a few moments, he responded with a series of celebration emojis. Quinn smiled. He was going to be a good dad.

Quinn clicked off her phone and jumped to her feet. She had three days to prepare to meet her daughter for the first time. She'd also be meeting Nora for the first time, though, too. And Nora's attorney. Did she own any outfits that announced, "I'm not a pushover" to the adults in the room? Or was it better to go with warm and maternal, for Emily's sake? Maybe something she'd wear to her job at the library that would be appropriate for getting down on the floor to play with a child. The navy blouse with the bird-print and a pair of jeans? Or the black and white cat cardigan with a pair of cropped pants? Quinn twisted her dark curls into a bun. Maybe she ought to consider getting her hair cut.

She was about to dial the number of her hair salon when she caught a glimpse of the mirror. A woman with wild, desperate eyes stared back at her. It was *not* a good look for a person about to meet her daughter for the first time.

Quinn lowered the phone. Helena had told her not to overthink it. The bird-print blouse would be fine, and she probably didn't need a haircut. The most important thing was to connect with Emily. To make her daughter feel comfortable and safe in her presence.

With that thought, Quinn spun around and crouched next to the bed, reaching under it to pull out her secret boxes of baby things. She flipped open the lid on the first box, and stared at the contents. So much of her collection was for a newborn, and Emily had long passed that stage. Quinn's heart ached at all she'd missed, but it wasn't the time to dwell on it.

Quinn reached into the box, and from under a pile of onesies and baby socks, pulled out the stuffed bear from her childhood. The fur was worn in places but, otherwise, the bear was in surprisingly good shape. *Things were of much better quality thirty or forty years ago.* She ran a hand over the bear's ears and gave its shiny plastic eyes a rub with the hem of her shirt. Helena had said not to bring any presents, but this bear wasn't just any toy. It was a special keepsake that might help Emily feel more comfortable with her.

Quinn got down on her elbows and leaned under the bed again, grabbing for another box, this one tattered and yellowed with age. She flipped open the lid to reveal a photo album with a faded 1980s paint-splatter print across the cover. Inside the album, Quinn found a series of photos of a couple sitting in a living room with a brown plaid couch and gold shag carpet. The woman had kinky brown hair and bangs curled off her face, and the man sported a Burt Reynolds mustache and matching mullet. They held a baby in white apron-front bloomers clutching a brown teddy bear. As Quinn turned the pages, the scenery varied. Sometimes the couple sat in the same living room; at other times, they'd moved to a backyard or a park. Gradually, the child grew from a baby to a toddler.

Quinn paused on the photo of the little girl standing about hip-high next to her parents, wearing a pair of jean shorts and striped T-shirt. The girl's dark hair had grown from soft baby-waves into shoulder-length ringlets. In one hand, she clutched the leg of the teddy bear; in the other, a popsicle. Quinn ran a hand over the almost four-decades-old picture of herself. She must've been about the same age in that photo as Emily was now. Quinn had inherited her mother's dark curls and her father's smile. Had she passed them on to her own daughter? She couldn't believe she was about to find out.

Quinn continued to flip through the photos. Her childhood had been a happy one, with two parents who'd loved her, and a warm, comfortable home. The only thing missing had been siblings, but her parents had tried for years for a baby before Quinn had come along. They'd called her *their miracle* and showered her with affection. Both of her parents were only-children, too, so when they'd died in a car accident when Quinn was a sophomore in college, they'd left her all alone. Of course, now she had James, but there was nobody she knew in the world related to her. Nobody with the same eyes or smile or unique set of genes.

Until now.

Quinn took one last look at the photo of the girl with her parents and the stuffed bear. Someday, maybe she would have a photo like that with her own daughter. Reluctantly, Quinn gently closed the album and slid both boxes back under the bed. She climbed to her feet, picked up the stuffed bear, and slid it into her oversized purse.

She'd bring the bear to the meeting with Emily, just in case. How could it possibly hurt?

———

That evening, Quinn picked up a bottle of wine and then swung by the grocery store for a crusty baguette and the ingredients for a fancy cheese plate. If there was one perk of not trying to get pregnant anymore, it was that she could abandon her gluten-free vegan diet for good. James would be elated. He'd put on a good face about it, crunching his way through hundreds of salads, pretending to enjoy roasted broccoli and hemp seeds. But Quinn knew that, deep down, he wished they could order a pizza once in a while.

Quinn wanted to surprise him with a little celebration. In just a couple of days they'd meet their daughter. It would only be a short visit, the first step in a very long process, but they hadn't had much to celebrate lately. She'd take a win wherever she could get it. Besides, it would be good for her and James to spend some time together.

Quinn set some candles on the bedroom dresser and dug through her underwear drawer for some of the lingerie she'd gotten as a bridal shower gift. After some indulgent food and a bottle of wine to loosen them up, she planned to steer the evening in a romantic direction. With all of Quinn's hormone injections and the stress of treatment schedules, it felt like ages since either of them had been in the mood.

Quinn put the finishing touches on her cheese plate, scattering candied walnuts among the fruit and triple-cream Brie, and then checked the time. If James wasn't working late—a situation that seemed to happen with more frequency lately—he was usually home by six. But it was past six-thirty, and she hadn't heard from him. He didn't usually forget to text her, but maybe he'd gotten caught up in a meeting.

Quinn opened her phone and called his number. It rang once and then immediately switched over to voicemail. She hung up the phone and found a playlist of mellow jazz for background music, and then she opened the bottle of wine to let it breathe.

At seven-twenty, Quinn called James again, and when he didn't answer, she sent a text. *Just checking in!* She didn't want to be dramatic about it if he was busy in a meeting, but she was starting to worry. Quinn poured a splash of wine in her glass and swallowed it in one gulp. They'd both been distracted lately and hadn't spent nearly enough time together. And they certainly hadn't put much effort into their marriage. Nothing was really wrong with it, but it had grown a bit neglected, like a garden that needed a good weeding. What if things were finally starting to look up for them, and then something happened to James? Her heart stuttered as her anxious mind gravitated to all the worst possible scenarios.

What if last year's situation was happening all over again?

Quinn shook her head. There was no reason to go there. James wasn't even an hour late, and he didn't know she'd been planning a surprise. He had no reason to rush home from work.

It was just that he usually texted if he was going to be late.

At 7.45 p.m., Quinn heard the front door swing open and the jingle of keys dropping on the hall table. She jumped up from the couch where she'd been working her way through a second glass of wine and followed the sound to the entryway. She found James standing by the hall closet, staring down at his phone.

"Hi."

He jumped at the sound of her voice and looked up. Quinn blinked in surprise. His hair was stuck up at all angles, as if he'd run his hand through it a dozen times, his face was pale, and his eyes bloodshot.

"Are you okay?" she asked.

He stared at her for a moment as if he were processing her question. Finally, he gave her a tired smile. "I'm fine. Just... a long day."

"Did you get my messages?" Quinn's eyes drifted to the phone in his hand.

"Yes. Sorry. I was in a meeting until fifteen minutes ago, and then I hopped right in the car and drove home." He stuffed the phone in his pocket. "I just checked my messages right now."

Okay, well that explained it. There hadn't been any reason to get worked up. It was just that everything felt so tenuous lately. So out of her control. But James was fine, just distracted. "You're working too hard lately. I know you feel an obligation to make sure we're secure financially." Her heart flipped. Especially because they might be supporting a child soon. "But I'm worried about how much you're taking on." Quinn reached out and took his hand. "We'll be fine. We'll be able to support Emily. Kids are expensive, but it's not like we have to buy diapers and formula." She gave him a wry smile. "I guess that's the one benefit of not having a baby."

Instead of laughing at her lame attempt at a joke, James rubbed his temples and seemed to grow even more tired. "Yeah... thank God we don't need to buy diapers," he murmured.

Quinn started tugging him into the living room. "Come in and sit down. I have wine and cheese."

He shuffled behind her, stopping by the couch to survey the platter on the coffee table next to the open wine bottle. "Wow. It's been a while since we had a drink together."

"Well, we're celebrating." She flashed him a grin. "We're about to meet our child."

James took a deep breath and blew it out slowly, nodding as he flopped down onto into the couch.

"Are you excited?" Quinn prompted, perching on the edge of her seat to pour him a glass of wine. She looked up to find him watching her with an affectionate, almost wistful expression on his face.

"Beyond excited." James reached out and tucked a lock of her hair behind her ear, and for a second, he looked like he might tear up. "I love you so much, Quinn. I want nothing more than to be a parent with you." He breathed out another sigh. "I hope you know that."

Quinn leaned in as his hand drifted from her hair to her

shoulder. "Of course I know that. I love you too." She set her glass on the table, then leaned in and kissed him. James kissed her back, slowly easing her back against the couch cushions and tugging her shirt over her head. Quinn reached up to pull him closer, and for the first time in a long time, she wasn't thinking about whether the timing was right for ovulation or if she'd remembered to take her fertility vitamins. The only thing that crossed her mind before she stopped thinking about anything at all was how lucky she felt to be with James. And how hopeful she was that they'd finally have the child they'd always dreamed of.

7

Quinn rubbed her sweaty hands on the legs of her pants and, for about the hundredth time, glanced through the conference room's glass walls to the elevators on the far side of the reception desk. Any moment, those doors would slide open and her daughter would walk out.

Her heart beat wildly, and she could hardly sit still. A thousand half-formed thoughts ricocheted through her head. Would Emily like her? What would she say to Nora? Would it be horribly painful and awkward? Quinn wished they hadn't agreed to a meeting in a stodgy law-office conference room. The space, with its sharp-edged glass table and rolling leather and chrome chairs, was no place for a small child. Why hadn't she asked Helena to arrange the meeting in a park or someplace that would feel more familiar to Emily? Someplace where they could all relax and get to know each other.

Quinn glanced across the table at Helena and her associate murmuring quietly to each other and occasionally typing something into their laptops. The presence of these lawyers was a terrible idea, too. Everyone would be staring at her and James, gauging their reactions, scribbling notes to use for or against them in their custody case. It should've been just her, James, and Emily. And Nora, of course. If the lawyers had insisted, they could have hired a neutral third party like a social worker. Quinn felt like she was about to sit for the most important test of her life, and she wasn't sure if she'd ever be well-enough prepared. Nora had all the advantages of having known Emily for her entire life. All Quinn had was biology.

But biology was powerful. Quinn took a deep, calming breath and blew it out slowly. She hadn't met Emily yet, and already she felt fiercely maternal toward her. Already, she understood the "mama bear" protectiveness that other women talked about, and she'd only been able to imagine.

James's hand settled on top of hers. "You okay?"

Quinn glanced at her husband. His face was calm, impassive, as if he were simply waiting for a bus or for his food in a restaurant. But his foot's rhythmic tapping beneath the table gave away his nerves. She flipped her hand around until she was holding his, and gave it a squeeze. No matter what happened, they had each other. Their impromptu celebration on Friday night had almost felt like the early days, before the heartbreak of infertility had taken over. Maybe the hard times were finally in the past, and this experience would bring them closer than ever.

"I'm fine." She gave James a tentative smile. "Just ready to finally meet our daughter."

She'd never grow tired of the wonder that slowly drifted across his face at those words. *Our daughter.* It was how she'd always imagined he'd look when he held their new baby for the first time.

This moment would be a first time, too. The first time they'd meet their child. Quinn was determined to cherish it.

"I wonder where they are." James glanced at his watch.

Quinn's gaze skated to the clock on the opposite wall. 9:07 a.m. Nora and Emily were supposed to arrive seven minutes ago. Was this some sort of power move on Nora's part? Was she intentionally making them wait? The meeting was stated to end at ten. Helena said Nora's team wanted to keep it to an hour, so it wouldn't be too stressful for Emily, and so Nora could get her back to preschool before nap time. Was Nora trying to exert her control over the schedule and shorten their time even more?

When the clock ticked to 9:09 a.m., Quinn turned to Helena. "They're almost ten minutes late. Should someone call them and make sure nothing happened on the way?" What if there'd been an accident? Her heart tipped sideways as a new thought occurred to her. What if Nora had decided to no-show? "Should we make sure they're still coming *at all?*" Her voice slowly rose with each word.

Helena held up a hand. "Let's give them a few more minutes before we panic. If they're driving in from the suburbs, they might have hit traffic. If they're not here in five minutes, I'll call opposing council." Helena nodded at the untouched plate of cookies on the conference room table—an offering brought in by Helena's assistant. "Would you like some coffee while you wait? Or maybe something to eat?"

Just looking at food made Quinn's stomach lurch, and she shook her head. There was no way she could eat at a time like this.

Helena's gaze tipped toward the door, and her mouth curved into a smile. "Ah, looks like we won't have to make that call after all. Here they are now."

Quinn jerked backwards and spun around in her chair. Into the conference room strolled a man and woman, each wearing suits and carrying briefcases. Opposing council, probably, but Quinn barely registered them. Because out from behind the attorneys walked an attractive blond woman about Quinn's age, holding the hand of a little girl.

Quinn had imagined this moment a hundred times, had walked through the different scenarios in her head. In each one, she remained composed, calm, even a tiny bit detached. But now that she was there in the moment, she gasped and lunged to her feet. "Oh," she murmured, clutching a hand to her chest and staring at the girl. "Oh, she's—she looks like..."

Quinn knew the exact moment that Nora saw it too, because the other woman's face crumpled.

Emily looks just like me.

If someone had snapped a photo of Emily with an old-fashioned photo filter and slipped it into Quinn's childhood album, she wouldn't have been able to tell the difference between the little girl in front of her, and her own childhood pictures. Emily's hair framed her heart-shaped face with Quinn's wild curls, and her big, brown eyes—the exact same shape as Quinn's —stared up at her.

Maybe the resemblance between Quinn and Emily wouldn't have been quite so striking if Emily wasn't standing next to Nora, whose straight, wispy blond hair and blue eyes declared her complete lack of genetic connection to the child.

Nora's blue eyes filled with tears, and one of her attorneys put a comforting hand on her shoulder.

"Well." Helena's voice cut in from somewhere behind Quinn. "Thank you all for coming, and for agreeing to this meeting." Quinn knew Nora didn't have a choice, and Helena was only being polite. "I suppose we should do introductions."

Nora's attorneys quickly jumped in to make the rounds and shake everyone's hand, and Helena did the same. The shuffle of bodies left Quinn and James standing on one side of the doorway, and Nora and Emily on the other. They stared across the narrow space at each other.

Finally, James cleared his throat. "Well, you must be Nora and Emily."

"Yes." Nora tugged Emily a little closer to her side and glared at James as if he were a creep on the playground.

"I'm James, and this is Quinn."

"I know who you are," Nora snapped, taking a step backward and pulling Emily with her.

Quinn's spine stiffened at Nora's obvious hostility. She didn't expect the other woman to welcome them with open arms—after all, she'd never wanted this meeting in the first place—but how was it possible that Nora had absolutely no understanding of their position at all? She'd gone through IVF, too, and knew the heartbreak of infertility better than anyone. What if the clinic had given *her* embryo to someone else? Surely Nora could understand the gravity of what Quinn and James had lost in this terrible mix-up.

Quinn's gaze slid from Nora's angry face to Emily's curious one. She took a deep breath to center herself. That little girl was the person who really mattered here. She didn't deserve to end up in the middle of their anger and resentment.

Quinn knelt down to the girl's level. "Hi, I'm Quinn. You must be Emily." For the first time, she noticed Emily had a stuffed bear tucked under her arm. "Who's your friend?"

Emily held up the bear. "This is Mirabel."

"From *Encanto*?" As a children's librarian, Quinn was familiar with the popular children's movies. Kids came in all the time looking for books about Pixar and Disney characters.

Emily nodded happily.

Quinn reached out her palm toward Emily's bear. "It's nice to meet you, Mirabel."

Emily dropped Nora's hand and inched toward Quinn. She held out the bear, and Quinn pretended to shake his paw. Then she held out a hand to Emily. "It's nice to meet you too, Emily."

Emily giggled as she slid her tiny palm into Quinn's. As soon as Quinn's hand closed around the girl's, her heart cracked open. How could this be the first time she'd ever touched her own child? Emily should have wrapped her tiny baby fingers around Quinn's on the day she was born. Should have clutched both of Quinn's hands while she toddled around on unsteady legs, learning to walk. Should have held out a fistful of dandelions she'd picked just for Quinn.

Instead, Nora had experienced those important moments with Emily. And Quinn could never have them back. Her eyes welled up, and she brushed at them with her sleeve. "I have a bear friend, too," Quinn said over the lump in her throat. "Do you want to meet him?"

"Okay!" Emily nodded.

"Over here." Quinn crossed the room to where she'd left her bag. She picked it up and sat down, pulling out the next chair for Emily. The girl climbed in and pushed off the table to give the chair a spin. Quinn laughed. Maybe the conference room wasn't such a bad choice after all. "These chairs are fun, right?"

Emily spun around again, lifting her arms as if she were on a roller coaster.

"*Careful, Emily.*" Nora's voice was sharp as she crossed the room and grabbed the back of the girl's chair, stopping it midspin. Then she directed an angry look in Quinn's direction. "She could fall off."

"Sorry. I didn't—" Quinn's eyes darted around the room at everyone watching this interaction. Her face flushed as one of Nora's lawyers scribbled something into his notepad. "Sorry."

Helena stepped in. "Why don't we all sit over here, and give Quinn and James a few minutes with Emily?" She gestured at the other end of the long conference table.

Nora hesitated for a moment before kneeling down in front of Emily. "Quinn and James are, um, friends of Mommy. They want to get to know you a little bit, just like we talked about at home." Nora kept her voice upbeat, but Quinn could tell every word pained her. "I'll be right over here, okay?"

Emily nodded, and Nora stood. She slowly walked to the opposite side of the conference table, her eyes glued to Emily the entire time. When Nora was safely settled across the room, James pulled over a third chair and sat down. "Hi, I'm James."

Emily eyed him more shyly than she had Quinn a moment earlier. Quinn remembered that Nora was a single mother and there wasn't a father in Emily's life. Even if there were other men in the family—Dr. Baxter had mentioned an uncle— Quinn's experience at the library had taught her that little kids were more comfortable with unknown women than with men. It was usually the moms who brought children to playgroups and story hour, and they all looked out for each other's kids. Quinn had always envied those groups of women, bonded by motherhood.

Though he'd always wanted to be a father, James didn't have much experience with children, and next to Quinn, he sat rigid in his chair, his foot tapping again. Quinn looked around the room for something to help both James and Emily feel more at ease. Her gaze settled on the plate of cookies in the middle of the table. She reached over and gave it a nudge in James's direction. "James, maybe you want to offer Emily a cookie? I see chocolate chips in there."

"*No.*" Nora jumped to her feet and rushed across the room again. "Emily can't have those." She grabbed the plate and pulled it out of reach. "If she wants a snack, I have fruit in my bag."

Quinn's skin went cold and then hot, a mix of mortification at being yelled at again, and anger at her own stupidity. It was nine in the morning. What had she been thinking, offering the girl a treat? Was everyone staring at her, silently judging? Were they jotting down notes for the custody hearing? *Feeds the child junk food at all hours of the day.*

"I'm so sorry." Quinn stammered. "I just didn't think... Of course it's too early for cookies." She pressed her hands to her burning cheeks.

Helena jumped in. "No harm was done. Maybe Emily can tell Quinn and James about school. Or do you do any activities? Sports? Arts and crafts?" She shifted in her shiny black heels, and her uncharacteristic discomfort made Quinn smile. Helena was clearly not a kid-person, but Quinn appreciated the effort.

But Emily didn't want to talk about her interests. She was still fixated on the plate on the table. "Mommy, I want a cookie!"

Nora huffed out a breath and shot an irritated look in Quinn's direction. One that clearly said, *Now look what you've done.* To Emily, her voice remained calm, patient. "Honey, you know you can't have one of those cookies. Let's look in my bag for a different snack."

Emily's head wagged back and forth, her brown ringlets bouncing. "I don't want fruit! I want a cookie!" Her eyes filled with tears.

A tiny ember of annoyance ignited inside Quinn. Was one cookie before lunch really going to hurt anyone? It almost seemed that Nora was being intentionally difficult, riling the child to make Quinn look bad.

"Emmie." Nora smoothed a wayward curl on the child's head. "I know you want a cookie, and when we get home, you can have one of your special ones after dinner. But right now—"

"Hey, Emily!" Quinn cut in. "I forgot to show you my teddy." She wasn't going to waste another precious second with her daughter, just because Nora wanted to be difficult. She'd missed enough already. "He really wants to be friends with Mirabel." Quinn fished around in her bag, pulling out her childhood bear.

Emily reached for the stuffed animal. "What's his name?" she asked, the cookies forgotten. Nora slowly backed away to her spot across the room.

"You know," Quinn said, ignoring Nora and focusing on the child, "I don't think he has a name. He was my friend when I was your age, and I just called him Brown Bear. Isn't that a silly name?"

Emily giggled. "He needs a real name."

"Why don't you and Mirabel go ahead and give him one?"

"We should call him Bruno!" Another character from the film, *Encanto*.

"Bruno the bear! That's perfect. Does Mirabel like it?"

With Emily's help, Mirabel gave an enthusiastic nod. "Do you have a bear, too?" She asked James.

James shook his head, sadly. "No, unfortunately, I don't. But maybe I could be friends with Mirabel and Bruno?"

Emily held out Mirabel and Bruno's paws to James. He solemnly shook hands with each bear and told them it was nice to meet them. Quinn's heart squeezed. He was trying hard, and Quinn knew he'd make a great dad with just a little bit of practice.

Emily took one bear in each hand and pressed them together as if they were hugging. "They like each other!"

Quinn smiled. "Of course they do! They'll be best friends. In fact..." She shot a quick glance over to the group at the other side of the room. Would they think she was overstepping? She focused on Emily and decided she didn't care. "If you want to take Bruno home with you so he can stay with Mirabel, I think he'd like that."

"Really?" Emily clutched both bears to her chest, and the smile that lit up her daughter's face showed Quinn she'd made the right decision. And then, even better than that, Emily hopped off her chair and gave Quinn a hug.

Quinn's breath caught as the little girl's arms tightened around her, and the lavender scent of baby shampoo drifted over her. She leaned in to hug Emily back, and she didn't want to ever let go.

Suddenly, a wail from the other side of the room had both her and Emily jumping backwards. Quinn spun in her chair in the direction of Nora and the attorneys.

"Please!" Nora stood, clutching her fists together in front of her chest, tears streaming down her cheeks. "Please don't take my baby away."

Quinn stood to face the other woman. "I—" She didn't know what to say. Because the look on Nora's face was—heartbreaking.

"Please, Quinn, James." Nora took a step forward, looking back and forth between them. "Please, she's my baby. I'm the only mother she's ever known. You can't know what it would do to her to if you took her from me." Her shoulders shook now, and she barely managed to get the last few words out over the crying and gasping. "Please... don't... do this to her. To us." Nora stumbled into a chair and put her head in her hands on the conference table, her whole body wracked with sobs now. "Don't take my baby."

Emily pushed past Quinn and ran to Nora. *"Mommy!"* She grabbed Nora's arm and yanked on it, her little mouth opening wide as she let out her own wail. *"Why are you crying, Mommy?"* And in the next moment, she flung herself on the floor in a tantrum, wailing and kicking her little sneakered feet on the carpet.

Quinn took a step toward Emily, but stumbled to a stop as Nora spun in her chair and knelt down on the floor next to the girl. Nora gathered Emily in her arms and rocked her back and forth while both their sobs echoed through the conference room. Quinn backed away, bumping into James. He put an arm around her and pulled her against his side.

Across the room, one of Nora's attorneys leaned in and said something sharply to Helena. Quinn couldn't hear Helena's response, but by the way Helena shook her head and waved a hand in the air, it was clear she and the other attorney were arguing.

Quinn hovered in the corner, watching Nora and Emily on the floor, and each wail and sob tore at her insides. Her eyes burned with unshed tears. This was horrible, the whole situation was a nightmare.

She'd had always dreamed of being a mother, ever since she was a child herself. When she was Emily's age, she used to dress up her dolls, comb their hair, and pull them around in her little red wagon. She'd gone to college and then graduate school to become a children's librarian because she loved being around kids, helping them learn, seeing the wonder on their little faces. She'd almost given up on the idea of having a baby of her own, and suddenly here in front of her was the child she'd always imagined.

All Quinn was asking was a chance to get to know her biological daughter. So, why did she feel like such a villain?

Across the room, Helena and the other attorneys exchanged a few more terse words, and then Helena gestured for Quinn and James to follow her through the door.

Outside the conference room, the sounds of Nora and Emily crying was more muted. Or maybe Nora had calmed down once she wasn't in their presence.

"Quinn, James, listen." Helena pressed a hand to her forehead as if this whole debacle was giving her a headache. "We're going to have to cut this short."

For a moment, Quinn was tempted to argue. They were supposed to have another half-hour with Emily. And they'd all been getting along so well until Nora burst into hysterics. Had she done it on purpose to end the meeting? She'd been hostile from the beginning. But Quinn quickly shook her head of that thought. Nora wouldn't have intentionally upset Emily. It was clear that Nora loved her deeply. "Okay." Quinn took a deep breath. "We can reschedule, right? The judge said we have the right to see Emily."

"Absolutely." Helena gave a reassuring nod. "There will be a hearing, and I expect the judge to grant a regular visitation schedule. And I've made it clear to opposing council that if these types of outbursts and interruptions continue, the judge will be hearing about it. You're entitled to see Emily, and if Nora isn't capable of remaining calm, I'll have to insist that a different chaperone be appointed."

James held out his palm to Helena. "Thank you."

"I'm sorry it went like this." The regret in Helena's voiced bolstered Quinn a little. They were lucky to have such a capable attorney on their side.

James put a gentle hand on Quinn's shoulder. "I think it's time we go now. Helena will call us with any new information."

Quinn glanced one last time through the wall of windows into the conference room. Nora was standing now, holding Emily on one hip, and talking to her attorneys. Emily looked exhausted as she leaned her cheek on Nora's shoulder with a thumb in her mouth and eyes still wet with tears. Near the conference table, Quinn's bag still sat on a chair. "I just need to get my things."

Back in the conference room, Quinn kept her head down as she grabbed her bag. She was about to turn and leave when part-way under the table she spotted Mirabel and Bruno. When Emily had started crying over Nora's outburst, she'd abandoned them on the floor. Quinn picked up the stuffed bears and settled Mirabel on a chair where Emily would see her. Quinn shot a glance in Emily's direction, and their eyes met across the room. Quinn smiled and held up Bruno. Then she carefully set him on the chair next to Mirabel. Emily immediately perked up, lifting her head from Nora's shoulder.

Quinn gave her a little wave, and Emily pulled her thumb out of her mouth so she could wave back, a smile stretched across her face now. Quinn hesitated for a moment before she turned and, heart aching, walked out of the room, leaving her child behind.

8

James was quiet on the way home, murmuring one-word answers as Quinn tried to talk to him about the furor at the attorney's office. About halfway into the drive, she finally gave up. *He's still in shock.* That morning had been a lot to take in, and James had never been one to go on about his feelings, at least not until after he'd had time to process them. Still, Quinn would have liked to talk about *her* feelings, because heartbreak and anger, joy and hope were currently waging a battle inside of her.

Couldn't he at least give her a smile, a squeeze of her hand, something to let her know that they were in this together?

When they finally pulled up in front of the house, James switched the car to park and got out, heading into the house before Quinn could even unbuckle her seatbelt. She followed more slowly, confusion building. When she stepped into the house, she found him sitting on the couch staring at the wall across the room.

She sank down next to him. "Can you talk to me about what you're thinking?" Just a few hours ago, she'd been reflecting on how close she felt to him. And now the cavern between them had opened up again. "I know today was difficult and emotional, but we're in this together, and we need to communicate."

James hesitated, running a hand through his hair. Finally, he sighed. "Are you sure we should continue with this?"

Quinn blinked. "Continue with what?"

He studied the painting hanging on the opposite wall. "Continue with..." His shoulders drooped. "Continue pursuing this relationship with Emily."

Quinn's mouth dropped open. "I—I don't understand."

"That was rough there in the conference room."

James was upset. *Of course he is.* Seeing both Nora and Emily crying like that had broken her heart. It would clearly cause Nora terrible pain to fight for Emily—but Quinn and James were in terrible pain, too. Nora had made it clear that she wasn't willing to work with them to have a relationship with their daughter, so what other choice did they have? "It was awful," Quinn admitted. "But it was one hard day. It doesn't mean we should just walk away. We agreed that this is in Emily's best interest. I still believe that. Don't you?"

He lifted a shoulder absently, and Quinn realized he still hadn't looked at her. She felt that familiar sense of despair, the one that had reared up every time another pregnancy test came back negative. The one that had nearly consumed her when she believed their embryo was lost and their chances of having a baby was really and truly over.

The discovery of her child's existence had been a lifeline. Suddenly, the years of disappointment and heartbreak were nothing if it brought Emily to her. And now that she'd met her child, heard her laugh, seen her face, so much like her own... Now that she'd experienced the absolute joy of Emily's little arms wrapping tightly around her...

How could she ever walk away? How could James even suggest it?

Quinn wrapped her arms around herself. "So, you just want to give up?" What about camping trips and baseball games? What about his dreams of being a father? None of this made any sense.

"Not give up." James finally met her eyes. "Maybe we should consider other ways of having a baby."

Quinn pressed her hands to her cheeks as frustrated tears welled up in her eyes. "What other ways? We tried IVF for years."

"And it never worked," James muttered. "It never stuck."

Quinn flinched like he'd taken a swing at her. She'd spent years fighting off the little voices in her head that whispered it was all her fault they couldn't have a baby. They'd had every test under the sun. James's sperm was just fine. Healthy. Vigorous. Perfectly capable of going for a swim down a fallopian tube and finding some genetic material to mix with. While her eggs were shriveled and her uterus was all dried up.

James knew about her insecurities around her fertility—or lack thereof. Why was he saying these things? What happened to *I want nothing more than to be a parent with you*? Quinn's eyes burned. "We never had a *chance* to see if the most important embryo would stick. It was given away to Nora."

James waved a hand helplessly. "You saw them in that conference room. Both Nora and Emily were hysterical over the idea of us being in Emily's life."

"Emily wasn't hysterical over the idea of being us in her life. She *liked* us. We had a real connection with her. *Nora* was the one who became hysterical, and she got Emily all worked up." Quinn swiped at her dripping eyes with her sleeve. "What is this really about? One rough day, and you're ready to give up?"

He raked a hand through his hair and flopped back against the couch cushions. "I wonder if you're losing perspective."

"What does that mean?"

"It means..." James hesitated for a moment. And then

finally, he said, "It means that you've grown so obsessed with the idea of having a child that it's all you talk about, it's all you think about. It's consumed your entire life."

For a moment Quinn was speechless. "Of course it's consumed my entire life. I was the one enduring the daily drives back and forth to treatments, the shots, the constant poking and prodding and teams of people literally up in my business. How could it *not* consume my entire life?"

"I know it was hard. But you turned into a—a—baby-making *machine*. Everything in our life revolved around getting pregnant. We could never go out to eat, could never have a drink and relax or do anything fun because you had to sip your fertility teas and go to bed early and get to acupuncture at the crack of dawn."

Quinn lunged to her feet. "We devoted our savings and years of our life to having a baby! Was I supposed to flush all that down the toilet and pretend it didn't matter? To go out and party and treat my body like a trash can?"

"No, of course not. But not every minute of every day had to be solely focused on getting pregnant. You stopped caring about us as a couple." James shook his head. "We couldn't even have sex without consulting a calendar or taking your body temperature or swallowing a handful of Chinese herbs first."

"So that's what this is really about?" Quinn dropped her hands to her hips. "You're angry about our sex life?" Was he forgetting about the other night on the couch? And then later in their bed? She'd thought that had meant something. That they had turned a corner, that they were connected and ready to face this together.

"No, it's not about sex. It's that I can see you getting that same tunnel vision with winning custody of Emily that you did with trying to get pregnant. You're losing perspective."

"Maybe it's not my perspective that's changed—it's yours." Quinn couldn't believe they were having this conversation.

"You were the one who proposed to me after only eleven months because you didn't want to wait to try for a baby. I didn't make the decision to do IVF all by myself. You were there, too. And when we found out about Emily—it was *your* idea to hire an attorney."

"Maybe that was a mistake."

He couldn't have hurt her more if he'd reached out and slapped her. "After everything we sacrificed, all the time and money and emotional energy, we're finally close to having the family we always dreamed of. And suddenly, you've changed your mind? You want to walk away?"

James stared down at his hands. "I'm not saying I want to walk away from having the family we dreamed of. There are other ways."

"We couldn't possibly afford adoption now. At least not unless Helena comes to some sort of settlement with the fertility clinic, and that could take forever. Besides, Emily is *our child*."

James sat up abruptly and grabbed her hand. "Quinn, hear me out and don't say anything until I'm finished, okay?" He took a deep breath, but just as he was about to speak, his phone rang with Helena's name.

For a second, he just stared at it.

"Answer the phone," Quinn prompted. "It could be important."

James swiped to answer, and set the phone to speaker.

"Hi, James." Helena's voice reverberated into the room. "Is Quinn with you?"

"I'm right here."

Through the phone, Quinn could hear Helena's manicured nails tapping on her keyboard. "I'm sorry again about how things played out today."

"Thanks," James murmured.

"But that's not why I'm calling. I have more news."

Quinn's heart stuttered, like it always did when Helena had news. She couldn't help it. Hope was a powerful thing. "Yes?" she whispered.

"Well, it's not really news, since the clinic had been certain of the switch. And of course, nobody can deny that Emily looks exactly like Quinn." Helena chuckled, oblivious to the tension on Quinn and James's end of the phone. "But it's official. The DNA tests came back, and you are completely, one hundred percent Emily's genetic parents."

"Oh," Quinn gasped, overwhelmed with emotion. "Oh, God." She put her head in her hands, unable to hold back any longer, and her shoulders shook with silent sobs.

Quinn had known Emily was theirs; she'd felt it before she'd even met the child. But now it was confirmed.

And James wants to walk away.

An arm slid around her shoulder and James tugged her against his side. "It will be okay, Quinn," he murmured into her hair. "I promise."

"James, Quinn, are you there?" Helena's voice cut in.

James cleared his throat. "Yes, sorry, we're here. We're just... We're taking it all in."

"Well, I'll let you go. Call me if you need anything." And in her no-nonsense way, Helena hung up.

Quinn leaned against her husband as her emotions swung wildly from longing for the comfort he provided, to anger and confusion at his sudden change of heart. Comfort won out, and she allowed him to wrap his arms around her while she sobbed against his chest.

"I love you, Quinn." James whispered. "We'll work this out."

Finally, her tears slowed, and she sat up and wiped her eyes. "James," Quinn said, sliding away so she could meet his gaze. "She has my mother's eyes. And your mother's smile. Did you notice that?"

James stared at her across the couch cushions, across a gulf that felt wider than physical distance. Quinn grabbed one shaking hand with the other as her heart pounded in her ears. If she couldn't change his mind, would that be the end? Quinn couldn't very well stand up in front of a judge and ask for custody while her husband and the man she shared a home with stood next to her saying, "No, thank you."

She could do it on her own, but—

Quinn's breath hitched. *Not if I want to stay with James.* She'd be forced to choose. Her husband, or her child. Quinn closed her eyes, picturing Emily smiling up at her as she held out her well-loved teddy bear. How could Quinn give up her own child and not spend the rest of her life resenting James for it? But James... he was the man she loved. The man she'd vowed to spend her life with, for better or worse.

The lines around his eyes deepened as he flinched from the pain of it. "She does have my mother's smile." He shook his head slowly. "God, I miss her."

"Our families might be gone." Quinn's voice shook at the memory of her happy childhood immortalized in photographs under the bed. Her parents were taken from her far too soon. But Emily—"Emily is their legacy. Don't you see that? She's all the best parts of us. We can't just walk away from her."

Quinn held her breath as James stared down at his hands. Finally, he nodded. "You're right."

Oh, God, she was going to cry again. *Oh, thank God.* "Does that mean you're in this with me?"

He swung his gaze up to meet her eyes. "She's our child. How could I not be in this with you?"

9

"Mommy, I want M&Ms!"

As Quinn strolled down the grocery store aisle, she passed a woman about her age steering a cart with one hand while tugging her young child away from a display of chocolate treats with her other.

"We don't need any more candy today," the mother said in an upbeat, sing-song voice. It was the same tone Quinn had heard mothers at the library use to distract their children from something they shouldn't be doing while trying to avert a temper tantrum. "Come on, honey. Let's go pick out some cereal."

The boy hesitated, probably weighing whether he should hold out for chocolate or take his chances on Lucky Charms. Finally, he turned and allowed his mother to lead him toward the cereal aisle. Quinn watched until he and his mother slowly made their way around the corner and out of sight.

Someday that could be me.

Quinn could imagine strolling around the grocery store with Emily's little hand tucked into hers. Smiling at the other mothers in solidarity. *Mine wants M&Ms too.* Quinn knew she'd be way too lenient and would probably say yes to both M&Ms *and* Lucky Charms, just to see the happiness on Emily's face. Not that she'd be a pushover, Quinn promised herself. And she'd make sure Emily ate her vegetables before she was allowed a treat.

Her heart ached with longing at the thought of spending a day with her child. Running errands and buying groceries and going home for a family dinner around the dining table. Ordinary, everyday activities that, when spent with her child, would feel like a gift.

From down the aisle another mother approached, this one pushing a cart that overflowed with groceries and children. She had a baby strapped into the child seat in front and two kids who looked to be twins around the age of three in the back with the food. One twin kept throwing things out of the cart onto the floor while his mother scrambled to pick them up. The other reached out and grabbed a handful of candy off the shelf.

"Simon, stop it." The mother chased a rolling orange and tossed it back into the cart. "Jackson, I said *no candy*." She grabbed a bag of Twizzlers from his hand.

The baby, who looked to be about a year old, picked up a box of crackers that her mother had wedged into the seat next to her and began chewing on it. "Lily, don't put that in your mouth, it's covered in germs." The mother tugged the box out of the baby's hand. Lily's little eyes widened in surprise, and then she opened her mouth and let out a piercing wail.

"Okay, okay. Never mind. Here you go." The mother handed the box to her child, and the girl quieted down and went back to gumming on one corner. Simon tossed another orange over the side of the cart.

Quinn picked it up and held it out to the mother. The woman sighed deeply, taking the orange as her gaze slid to Quinn's. "Sorry."

"No problem." Quinn gave her a sympathetic smile. "You look like you have your hands full."

"You could say that." The mother snatched another package of candy from Jackson's hand. "Any chance you want to take one off my hands?" she said, with a laugh. "I'll sell them for cheap. In fact, I'll pay *you* to take them."

Quinn forced a smile. "I really wish I could." She tried for the woman's joking tone but couldn't quite mask the wobble in her voice. The back of her throat began to ache. "Excuse me." Quinn turned abruptly and took off down the aisle. She didn't stop until she was all the way across the store in the feminine hygiene section.

The only other customer in the aisle was a college-aged girl comparing boxes of tampons. Quinn let out a relieved sigh to be away from all the children, and leaned on a shelf for support. The woman back there was only joking. Quinn was sure a mother like that loved her kids, and she had to admire how the woman had managed to juggle all of that and still keep her sense of humor. But she had no idea how lucky she was. Quinn would've given anything to be chasing oranges around the grocery store with a cart full of kids. To go home to chaos and sticky fingers and laughter instead of a quiet, empty house to wait for James to return from work to have the same conversation about their day they always had, staring at the same spot at the table where a child should have been.

Even though she knew parenting wasn't easy, Quinn vowed that she'd never be one of those tired, stressed-out mothers snapping at her kids and joking about giving them to strangers in the grocery store. The ones who always looked like they wished they could be somewhere else. If given the chance, Quinn would cherish every moment with Emily.

Her phone buzzed, and she fished it out of her bag to find Helena's name lighting up the screen. "I have news," Helena said, as soon as Quinn swiped to answer.

Quinn appreciated that they'd hired an attorney who got right to the point. She had no interest in chit-chatting; she only wanted to know when she could see Emily again.

"As I mentioned previously, I made a motion for a regular visitation schedule with Emily until a permanent custody agreement can be reached. The judge scheduled a hearing for next week."

Quinn gripped the phone tightly in her suddenly sweaty palm. "Oh," she said, breathlessly. "We have to go in front of the judge?" She knew they'd probably have to eventually, but she didn't know it would be so soon. She'd never been in a courtroom in her life. "Will James and I have to go up on the stand? Will they question us?"

"No, nothing like that," Helena reassured her. "Opposing council and I will do all the talking. Their side will argue against visitation and probably try to convince the judge that spending time with you and James would be disruptive and confusing for Emily. And we'll make the argument that you have a right to get to know your biological child."

"And what are the chances you'll win that argument?"

"The rights of biological parents tend to hold a lot of weight in a court room. Unless opposing council can convince the judge that Emily's safety or well-being would be threatened by spending time with you and James, it's likely we'll win this one."

"Of course she'd be safe with us. We would never hurt her."

"We have nothing to worry about," Helena assured her.

"How much time will we ask for? How often will we get to see her?"

"Obviously, we'd love to get you as much access as possible. An evening during the week, plus a day on the weekend if we can. But a lot depends on Emily's schedule. The judge won't want to disrupt her regular routine."

"That would be wonderful. The library closes at five, and

we have a weekend librarian except when I have special events. So, I can be flexible."

"And James?"

James's availability was a bit more of an unknown. He traveled for work a lot and had had quite a few late nights recently. But surely, he'd make visits with Emily a priority. "James will be fine with whatever is decided."

"Wonderful." Helena promised to email over some more information about the hearing, and hung up.

Quinn made her way to the front of the store to pay for her groceries. The woman with the baby and twins waited for her turn at one end of the checkout area, so Quinn veered to the other side of the store. She lined up behind a younger woman and older man, neither of whom seemed to be there with kids. The older man paid for his groceries, and then the younger woman stepped forward so the cashier could ring up and bag her items. Quinn finished unloading her cart onto the belt, and looked up just as the younger woman turned to slide her credit card through the machine. Quinn sucked in a breath.

Strapped to the woman's chest was a tiny baby no more than two or three weeks old. Its fuzzy little head peeked out from the top of the carrier, and one tiny hand slid out the side, clutching a fistful of its mother's shirt. Quinn stared at the baby as its eyes fluttered shut and mouth twitched like it was sucking on an imaginary bottle of milk.

Her heart crumpled. She'd never have what that woman in front of her had. Never carry a tiny baby on her chest, never feel her warm breath against her neck or tiny hand holding onto her. Her chance had been stolen the moment that Emily's embryo was given to Nora. And now Emily was almost four years old. Her baby years were gone, and Quinn would never get them back. And instead of having a chance to make up for all that time she'd lost, Quinn was fighting for the right just to *see* Emily. Fighting for a few supervised hours a week in an attorney's conference room, like she was some sort of criminal or abuser who couldn't be trusted with her own child.

The cashier, an older woman with graying hair and a button with her name pinned to her sweater cooed at the baby. "Ohhhh, look at you. What a little darling."

The baby's mother gave a tired smile. "Thanks."

The cashier ripped a receipt from the register and handed it to the baby's mother. "Enjoy every minute. It goes so fast."

The baby's mother winced as she picked up her bags of groceries. Probably sore from having just pushed out a baby, or maybe she'd had a C-section that was still healing. She didn't look like she was enjoying any moment at all as she turned and shuffled toward the exit.

The cashier turned to Quinn. "I remember those days like it was yesterday. Mine are all out of the house now. My youngest is in college, the oldest just got married last month."

"That's wonderful." Quinn said. "Congratulations."

"I had four within seven years of each other. Those were the days." The cashier shook her head. "The house is so quiet now. I miss them like crazy."

"I bet you do." Quinn gave her a genuine smile. She usually found it painful to hear women talk about how easy it had been for them to have kids. She and the women on her infertility message board used to commiserate about getting stuck in those conversations. *Four* children! In seven years! But for once, Quinn didn't mind. It was nice to encounter a mother who appreciated what she had. Who cherished the time when her kids were young instead of wishing it away. Quinn was willing to bet the cashier wouldn't have joked about selling her kids to a stranger in the grocery store.

The cashier picked up a can of beans and ran it through the scanner. "Do you have any kids?"

"No," Quinn said. It was an automatic response she'd been saying to prying older ladies in the grocery store or at work for the past decade and a half. But then she pictured Emily's shining eyes and bouncing curls and smiled. *I am a mother. I do have a child.* But she couldn't quite bring herself to say that, for fear that she would jinx it. She finally settled on, "Well... not quite yet."

"You married?"

"Yes."

"Well, what are you waiting for?"

Quinn blinked. It shouldn't have surprised her. People always seemed to want to give women advice about their reproductive choices. As far as she knew, nobody had interrogated James about why he hadn't fathered any children yet. But then, *his* biological clock wasn't about to tick down to zero.

"I—"

The cashier cut her off. "So many women put off having kids these days." She weighed a bag of grapes. "You're all so busy focusing on your careers, you think you'll be able to get pregnant forever."

The air whooshed from Quinn's lungs, taking all of her kind thoughts about the cashier right along with it. She should have known better than to engage in this conversation. The women on her infertility message board would shake their heads if they knew. *What were you thinking?* Some women had no concept of the fact that not everyone could decide to have a baby and it would just happen. Multiple times.

"Things start to get old in there, if you know what I mean." The cashier looked at her sideways, shaking her head with judgement masked in friendly advice. The woman waved a hand at the general direction of Quinn's abdomen. "You'd better start trying, or you're going to miss your chance."

Quinn blinked back tears as a cavern opened up inside her, as hollow and empty as the contents of her womb. *I've been trying. I've been trying so hard.* People had no idea the pain of it, the heartbreak. It wasn't only the failed cycles and negative pregnancy tests. It was the comments that implied she hadn't prioritized the right things, the assumptions that if she didn't have kids, it was her own fault. It was people judging her, thinking they knew best, acting superior simply because they'd won the fertility lottery.

All you had to do was have sex, Quinn wanted to shout. *How hard is that?*

But as James had bitterly reminded her in the heat of their fight, it *was* hard. She'd made it hard by turning sex into an obligation. A chore. James had clearly dreaded it and, for months, maybe years, his heart hadn't been in it. So, she'd failed at that too.

At that moment, the woman from the candy aisle walked into her line of vision, slightly blurred through Quinn's unshed tears. As the woman pushed the grocery cart with one arm, she balanced the baby on her hip with the other. The twins wiggled around, and as she walked past, Quinn could hear her scolding them to sit down and leave the bags alone. "God," the woman muttered to herself, shaking her head. "As soon as your father gets home from work, I'm pouring myself a glass of wine and hiding out in the bathtub."

With that, Quinn's tears spilled over. It was all too much. Her shoulders shook, and a sob escaped. And then another one. The grocery belt whirred as her milk and vegetables rolled toward the bagging area, but Quinn stood frozen there, crying openly now.

Several people in the next checkout line turned to stare, but Quinn didn't care. She couldn't have stopped even if she tried.

"Is she okay?" another store employee called over from his register.

Quinn's cashier lifted her hands in a helpless gesture. "We were chatting, and then all of a sudden..." She waved a hand at Quinn. "I don't know what happened. You okay, honey?"

Quinn swiped at her eyes with the back of her hand. Of course the cashier had no idea the pain her words had caused.

She shook her head. Her child had been taken from her, and she'd been robbed of four years. Four years. *But please, tell me how I've been too focused on my career.* A wave of hopelessness crashed over her, and another sob escaped. Through her tears, Quinn groped for her purse in the bottom of her shopping cart. Her hand closed over the strap, and she yanked it onto her shoulder. Leaving the groceries on the belt and the cashier gaping at her, Quinn turned and walked out of the store.

10

The courtroom was colder than Quinn had expected. She'd worn her most conservative dress, cap-sleeved with navy and white stripes—*no bird or cat prints today*—but with the eighty-degree temperatures outside, she hadn't thought to bring a matching cardigan. Quinn crossed her arms over her chest, rubbing her hands across the goose-bumped skin on her shoulders. Some of this was just nerves. As soon as she and James had parked the car in a downtown garage and crossed the street to the family court building, Quinn's adrenaline had begun buzzing like she'd chugged a triple shot of espresso on the drive over.

It hadn't helped that the Allegheny County Courthouse looked like something out of *Game of Thrones* with its antique stone walls, rounded archways, and circular turret at one end. Quinn remembered reading that many downtown government buildings had been built in this medieval style, and she imagined the architect intended to command respect from anyone who entered through the mahogany doors into the stately, echoing vestibule on their way to their hearing.

At least the actual room where family court hearings took

place had the design of a more modern—if somewhat generic—government building. Unflattering fluorescent lights hummed overhead as Quinn sat with James and Helena behind a basic wooden office table, waiting for the hearing to begin. But she couldn't help but stare at the bench looming in the front of the room, complete with a gavel and some sort of Latin seal on the wall. At any moment, the judge would come out from the side door and decide her fate. The fate of her family.

Quinn took a calming breath and remembered that this wasn't a hearing for custody of Emily. That would come later. Today, they'd be petitioning for visitation rights, and Helena had been confident that the judge would rule in their favor.

Quinn dragged her gaze away from the bench and snuck a peek at Nora sitting with her attorney at the next table over, just across a narrow aisle. After agonizing over what to wear that day, Quinn had obviously chosen correctly, because Nora's outfit—a navy dress with a white and navy striped belt—was so similar to Quinn's that it was almost as if they'd called each other to plan what they were going to wear.

Nora remembered her cardigan, though. Quinn gave an immature huff. She couldn't help feeling that she and Nora were locked in a silent competition where every part of them would be judged, and the prize at the end was Emily. Nora already had a leg-up, having spent the past four years with the child. But Helena had said judges considered biology as a major factor in their decision-making. So, it was impossible to know which way the judge would lean.

In the meantime, Quinn was determined to outshine Nora in ways that she could control; with her calm demeanor in the courtroom, the right conservative clothes, her job as a children's librarian. Helena had said Nora worked as an accountant for a local health conglomerate. It wasn't exactly a profession that screamed *I love children.* Quinn, on the other hand, had a knack for making a connection with pretty much any kid that came

through the library, even the shy ones. That had to mean something to the judge.

On some level, Quinn knew that making these kinds of
comparisons between her and Nora wasn't rational. The judge
probably didn't care what kind of work they did, as long as they
could keep Emily fed and put a roof over her head.

But these details were all Quinn had to hold on to. If she
spent an afternoon trying on every outfit in her closet to find the
perfect thing for the hearing today, that was one afternoon
when she didn't have to think about what she'd do if they lost.

Quinn wished that James had made a little bit more of an
effort, too. She sighed in frustration, remembering the argument
they'd had when he'd come downstairs that morning in a pair of
khakis and a pale blue button-up shirt. He'd looked perfectly
appropriate for an ordinary day as a sales manager at a tech
company. But this wasn't an ordinary day.

"I thought you agreed you were going to wear a suit." Quinn
had set the spatula she'd been using to stir the eggs onto the
counter.

"All my suits are at the dry-cleaners." James had shrugged,
unconcerned, as he worked the button on the cuff of his shirt.

"But..." Quinn had sputtered in disbelief. "We talked about
this a week ago! I offered to pick up your suits, and you said
you'd do it."

"I forgot, okay?" James had turned away to grab a mug from
the cabinet and pour himself a cup of coffee. "I had a lot on my
mind, and I forgot to pick up my goddamn suits."

Quinn had sucked in a breath. What could he possibly have
on his mind? The stakes couldn't be higher for this hearing. If
they weren't granted visitation rights—a chance to spend time
with Emily—how would they ever get custody of her? Yet James
couldn't even be counted on to pick up a suit.

James had scrubbed a hand through his hair, making it stand
on end, and Quinn had hesitated. For the first time she'd

noticed the dark circles under his eyes, the fine lines around his mouth. Quinn's heart had tugged. Maybe their struggle over infertility had been harder on James than she'd thought. She'd been so wrapped up in her own pain, maybe she'd missed how it was affecting him. After all, he'd shouldered the worries over how to pay for treatments. And although he hadn't had to go through all the needles and procedures, he'd held her hand, at least in the beginning, and put on a good face to keep her spirits up. It must have worn on him more than she'd realized.

"Never mind about the suit," Quinn had said.

Now that they were in the courtroom, Quinn had to admit that the suit didn't really matter anyway. The judge would never even notice it from all the way up there on the bench. *Or,* she realized with a stab of panic as James's phone buzzed, *if he's not in the room at all.*

Instead of muting it and shoving it back into his pocket, he pulled it out and checked to see who was calling. Quinn tried to get a look over his shoulder, but he stood up quickly, swiping to answer as he headed down the aisle toward the back of the courtroom.

"*James,*" Quinn hissed, her gaze swinging wildly from her husband to the door where the judge was supposed to appear any minute, and then back to James. "We're about to start."

But he simply held up a finger—*I'll only be a minute*—and kept walking out the door.

Quinn turned back around in her seat, sneaking a look at Helena who was watching her with an inscrutable expression on her face. Quinn forced a smile. "He'll be right back."

Helena gave a nod and went back to the leather-bound notepad in front of her. Quinn shifted in her seat and glanced back at the door where James had disappeared. *Where is he?* She pulled out her phone and sent him a text under the table. *Where are you? You need to come back NOW.*

At that moment, the mood in the courtroom shifted. Nora

and her attorney, who'd been murmuring to each other, went silent. Quinn looked up from her phone as the side door behind the bench opened up, and a man in a black policeman-like uniform came through it. Quinn had watched enough TV law dramas to guess he was the bailiff whose job it was to stand guard over the proceedings. The bailiff was swiftly followed by a tall, imposing woman in a long black robe. Quinn followed Helena's lead and stood as the judge made her way to her seat.

Helena had said that Judge Guerrero was known to be fair and reasonable, but all Quinn could see was the set of her jaw and frown lines between her eyes. Her gray hair was cut into a short, severe bob, and she wore a pair of reading glasses perched on her nose. This woman looked like she'd seen it all, and certainly wasn't about to allow any nonsense in her courtroom. Quinn's heart began to pound. *Oh my God, where is James?* If they started off on the wrong foot with the judge, how would their case recover from that? And if he was having second thoughts about fighting for Emily again, how would their relationship recover?

Quinn looked over her shoulder and breathed a sigh of relief as James slipped back through the door of the courtroom. Thankfully, everyone was still standing while the judge was settling into her seat, and nobody seemed to notice as James slid into place next to Quinn. She shot him an irritated look, but quickly smoothed her face into a neutral expression as Judge Guerrero's gaze slid from Nora's table to theirs.

Someone in the back of the room cleared their throat, and a pen scraped on a pad of paper, but otherwise the room was silent. Judge Guerrero flipped through a pile of bound papers, giving a vague nod every now and then. Finally, she looked up.

"I've read the plaintiff's petition requesting visitation with the minor child, Emily Robinson, pending the custody hearing scheduled for August the twelfth." Judge Guerrero's voice reverberated across the courtroom. "Genetic tests have been administered, and it has been established that the plaintiffs in the case, James and Quinn Marcello—" She glanced over at their table, and Quinn sat up straighter in her chair. "—are the genetic parents of the child. Whereas, Nora Robinson—" Across the aisle, Nora's shoulders tensed. "—is the gestational mother who has raised the child for approximately the past four years. Is that correct?"

"Yes, Your Honor." Helena answered for everyone.

"And this custody dispute is the result of a mix-up at an infertility clinic, in which the embryo of Mr. and Mrs. Marcello, the genetic parents, was inadvertently transferred to Ms. Robinson, who later gave birth to the child."

"Correct, Your Honor." Nora's attorney responded.

Quinn studied Judge Guerrero, searching for any sign of her opinion. Would the judge take Nora's side because she'd been the one to raise Emily? Or did she sympathize with Quinn and James who'd lost their chance due to a terrible mix-up? The judge kept her voice neutral, carefully measured, and it was impossible to know what she was thinking.

"And now the genetic parents are seeking custody of the child," the judge continued.

"That's correct." It was Helena's turn again. "The embryo was transferred to Ms. Robinson without my clients' knowledge or consent. Their intent to parent the child has been well established. We'd like to submit for the record an affidavit from the plaintiffs' fertility doctor who can attest to the fact that Mr. and Mrs. Marcello underwent almost five years of fertility treatments with the design of parenting any offspring that were a result of said treatments."

Helena held out a document, and Judge Guerrero nodded at the bailiff to retrieve it. He crossed the courtroom, took the paper from Helena, and handed it over. As the judge peered down at the document through the glasses perched on the end of her nose, Quinn shifted in her seat. She wished she'd thought to ask Helena if she knew anything about Judge Guerrero's personal life. Was she married? Did she have children? Judging from her gray hair, she could be a grandmother by now.

Quinn tried to calculate whether it would be better or worse for their case if Judge Guerrero was a mother. It probably didn't do any good to speculate, but she couldn't help herself.

Judge Guerrero handed the document back to the bailiff. "Please enter this into evidence."

"Your Honor," Helena continued. "My clients were not only denied the opportunity to give birth to their biological child, but to nurture her and raise her for the past four years. We're asking that they be given the opportunity to get to know her now. That they not be robbed of any more time now that this grave error has come to light."

The judge's gaze swept across Quinn and James. Quinn sat up straight in her chair and met the judge's eyes. *Please.* Quinn pleaded silently. *Please let me see my child. Don't make us miss any more time with her.* And to her horror, Quinn's eyes filled with tears.

Oh God, not now.

Quinn quickly fished a tissue from the side pocket of her purse and swiped at her eyes with it. Would it anger the judge if she started crying? If she expected decorum in her courtroom, she probably wouldn't tolerate outbursts of emotion. But when Quinn peeked up at the bench, Judge Guerrero was watching her with an expression of... could it be compassion? The hard lines on the judge's face had softened, and she gave Quinn a hint of a reassuring smile.

"I'm inclined to grant the plaintiffs' request," Judge Guerrero said, picking up a pen and making a note.

Quinn's gaze swung to Helena as if to ask, *We're the plaintiffs, right?* Helena gave her a reassuring nod. Quinn's shoulders relaxed, and she blew out the breath she'd been holding.

Judge Guerrero turned to Helena. "I see here that you've requested bi-weekly visits?"

"Your Honor," Nora's attorney cut in, "Emily Robinson attends preschool on Monday through Friday, and she participates in a number of activities after school, including swimming lessons and gymnastics. She looks forward to both of these activities, and they're beneficial to her health and safety."

"What is your point?"

"Adding a weekday visit to her schedule, especially with two people who are virtually strangers to her would not only be disruptive but exhausting. We believe that this would not be in Emily's best interest."

Judge Guerrero peered over her glasses at Nora's attorney. "What does council recommend would be in the child's best interest?"

"Well, as I mentioned previously, Quinn and James Marcello are virtual strangers to Emily. While they may have a genetic link to the child, they have no other connection with her, and we believe it would be confusing for Emily to suddenly be required to spend time with—"

Helena slapped a hand on the table, cutting off the other attorney. "This is precisely why we're asking for visitation rights. My clients deserve the chance to get to know their genetic child."

Yes! Quinn nodded in agreement, making a mental note to send a bottle of wine to James's colleague who had recommended Helena to them.

The judge raised an eyebrow at Nora's attorney. "Less than a minute ago, you heard me grant visitation rights to the plaintiffs. Therefore, I'm quite sure you're not suggesting that I walk that back, are you?"

"No," Nora's attorney quickly jumped in. "No, of course not. However, we request that you limit visits to only one day a week, on weekends."

Judge Guerrero glanced through her stack of papers again. "Visits will be Saturday afternoons for three hours."

Quinn grabbed James's hand and gave it a squeeze. Three hours a week with Emily. It wasn't quite as much time as she'd hoped, but she'd take what she could get for now. And maybe soon, they'd be seeing Emily more. A lot more. Twenty-four hours a day, seven days a week more.

Nora's attorney cleared her throat. "We would like to request that Ms. Robinson or another family member be present for these visits. Emily is not quite four yet, and it will be incredibly upsetting for her to go alone with complete strangers." The scathing glance the attorney shot at Quinn and James implied they were criminals and child molesters. "Especially when we know nothing about their backgrounds or ability to care for a child."

Quinn flushed with indignation. Nobody would question their ability to care for Emily if they'd been allowed to give birth to her. Besides, she was a children's librarian. They wouldn't allow her to do that job is she had a record of harming children.

Judge Guerrero focused her gaze on Quinn and James. "The plaintiffs will submit criminal background reports and child abuse clearances to the court. In addition, I'm ordering a home visit be conducted by a court-appointed social worker within the next sixty days. In the meantime, visitation with the child will be supervised by the gestational mother or another suitable family member."

Then her glance slid to Nora, and her eyebrows raised. "I'm aware of your... emotional reaction at Emily's first meeting with Mr. and Mrs. Marcello. While understandable, you must make sure it doesn't happen again."

"Of course, Your Honor," Nora whispered.

"Good. Visits between the plaintiffs and the child will begin this Saturday."

Across the aisle, Nora grabbed her attorney's arm, and the

two began a whispered exchange. Quinn shot a questioning glance at Helena, who shrugged.

"Is there a problem?" Judge Guerrero asked.

Nora's attorney cleared her throat. "This Saturday is Emily's fourth birthday party. Friends and family were invited weeks ago, and it's all Emily has been able to talk about."

"Well," the judge said, gathering up her papers. "It sounds like Mr. and Mrs. Marcello will be attending a birthday party this Saturday. Thank you, council. That will be all." And with that, she stood up.

"All rise," the bailiff called across the court room.

Quinn jumped to her feet, and as soon as the judge disappeared behind the side door, she grabbed Helena in a hug. "We did it!"

Helena patted her awkwardly on the back. "We couldn't have expected better. It's great news, and I was encouraged to see the judge was sympathetic to your situation."

James held out his hand. "Thank you, Helena. You did a fantastic job."

Quinn smiled at James. She was still upset about his disappearance earlier. How could she not be? But this wasn't the time to bring it up. She could talk to James tomorrow, ask him to be more mindful, to be present, for Emily's sake. But today was a major victory, and now they had something to celebrate.

As they made their way to the door, Quinn glanced at the table across the aisle. Nora sat alone, her face pale and her head bent over her hands. She looked so forlorn that for a moment, Quinn was tempted to sit down and reassure her that everything would be okay. But what could she say that would be any consolation at all? Their goals were entirely at odds. If Nora won custody of Emily, it meant Quinn and James lost. And if Quinn and James won, well...

Heart aching, Quinn watched Nora swipe at her eyes with

the palm of her hand, and doubts crept in. Was it right what they were doing? Fighting for Emily like this?

Helena's voice cut into her thoughts. "If you could come with me, Quinn, I have some paperwork for you and James to look at."

Quinn spun to face the attorney, and forced a smile on her face. "Great. I'm right behind you."

If they didn't fight for custody of Emily, they'd have absolutely no access to her. Nora had made that clear when she'd refused to even discuss some sort of shared custody agreement with them. And now, her attorneys were arguing about three measly hours a week. If Nora believed that denying Emily access to her biological parents was a good idea, it was better that she and James stepped in.

With that thought, Quinn headed up the aisle toward the door without a backward glance.

11

Nora's home couldn't have been more charming. Considering its location in one of the more upscale suburbs near the city, the house wasn't especially large. But it had an expansive front yard populated with flower beds and mature trees, a stone path leading to a small portico over the door, and dormer windows that gave the effect of a small country cottage.

Quinn sat in her car and gazed down the street to the cul-de-sac where a group of children were riding their bikes. *Nora sure had picked an idyllic setting to raise Emily.* When Quinn had steered her car into the neighborhood a few minutes earlier, she'd even passed a brick elementary school with a playground and baseball diamond.

Quinn couldn't help but compare Nora's home to where she and James lived in the city. Highland Park was a sought-after neighborhood, centrally located, with beautiful old Victorian houses and a reservoir with walking trails and a playground. But their house was a row home with neighbors on both sides, and their yard was no more than a postage stamp in the back of the house. City schools were chronically under-funded, and pedestrians had to watch for traffic even on the side roads, so smaller children couldn't roam without parent supervision.

None of the problems of the city had ever bothered Quinn before. She loved having the ability walk to cafés and shops instead driving everywhere. There were museums, libraries, and universities to explore. And diversity. People from all walks of life gravitated to the city.

But that competitive feeling reared up again. Did Nora have the better home for a child? Would the judge care if Quinn and James didn't live on a quiet street that was perfect for children to bike and play with the neighbors?

Quinn turned off the engine, grabbed Emily's gift from the passenger's seat, and climbed out. It was useless to get bogged down in these kind comparisons. Short of putting their house on the market, there was nothing she could do about where they lived. And Nora's suburban life might look like Pleasantville, but that didn't make it any better than hers. Quinn wasn't going to let her insecurities ruin this special day.

But as Quinn followed the sounds of laughter drifting over the six-foot wooden fence that cordoned off the back yard, her nerves bubbled to the surface again. She slipped through the gate and hesitated, taking in the scene. If a more stereotypical kid's birthday party existed, Quinn couldn't imagine it. Bouquets of helium balloons bobbed around the yard, their long ribbons tied to the ends of picnic tables covered in brightly colored cloth. A separate table held an impressive spread of finger foods and a cake in the shape of a unicorn. On another table, a tower of presents waited for Emily to dive into them.

Quinn had pictured a small gathering, maybe four or five children from Emily's preschool playing games and eating cake. But Nora had invited an entire crowd—at least forty party guests of all ages were scattered around the yard. The adults sat in small groups of lawn chairs, chatting while they nibbled on hors d'oeuvres and drank bottles of beer or cups of lemonade.

Across the yard, a gaggle of children of varying ages blew bubbles, chased balls, and took turns swinging a stick at a piñata. In the center of it all, a man in a striped suit with a colander on his head juggled bowling pins and balanced a spinning plate on his nose.

Quinn hovered at the edges of the party, desperately wishing James had been able to come today. But he was traveling for work and his flight to Miami had left that morning. Quinn couldn't believe that James was missing Emily's birthday party, and they'd fought about it on the drive to the airport.

Can't you change your flight and go tomorrow? This is important.

I have meetings with clients tomorrow. That's important, too.

You're golfing with clients tomorrow. It's not the same thing.

Quinn sighed. It seemed like everything was an argument lately. James was so distracted, always on his phone when he wasn't working late. After talking him down from his hesitation a few weeks ago, she'd thought he was 100 percent committed to Emily and their family. But although he'd insisted that he was all-in, he wasn't making as much of an effort as she was. Quinn couldn't help feeling like he'd abandoned her, especially now that she was on her own surrounded by dozens of Nora's family and friends.

She had no idea what Nora had told everyone at the party about their situation. Would they know that Quinn was Emily's biological mother? Or that she was trying to get custody of Emily? Getting the story straight hadn't mattered much when she'd thought the party would be a group of four-year-olds. But what was she supposed to say to all these people? Would they be staring at her? Sizing her up?

She crept forward, scanning the crowd for Emily. When she spotted the little girl sitting on a bench in a bright pink tutu,

Quinn's mouth curved into smile. This was why she was at the party. No one else mattered.

"Happy birthday, Emily," Quinn said as she approached. Emily looked up from her juice box and blinked, a blank look on her face. *She doesn't recognize me.* "We met last week," Quinn prompted. "I'm Bruno's friend?"

Emily's face lit up. "I remember you!" She hopped to her feet, deposited the sticky juice box on the bench, and ran into the house. Before Quinn could wonder what had happened, Emily emerged a moment later with Bruno. Quinn's heart squeezed at the sight of the little girl running across the yard, waving Quinn's childhood bear. And then she noticed that Emily had wrapped a small scrap of tulle around Bruno's stomach and secured it with a safety pin so it flared out in a similar fashion as her own tutu. "Bruno wanted to come the party, too."

"Hi, Bruno!" Quinn reached out to touch the tulle. "I love your dress. I wish I'd known everyone was in tutus. I would have worn mine, too."

Emily giggled. "You have a tutu?"

"Of course. Doesn't everyone?"

"Mommy doesn't."

"Mommy doesn't what?" a voice said from behind her.

Quinn turned around to find Nora approaching with a paper plate in her hand.

"Oh," Nora said when she spotted Quinn, "I didn't realize you were here yet."

"I just arrived."

"Well... welcome, I guess." Nora's tone implied Quinn was decidedly unwelcome.

"Thank you," Quinn said with false cheer, determined to ignore Nora's lack of manners for Emily's sake. "I was just about to find you to say hello," she lied.

"Well, no need to now." Nora glanced around the party and then focused back on Quinn. "Where's James?"

"He..." What would James' absence say to Nora? "He hated to miss it, but he had a work trip." Would Nora mention to her attorneys that James had bowed out of the party, not to mention their very first Saturday visit? "He wanted me to send his love to Emily and tell her he can't wait to see her next week."

"Right. Well..." Nora shrugged, and then turned to take Emily's hand. "Em, come with Mommy. I made you a plate. You need to eat a little something."

"I don't want to eat." Emily tried to tug her hand away. "I want to go play."

"You can play after you've had a few bites. If you don't eat, your tummy will hurt."

"I'll eat later," Emily whined, gazing across the yard at the kids blowing bubbles.

"Emily..." Nora said in that voice that Quinn had heard mothers use a thousand times at the library. The one that said *I'm not arguing about this.*

"I don't *want* to."

"Hey, Emily," Quinn jumped in. "I noticed Bruno looks hungry. Maybe you could share your carrots with him? I don't think he's ever had carrots before."

"He hasn't?"

"Nope. Could you show him how to eat a carrot?"

Emily lifted a baby carrot from the plate Nora was holding. "Here, Bruno. You just bite it like this." She chomped into it with an extra loud crunch. Then she held the end to Bruno's mouth. "Now you try."

"Oh, I think he likes it," said Quinn, encouraged. "Maybe he wants to try a piece of cheese too?"

"Bruno, do you want cheese?" Emily took the plate from Nora's hand and settled onto the bench a few feet away. She ate a bite of cheese and offered the other half to the stuffed bear, then did the same with a strawberry.

Quinn looked away from Emily to find Nora glaring at her. What was her problem? She'd wanted Emily to eat. Well, Quinn had gotten her to eat.

"I don't need your help." Nora crossed her arms over her chest.

It kind of looks like you do. But Quinn couldn't say that, as much as she wanted to. She didn't want to ruin Emily's birthday party by picking a fight. And it probably wouldn't go over well with the judge either. So, instead, she forced a pleasant smile. "Well, thanks for having me at the party."

"It's not like I had a choice," Nora muttered under her breath. She shot a glance at Emily, who was chattering at her stuffed bear while she nibbled on her snack. Then Nora shuffled a few feet away and waved at Quinn to follow. "You know you're only here because the judge ordered it," Nora said in a low voice, leaning in so Emily wouldn't overhear. "Don't start thinking you're welcome."

Quinn blinked. She'd expected Nora to at least be civil. "Look, I'm not any happier about this situation than you are."

"Aren't you?"

"What is that supposed to mean?"

"It means an opportunity just fell in your lap when you found out about Emily, didn't it? IVF didn't work out, but, lucky for you, there's suddenly a child that you can lay claim to."

Quinn was reeling. Was Nora really doing this now, in the middle of her daughter's birthday party? "*Lucky?*" Quinn hissed. "You think this situation makes me feel lucky? Emily isn't some random child I'm trying to move in on. She's my biological child."

"But that's all she is to you. You don't know her. You don't know her favorite book, or what she likes to eat, or how she likes to be tucked in at night." Nora's voice cracked, and she took a deep breath. "You haven't been there when she was hurt, or cried, or called for her mother. *I was there.*"

Quinn's chest tightened. She would have given *anything* to be the one Emily relied on these past four years. "I didn't have a choice to be there."

"Well, I am sorry for that. But it's too late now—you can't just show up four years later and expect to be her mother. She has a mother."

Quinn couldn't believe the unfairness of this conversation. Did Nora really believe that Quinn had no claim whatsoever to Emily? "What would you do if she were your biological child?"

Nora's eyes skated past Quinn and landed on Emily. She hesitated for a moment, and then finally said, "I'd walk away. For her sake."

Quinn shook her head. "I don't believe it for a second—"

Before she could say anything else, Quinn was interrupted by a gray-haired woman approaching. "Nora, how are you dear?"

"Aunt Susan," Nora said, her irate expression rapidly morphing into a pleasant smile. "It's so nice to see you."

Nora didn't introduce her to the older woman, so Quinn hovered there awkwardly until Aunt Susan noticed her standing there. "Hello, I'm Nora's aunt, Susan."

"Quinn Marcello." Quinn held out her hand to shake the older woman's, but didn't give any further explanation. She was at a loss for what to say.

"And how are you two acquainted?"

"Um." Quinn looked to Nora.

"Old friends," Nora chimed in, with a too-wide smile.

"Oh, how nice that you could come." Aunt Susan turned back to Nora. "Would you mind terribly if I stole Emily away? Uncle Wesley has been practicing his magic tricks again, and he's dying to pull a coin out of her ear." Aunt Susan rolled her eyes with an indulgent smile, like she'd been watching Uncle Wesley pull coins out of children's ears for forty years.

"No, of course not." Did Nora seem a bit too eager to send Emily off with someone who wasn't Quinn? "Emily, come here, sweetie. Aunt Susan wants to take you to say hi to Uncle Wesley."

Emily abandoned her plate on the bench and ran over.

"Oh, look at you in this dress." Aunt Susan reached out to smooth an imaginary wrinkle on Emily's shoulder. "Could you be cuter?"

"Thank you," Emily said, giving a princess curtsey, and then holding Bruno up so he could curtsey, too.

Aunt Susan smiled at Nora. "She's really taken to that old bear, hasn't she? What happened to the other one—what was its name? Marigold?"

"Mirabel." Nora waved a dismissive hand. "Kids are fickle with their toys. She'll be in love with Mirabel again by next week."

"No." Emily shook her head. "I love Bruno."

Quinn's chest swelled with happiness. Nora was probably right—kids were fickle. But it had to mean something that Emily had formed an attachment to *her* bear.

Aunt Susan shook her head. "Nora, we were absolutely thrilled when you changed your mind and decided to throw a big family affair for Emily's birthday. She can have small parties with her friends when she's older."

"Y-yes—" Nora stammered, shooting a glance at Quinn. "That's what I was thinking, too."

"I'm amazed that you were able to put this all together in a little over a week." She gave Quinn a wide grin. "And even your old friends could come."

Quinn gave her a weak smile in return, but inside, she was reeling. *A little over a week?* Nora had planned this massive party *after* their hearing about visitation? And after the judge had said that this afternoon was supposed to be Quinn's time with Emily? Nora had insisted that the party had been planned for weeks, and the judge had gone along with it.

Had Nora brought in her huge family to intimidate Quinn? Or maybe she thought the bigger the party, the less time Quinn would get with Emily? It certainly seemed like Nora's plan was working. Quinn grew hot with anger. The judge had told Nora not to interfere. But what could Quinn do about it? The timing of the party was suspicious, but it wasn't like she could prove anything.

"Even your cousin Troy is here." Aunt Susan waved a hand into the crowd. "I'm surprised he made it. He's unemployed again, you know."

Nora nodded. "I heard."

"He's been staying in our garage apartment. How could we turn him away? And your uncle has been trying to get him a job as a caddy at the country club. But who knows if it will stick?" She shook her head, silver bob swinging. "Oh, well. Come on, Emily. Uncle Wesley has been practicing his magic tricks, just for you." She took the girl's hand and shuffled off to find Uncle Wesley.

Nora busied herself with cleaning Emily's plate of half-eaten vegetables and cheese off the bench. "Please excuse me. I'll need to get back to my guests." With that, she turned and walked away, leaving Quinn standing there alone.

12

Quinn found a drink in a cooler and settled into a lawn chair on the deck, apart from the rest of the guests. For about the hundredth time, she wished James was there. Quinn had always been a bit shy when it came to social gatherings where she didn't know anyone. She wasn't someone who could just walk up to a group and introduce herself, especially now, when she didn't know what to tell them about who she was or how she was connected to Emily. James was the sales guy, the one who could talk to everyone—he'd have known how to navigate this party.

But James had decided to go golfing in Florida rather than spend time with his child. What did that say about him as a parent?

Quinn mentally shook herself. James was working to close a deal. He was doing it for their family.

Across the yard, she spotted Emily with an older man waving a large gold coin. Well, that could only be Uncle Wesley. Quinn wondered if the younger guy next to him was the unemployed cousin, Troy. There were so many family members there, she didn't know how Nora kept track of them all.

Emily clearly loved the magic tricks, jumping up and down each time Uncle Wesley produced the coin from behind her ear. When he'd exhausted his tricks, Nora seemed to appear out of nowhere to take Emily's hand and coax her over to the next group of family and friends. Quinn sipped her seltzer water and waited for an opening where she might get another moment or two with her daughter, but it seemed that every time Emily finished with one group, Nora swooped in to occupy her with the next one. Quinn didn't know if it was deliberate, or if there really were that many people in this family who were dying to give Emily hugs, throw her in the air to make her giggle, and generally dote on her.

Short of following Emily around the party, there wasn't much Quinn could do. If Nora was trying to make her feel left out, or to prove that Emily didn't have any more room in her life for more family members, she was doing a great job of it. Would the judge look into their families and note that James and Quinn's were woefully lacking? James had an aunt who lived in Tennessee, but they only saw her on an occasional holiday, and there wasn't anyone else on his side. And of course, her parents had been only children, and they'd passed away years ago.

Quinn had always wanted children, and her longing had only become stronger after her mom and dad's accident. During all the holidays and birthdays she'd spent tagging along with friends in her twenties and early thirties, she'd imagined her own house full of kids at Christmas, and a Thanksgiving table surrounded by family.

This party only reminded her of how that dream was slipping away.

Quinn was pulled from her thoughts by movement on the other side of the deck. A small, dark-haired boy about five years old had wandered up the stairs holding a Lego figure and making *beep-bop* noises. He rolled his toy along the railing until he got to where Quinn was sitting.

"Hi." Despite her dark thoughts a minute ago, she couldn't help smiling at the boy's sticky-uppy hair and face smudged with chocolate. "Who do you have there?"

"This is my robot, Bot-ster." He spun the figure around on its rubber treads, and it stared back at her with glowing blue eyes. The boy waved one of Bot-ster's mechanical arms at Quinn.

"Did you build that by yourself?"

"Yep!" He drove Bot-ster a few feet down the rail and then back to Quinn. "My dad helped a little."

"Cool, I love robots." Quinn had read at least a dozen children's books on the subject during story hour, and robot crafts were some of her most popular.

"They make robots in Pittsburgh, you know," the boy said, eyes wide with excitement behind his blue glasses that had gone slightly askew. "There's a whole *school* for it." His shoulders drooped a little now. "But you have to be a grown-up."

"Carnegie Mellon, right?" The university was famous for its robotics department.

"My dad says I can go when I'm older."

"I bet you'll invent a really cool robot someday."

The boy smiled up at her with his chocolatey grin, and Quinn's heart pitched a little. "I'm going to invent a robot that cleans the whole house. That way my dad won't have to, and we can go out and play more."

"I would *totally* buy a robot that cleaned my house."

"So you can go out and play more, too?"

"Yes, I'd love to go out and play more." Quinn's smile faded as she gazed out into the crowd of kids running through the yard, chasing balls, and blowing bubbles. She could imagine spending her weekends pushing a small child on the swing or helping her across the monkey bars, and when she got older, throwing a ball or going for hikes in the park.

"You could play robots with me if you want."

Quinn glanced out into the yard where Emily was occupied with yet another relative, and then turned back to the boy. "Sure. I'm Quinn. They call me Miss Quinn at the library where I work."

"I'm Connor." His expression turned serious, and he held out his little hand to shake hers. "It's nice to meet you."

Charmed, Quinn shook his hand in return. "Nice to meet you too." She looked around the deck. "Now, what would Botster like to do today?"

Connor found a bucket of plastic dump trucks and tractors by the back door of the house, and they spilled it on the deck to make an obstacle course for the robot to climb over.

"So, how do you know Emily?" Quinn asked, after they'd spent a few minutes lining up trucks across the wooden floorboards.

"She's my best friend." He placed Bot-ster in the back of a dump truck. "We play every day together."

Quinn was happy to think her daughter had this sweet, earnest boy as her closest friend. And happy that he had Emily, too.

After a few more minutes of obstacle-course building, Quinn heard footsteps tap on the wood behind her. Connor looked over Quinn's shoulder and smiled. She turned to find a man walking up the steps from the yard below and, for a moment, shyness took her over. He had the kind of rugged good looks that were more common in catalogues for outdoor clothing than in real life, and she couldn't imagine what a man like that was doing at a kid's birthday party.

Quinn rolled her eyes at her own ridiculousness. *You're married. Quit admiring this stranger.* But she couldn't seem to help herself. What was the harm in enjoying a beautiful view? Surely James had admired other women on occasion.

She was sure of it, in fact.

Quinn shoved that thought from her mind, her gaze dropping to the camera in the man's hand. It was the professional kind, with all sorts of dials she'd have no idea what to do with, and an oversized lens attached to the front.

Oh, that explains it. Nora had hired a photographer. But then the photographer approached Connor and said, "Hey bud, they just cut the cake. Why don't you clean up here and go and get some?"

With that, Quinn worked out that this stranger was Connor's father, and the realization made her feel less awkward. He was just another parent at the party, and his wife was probably one of the moms handing out plastic forks to the swarm of kids vying for dessert.

Connor quickly dumped the trucks back into the bin. "Thanks for playing, Miss Quinn!"

The man watched Connor run off and then turned his gaze to Quinn. "I'm sorry if he was bothering you."

"Oh, he wasn't bothering me," Quinn said with a smile. "He's a really sweet boy, and I love kids. Playing with them is pretty much my job."

The man tilted his head, and a lock of hair flopped over his tanned forehead. "You're Emily's preschool teacher?"

"Oh—n-no," she stammered. Emily's preschool teacher probably *was* at the party, though. It seemed like Nora had invited every person who'd ever spent a moment with Emily. Quinn wondered if the doctor who'd delivered her was there too. "I'm not a teacher. I'm a children's librarian."

"Ah, got it." He nodded. "Nora and Emily are at the local library every weekend. Emily is a real book lover."

Quinn couldn't help but smile at that. She'd always been a

book lover, too. Maybe Emily had inherited more than Quinn's curly hair and brown eyes.

"But I guess you probably knew that already," the man said with a grin.

Oh. He thinks I know Emily from the library. Quinn worked at the branch in the city, not out there in the suburbs. She really should set the record straight, but then what was she supposed to tell him about why she was there? A conversation like that was too fraught for an afternoon birthday party. And she'd had enough fraught conversations for one day. "Oh, um. Yeah," she finally stammered.

"Well, even if you like kids, you need a break every once in a while. Especially at this party. It's..." He paused as if he were searching for the right words. Finally, he settled on, "It's a lot."

A lot was exactly what it was. Only Quinn was finding it a lot for such different reasons. "I guess this isn't a typical party for the preschool crowd?"

"Not so much. Nora really went all-out on this one." He gazed out at the kids in the yard, and Quinn wondered about the dark expression that flashed across his face. Before she could spend too much time analyzing it, his smile was back in place. "The kids are loving it, though."

"They sure are." Even from all the way over there, Quinn could see that Emily was having the time of her life. The little girl was sitting across from Connor at a picnic table, laughing hysterically at the faces he was making, unconcerned with the pink icing smeared all over her mouth.

The man pulled a camera lens from his back pocket and gestured to the Adirondack chairs. "You want to sit...?"

"Sure," Quinn said, glad to finally have some company.

"I'm Liam, by the way." He held out a hand in a familiar gesture, and Quinn saw where Connor had learned his manners. "Nice to meet you."

"Quinn." She reached out take his palm. "So, how old is Connor?"

"He turned five a couple of weeks ago." Liam sat down across from her.

Quinn gazed out at the yard, wondering which of the women was Connor's mother. But nobody hovered around him the way Nora hovered around Emily.

"So, what kind of birthday party did he have?"

"You just spent ten minutes with Connor." The man lifted an eyebrow. "I bet you can guess."

Quinn pretended to think. "Robot-themed?"

"Exactly." He leaned back into the chair, crossing one leg over the other, and set his camera and lens on the table next to him.

"So, are you always the photographer for birthday parties?"

"I can't seem to help myself." Liam laughed. "Photography is my job. But I should take a break once in a while." He lifted a shoulder. "Somehow, I make it about ten minutes, and then I end up behind my camera again." He picked up his camera and angled it so he could look at the little screen in the back. "I think I got a couple of nice photos of you and Emily from earlier, actually."

Quinn blinked. He'd noticed her earlier? And specifically remembered snapping a photo? But then she shook it off. He'd just said a minute ago that photography was his job, which meant that he'd naturally be more tuned into the party guests than the average parent. And if he'd been walking around photographing everything, then of course she'd ended up in a picture or two.

Liam fiddled with the buttons for a couple of seconds, and then slid his chair closer to Quinn. He held out the camera so she could see the screen with a photograph of her smiling while Emily ran toward her holding up the tutu-clad bear.

"Oh, it's beautiful," Quinn said, her heart squeezing at the image of Emily's joy at sharing her childhood toy.

Liam frowned at the photo. "I think it's a bit too far away."

"No, you're being too critical. I absolutely love it. In fact—" She dug through her purse, looking for a pen and scrap of paper. "Could I give you my email address? I'd love to buy a copy from you. It's nice to have some photos of me with..." She trailed off. "My favorite kids." Of course, he'd think she was talking about kids at the library. But it wasn't like she'd lied. Emily *was* her favorite kid. Just not in the way he thought.

"I'm happy to send it to you, but there's no need to pay me. Birthday party photos are purely for fun."

She scribbled her email address on the back of a receipt and held it out to him. He took it and went back to his camera. "I switched to a longer lens after I took this shot, so I might have a better one. Let me see if I can find it."

While Liam flipped through his photos, Quinn eyed the camera. She was dying to see some baby photos of Emily, to catch up on all she'd missed out on, even if it was just through pictures. Quinn had been hoping to ask Nora about it at the end of their first meeting in Helena's office, but that meeting had ended... rather abruptly. And after their contentious discussion at this party, it looked like Nora was planning to get in her way at every opportunity. It seemed unlikely that she'd agree to hand over anything having to do with Emily.

But if Liam's son was Emily's best friend, maybe Liam would have some photos of Emily and Connor posted on Instagram, or in a portfolio on his website. "Make sure you give me your website address when you email me," Quinn said. "I'd love to check out your other work."

Liam nodded absently, still flipping through his photos. "It'll be in my email signature—oh, here's the other photo." He held out the camera to Quinn and she took it so she could get a better look. What she saw took her breath away. Liam had captured a close-up shot of Quinn crouching down to Emily's height. Their heads were tilted together, the dark curls of their hair almost touching as they gazed down at Bruno with twin smiles on their faces. But more than just their images, Liam had captured their emotions: Emily's unabashed joy, and the love and longing that Quinn thought she'd been doing a good job of hiding until she saw it there in the photo, displayed all over her face.

It was the kind of shot Quinn wanted to frame and hang in her living room. The kind that everyone who walked by would stop and remark at how alike she and Emily looked.

The moment it registered with Quinn, Liam sucked in a breath. Her gaze flew to his as a hurricane blew across his face.

Oh God, he knows.

He slid his chair back away from her as if she'd crack the camera if she came too close. "You're Emily's biological mother." His voice was measured, but a muscle in his jaw twitched.

"I—"

"I thought you were the children's librarian."

"I *am* a children's librarian."

"*Don't pull that.*" Liam raked a hand through his hair and stood up. "You know what I meant. You let me think that you knew Emily from seeing her at the library every week." He paced across the deck, and when he got to the opposite side, he paused there, leaning against the railing and looking out into the yard. Quinn followed his gaze to the picnic table where Nora knelt next to Emily, smiling affectionately as she gently wiped icing from the little girl's face.

Liam whirled back around. "Do you have any idea what you're doing to my sister?"

"*Your—*" Quinn's eyes widened. "You're Nora's brother?"

"Yes, and Emily is my niece. And I can't believe you'd show up to her birthday party and trick everyone into thinking you're some kind of *friend*, while the whole time you're trying to steal her away from her family." He shook his head. "From the mother who raised her."

Quinn lunged to her feet. "First of all, I wasn't trying to trick you. *You* came over and started talking to *me*. And, second of all, I have as much right to be here as anyone. This is my *court-ordered* time." She dropped her hands to her hips. "I'm Emily's biological mother. I've missed out on three birthdays before this. Four, if you count the actual day she was born."

"Why are you doing this?" The lines around his eyes deepened as if this conversation was causing him pain. "I get it that you're biologically related to Emily. But, so what? That's just a few clusters of genes. That's not a real connection, not like the kind you get from being there, day in and day out." Liam paced across the deck and back again, his voice rising with each word. "The kind of connection you get from bandaging knees, and sitting in the ER with a kid who has a hundred and four fever, and staying up half the night to make a Pilgrim costume for the school play."

Quinn's mouth dropped open. She'd never had the opportunity to do those things. "You think I didn't want to bandage knees and make costumes? Everyone acts like I gave Emily up for adoption, and then I changed my mind." God, how many times was she going to have to say this? "*I didn't give her up.* You think I'm trying to steal her away? She was stolen away from *me*." Quinn's voice cracked with emotion.

"I'm sorry that happened to you. I really am. But you can't right that wrong by taking her back four years later. It's too late. *Emily doesn't want you.* She wants her mother. All you'd be doing is ruining everyone's life."

If he'd turn around and kicked her, it would have hurt less than those words. Quinn pressed a hand across her mouth, trying to hold back a sob as her eyes filled.

Liam closed his eyes. "Shit," he muttered under his breath.

A tear spilled over, and she spun on her heel and grabbed her purse from the chair so he wouldn't see it fall.

"Look, Quinn..." Liam said in a low voice, dropping his hands to his side.

"Don't." Quinn shook her head. "I think you've said enough." She looked around for an escape route, and her gaze fell on Nora out in the yard with Emily on her lap. Emily was engrossed in tearing the paper off a gift, but Nora's eyes were frozen on Quinn. Then slowly, deliberately, she turned away, leaning in to give Emily a kiss on the cheek.

Quinn pushed past Liam and took off down the porch steps. By the back gate, she hesitated for a moment. Maybe she should say goodbye to Emily, but that would mean wading into Nora's territory, not to mention the whole group that had gathered around to watch Emily open her gifts. She couldn't handle it if one more stranger told her what a terrible person she was for wanting to be a part of her own child's life. Quinn's chest heaved as she tried to hold in a sob. It wasn't like Emily would notice that she was gone, anyway.

Maybe Liam was right. Emily didn't want her, and maybe she never would.

13

For the past four summers, Quinn had been meaning to buy patio furniture. Their little postage-stamp garden wasn't large, even by city standards, but it had a lot of potential. A six-foot privacy fence separated it from the neighbors on both sides, and the woman who'd lived there before them had planted bushes along the garage wall that flowered fiery red in spring. The brick patio outside the kitchen door was a perfect spot for a grill, maybe a small café table, and some comfortable chairs for lounging. She just needed to stop at Home Goods and get around to finding some.

When they'd first bought the house, Quinn had made big plans for the little space. She'd found books at the library about growing her own vegetables, and sketched out a design for raised beds where she could plant zucchini and tomatoes. Her Pinterest board had dozens of photos of whimsical perennial gardens full of lavender, salvia, and coneflower in shades of purple and white. And she'd pictured a string of fairy lights hanging over the patio, casting a warm glow while she and James dined outside in summer.

And then, just like everything else in her life, the fertility treatments had taken over, and all she'd managed to accomplish in the backyard was to weed around the bushes and remind James to cut the grass. But on the Sunday after Emily's birthday party, Quinn took a good look around the yard for the first time in as long as she could remember. Nobody was going to play a game of ball out there, but with a little effort, her little city garden could be just as inviting as any suburban yard. Why was she letting herself get so intimidated by what Nora had, instead of working to make her own space better?

Emily's uncle had accused her of trying to ruin everyone's lives. But Emily could have such a happy life here with parents who would be grateful every single day to have her.

Quinn gazed at the spot where she'd imagined the raised beds. If she planted peas and cherry tomatoes, Emily could pick them right off the vines and eat them. One of her books had suggested it as a way to get kids excited about eating more vegetables. Maybe they could fit a small sandbox in the back corner, under the tree, where Emily might play in the shade while Quinn read a book on the patio and James cooked dinner on the grill. And on the hottest days, there was plenty of room in the grass for a kiddie pool or a sprinkler to jump through.

James was still out of town for work, and Quinn would need another person to help to build a raised bed and sandbox, but she could certainly start on her perennial garden now. Maybe she'd run over to the garden center and pick up a few things. And then on the way home, she could check out some patio furniture. If she ordered it now, it might be delivered by the end of the week. Once they had someplace to sit, it would be fun to see if Elise and her husband wanted to come for drinks on Friday night. She and James hadn't hung out with another couple in ages. *And then maybe, once the yard is complete, Emily can come to our house for one of our Saturday visits.*

Quinn jumped to her feet and headed inside to find her car keys, feeling better than she had since she left the party yesterday. Just because Liam had said those awful things didn't mean they were true. Or at least not the way he'd meant them. Maybe Emily didn't want to be with her as much as Nora, but that was because Emily didn't know her as well. It was time to stop sitting around feeling sorry for herself and work toward making their life a place where Emily felt welcome and comfortable. A place that was just as good as anything Nora had to offer.

A place that was even better.

————

The next evening, Quinn was up to her arms in potting soil when her phone rang. She reached for it, thinking it might be James calling to check in. But instead, Nora's name appeared on the screen. Helena and Nora's attorney had made sure Nora and Quinn had each other's phone numbers so they could coordinate visits. But Quinn hadn't expected to hear from Nora so soon.

"Hello, Quinn." Nora's voice was cold and business-like.

"Hi." Quinn wiped her hands on her T-shirt to get a better grip on the phone. "How is Emily? Did she enjoy her party?"

"Emily is fine." Nora cleared her throat. "She had fun at the party."

"I'm so glad."

"She liked the books you brought." Nora sounded pained, almost as if it hurt her to admit it.

Quinn had picked out a handful of books for Emily that were some of her favorites to read during story time. She was excited to start introducing her daughter to some of the books she'd loved as a child.

"Liam mentioned that you and Emily are regulars at your local library," Quinn said, hoping that Nora might share a little more about her daughter.

"Yes, we try to go every *Saturday afternoon* for story time," Nora said curtly.

Did Nora mean to imply that now that Quinn and James had their visits on Saturday afternoons, she could no longer take Emily to story time? Quinn tried not to let it bother her that she was depriving her daughter of one of her favorite activities. Nora wouldn't have had to go to court, and the judge wouldn't have had to order their visits on Saturdays, if Nora would have agreed to cooperate with them.

"The dollhouse you bought her was too much, though." Nora's voice was laced with disapproval. "We really don't have room for it."

Aside from the gift bag of books Quinn had brought for Emily to open at the party, she'd ordered a dollhouse on Amazon and had it sent directly to Nora's house. Quinn couldn't believe it when she'd found a miniature replica of the house from the movie *Encanto*, complete with furniture and little figurines of all the characters. She knew it was way too much when she'd ordered it, but she couldn't help herself. She only wished she could've been there to see Emily open it.

Quinn bit back her suggestion that if Nora didn't have room for the dollhouse, Emily could play with it at her house. *Soon enough*, she told herself, gazing around at the garden that was already looking better thanks to the plants she'd picked up at the garden center.

Through the phone, she heard a small voice say something she couldn't quite decipher. After a moment, Nora murmured, "I told her it's your favorite present... Mmm-hmm... She knows you love *Encanto*."

Quinn's heart almost burst out of her chest. It was Emily, and from the sound of it, she loved the dollhouse. It was a small thing, but it meant so much.

Nora kept murmuring to Emily. "I know we have to put it together, but tonight is bath night."

Oh... Quinn hadn't realized until now that Emily couldn't just start playing with her gift. The dollhouse had been packaged in a flat box. Someone was going to have to assemble it. It was something seasoned parents probably knew all about, but that never would have occurred to her.

"I wasn't thinking about the fact that it might be a lot for you to put together on your own," Quinn admitted, feeling bad that she'd stuck Nora with such an arduous task. It would take an entire afternoon, and Nora probably didn't have time for that. "I'd be happy to come by and help you." Quinn realized she wanted to help. It felt like another one of those rites of passage she'd missed out on. In the movies, there was always a scene where the soon-to-be parents assembled the baby crib together. She and James had never gotten to experience that, so a dollhouse was the next best thing.

"I don't need any help," Nora snapped. At her tone, all Quinn's goodwill flew out the window. "I'm a single mom. I know how to use a screwdriver."

"I wasn't implying—" Quinn abruptly stopped talking. She was only trying to be nice, but if Nora wanted to assemble the damn dollhouse by herself, fine. Quinn had a garden to get back to. She picked up her brand-new trowel and stabbed it in the dirt. "Never mind. Was there a reason you were calling?"

"Oh. Yes." Suddenly, Nora had smoothed out the hard edges to her voice. "Actually, I was wondering if you could switch the dates around for your next visit. Unfortunately, I have to work next Saturday."

Quinn took another stab at the dirt, harder this time. She'd only had one Saturday with Emily and had barely gotten to see her. And now, Nora wanted to reschedule their second visit? Not a chance.

But as Quinn opened her mouth to turn down the request, she found herself saying, "Fine. We can do Sunday." Damn it. There was that guilt again. It probably *was* hard being a single mother holding all the responsibility of caring for a child. Juggling work and all the activities Nora's attorney had mentioned that Emily participated in. Quinn sighed, grateful that she'd always had James to rely on. Suddenly, she regretted making such a big deal about him missing Emily's party for his trip. Working hard at his job was his way of making sure their family had security. Why did she have to make him feel guilty about it?

Nora blew out a relieved breath. "Okay. Thanks. I really appreciate it."

They said their goodbyes, and at the last minute, Quinn added, "Give my love to Emily."

"Mmm-hmm." Nora murmured vaguely. "Sure."

There was no way Nora was going to relay the message. Quinn shrugged. She'd say it herself soon enough.

After she hung up with Nora, Quinn hit the button to dial James. He answered on the first ring.

"Hi, honey." His voice radiated warmth. "I'm just sitting here missing you."

Quinn smiled. "I miss you, too. How was golf yesterday?"

"It was great. The client is going to place a significant order with us, and I think he's considering an even bigger order for the fourth quarter."

A significant order meant a significant bonus. They could use the money. What if he'd stayed home like she'd asked and hadn't been able to close the deal? "I'm so glad you could be there."

"I'm so sorry I missed the party, though. How was it?"

Quinn told him about Emily dressing up Bruno and how she'd loved their gifts, leaving out the parts where Nora had seemingly tried to keep Emily away from her. And she definitely didn't tell him about Liam's angry words. It would only make James feel bad for not being there to defend her. And besides, she didn't want to think about that conversation or the contempt on Liam's face anymore. Hopefully, she'd never have to see Liam again.

"Unfortunately, we had to switch our visit next week," Quinn told him. "Nora has to work, and I figured she wouldn't agree to let us take Emily on her own. So, we're going to meet with Emily on Sunday instead of Saturday."

"Oh." James's voice dipped. "Oh, honey. I have to come back here to meet the client again on Sunday. I really need to close this deal."

Quinn's heart dropped to her stomach. James would miss another visit with Emily?

"The client requested Saturday," James continued. "But I said I absolutely couldn't because we were going to see Emily that afternoon. I'm scheduled to head to the airport and fly out Saturday evening, as soon as the visit was going to be over."

Quinn sighed. But what could they do? She'd already told Nora they could switch, and she didn't want to get in a fight about it. The next time they stood in front of a judge, Helena would be able to point out all the ways they'd been flexible and accommodating. In contrast to Nora.

"I'm so sorry," James murmured. "I'll be there next time, I promise."

Quinn's shoulders relaxed. "I know you will."

14

It had been a whole week since she'd seen Emily—*a week and a day*, Quinn reminded herself—and she was desperate to spend some time with her daughter. But at the same time, her stomach churned with nerves. Nora would be there again. Nora, whose attorney had argued that these visits should be supervised. Nora, who had thrown Emily an impromptu party full of people just to keep Quinn away from her, and was trying to interfere and sabotage their relationship at every turn. It didn't help Quinn's mood that James couldn't be there again. Thanks to Nora insisting they switch days, he was missing out on their precious time with their child.

Quinn parked her car and stepped out into the parking lot. At least they were meeting in a playground today, on slightly more neutral ground, even if it *was* in Nora's perfect Pleasantville neighborhood.

Across a ballfield and situated under a circle of mature trees, Quinn spotted the telltale green metal bars of a jungle gym and swing set. She headed over, scanning the playground for a small girl with dark curls, but there was only a mom pushing a toddler in a baby swing and a couple of teenagers flipping through their phones, so she settled on a bench to wait. Quinn had left the house almost an hour early for the twenty-minute drive, worried about hitting traffic. For all she knew, Nora would tell the judge she no-showed if she was even a minute late.

Quinn scrolled through her phone, doing her best to focus on the parenting article she was reading and not the baby waving his arms with joy as his mother pushed him back and forth on the swing. Emily was past the baby stage, and she probably wouldn't even fit in a swing like that anymore.

Before Quinn could spend too much time dwelling on it, someone skidded to a stop in front of her. "Hi, Miss Quinn!"

Quinn looked up to find Connor standing on the rubber playground turf with a basketball under his arm. "Connor! Hi, I didn't expect to see you here."

"I came to play basketball. It's my favorite sport." Connor dribbled the ball somewhat unsteadily, but by the way his little eyebrows knit together behind his glasses, she could see that he was trying hard.

"Well, I can see why. You're pretty good at that."

He gave her a toothy grin, except there was a gap where one of his front teeth used to be. "Well, look at you," Quinn said, matching his smile. "Looks like someone stole your tooth."

"I lost it! And the tooth fairy came."

"How much does a tooth go for these days?"

"Five dollars."

"Five! In my day, it was a dollar. But I guess I sound pretty old saying that."

"It's still a dollar," said a now-familiar voice as an equally familiar male frame dropped onto the park bench next to her. "You only get five when the tooth fairy forgets to come."

"Oh. Hi." Quinn took a deep breath as her eyes met Liam's. The last time she'd seen him, he'd said awful things to her. But she couldn't very well give him the cold shoulder in front of his son or get up and walk away. Connor was a sweet kid who didn't deserve that. It wasn't his fault that his father was a jerk.

"The tooth fairy *always* forgets to come," Connor pointed out, not sounding the least bit put out about it.

Liam sighed, shooting a contrite glance in Quinn's direction. "The tooth fairy is a very busy fairy with a lot on her mind."

Quinn looked at him sideways. What about Connor's mother? Didn't she ever do tooth fairy duty? Maybe she worked the night shift, or maybe Liam was actually one of those men who took on half the parenting duties. But that would mean she had to think something nice about him, and she didn't want to do that. She'd rather believe his wife worked the night shift.

"You want to play basketball with me, Miss Quinn?" Connor asked, bouncing the ball again.

"Oh, Connor, I'd love to. But I'm actually here to meet Emily. She's supposed to come with your aunt, Nora."

Connor shook his head. "Aunt Nora couldn't come. She had to work. So, Emily came with us."

Quinn sat up in her seat, her gaze swinging to Liam. "Seriously? Do you know we rearranged our schedule and James had to miss this because Nora said she had to work yesterday?"

"I know." He held up his hands in a motion of surrender. "She has a big project on deadline and ended up having to work today, too. Give her a break, okay? It's not easy being a single parent."

Quinn's shoulders slumped. There was that guilt again. The truth was, James had missed visits because he had to work, too. But they were lucky that Quinn could still be there. Nora didn't have a co-parent to send. "Fine. Whatever." She looked from one side of the playground to the other. "So, where is Emily?"

Liam hitched his head backwards, in the direction of the ballfield over his shoulder. "Picking dandelions."

Quinn turned around in her seat and spotted Emily running across the grass with a fistful of the bright yellow flowers clutched in her hand. When she got to the park bench, she held them out to Quinn. "Uncle Liam said they're your favorite."

Quinn took a shaky breath as Emily handed the dandelions over. Hadn't she been thinking just a few days ago that she'd missed out on these small moments with Emily? Quinn clutched the flowers to her chest as if they were a bouquet of long-stem roses. "Oh, he's right. I love them." She shot a glance at Liam, trying to work out why he'd encourage Emily to do something nice for her, when he'd made it clear he had nothing but contempt for her just last week. "How did you know I love dandelions?"

"Oh, I just had a feeling." He waved a hand. "In addition to making excellent gifts from little girls, I've heard they're good for apologizing, too." His lips curved into a tentative smile as he held out another wispy yellow bundle, smaller than Emily's. "I can't say I feel any differently about this situation. But I'm sorry for the way I blew up at you."

Quinn took the second bouquet from Liam, unsure of how she felt in this moment. It certainly didn't make up for what he'd said to her at the party. But she appreciated that he'd made this small moment with Emily materialize. Quinn held the dandelions up to her nose. They smelled like cut grass and spring. "Thank you."

All of a sudden, the hand holding the bundle Liam had given her began to vibrate, and a low hum came from somewhere in the same direction. "Uh…" Quinn said, holding Liam's flowers farther away from her. In the next moment, a bee made its way out from between the yellow petals of two flowers. "Oh, my God." Quinn jumped about a foot in the air and dropped the bouquet on the bench between them. "There's a bee in there!" The bee poked around the dandelions for a few seconds longer and then flew off.

"Daddy!" Connor admonished. "Someone could get stung."

"Someone meaning me," Quinn said, giving Liam a wide-eyed stare.

He looked back at her with equal surprise. "I know you're not going to believe me, but I swear I did not mean to give you a bouquet with a bee in it." He raked a hand through his hair. "I don't know how I'd even plan something like that."

Quinn studied him with narrowed eyes.

A thin sheen of sweat had broken out on his forehead, and his face looked stricken. "I know how this looks..." He held up a hand.

Suddenly, the hilarity of the whole situation hit her, and a chuckle rose up in her throat. He was right, there was no way he could have planted a bee in her flowers, so the only thing to do was laugh.

Liam ran another hand through his hair with a heavy sigh. "I really am sorry. About the other day..." He gave the dandelions on the bench a disgruntled poke. "And about that damn bee."

"It's okay. But remind me to look for snakes the next time you're around."

His shoulders shook with laughter. Quinn's annoyance with him melted away, and she almost wished it would come back. It was better to stay angry and to keep her distance. She and Liam were on opposite sides, and if she let her guard down, he might use it against her. Quinn reminded herself that Nora, and Liam by association, were the ones who'd refused her contact with her own daughter. They were the ones who'd forced her to go to court to fight for custody.

Connor plunged a hand into his jacket pocket and pulled out a couple of miniature peanut butter cups. "I won two treats at school on Friday for helping to clean up after recess, and I saved them to eat with Emily. Daddy, can we have them?"

Quinn smiled at Connor's eagerness to share his reward with his cousin, but Liam quickly shook his head. "You know Emily can't have that, buddy. Why don't you save them for after dinner?"

If the children hadn't been standing right in front of her, Quinn would have rolled her eyes. Nora's rules around sugar and treats were starting to get out of hand. Wasn't it more important to allow Connor to share with his cousin than it was to keep Emily from eating a tiny piece of chocolate? Besides, everyone knew that the more you denied kids candy, the more they'd just sneak it later. It was just one more example of where she and Nora would never agree on how to parent Emily.

"What do you think, Emily?" Quinn lunged to her feet with a smile, hoping to ward off a tantrum when Emily realized she'd just been denied a treat. "Should we go throw the ball with Connor?"

Emily and Connor jumped up and down with excitement.

"Are you coming too, Daddy?" Connor dribbled the ball again.

Liam's eyes met Quinn's, and then he looked away. "No." He leaned back against the bench. "I think I'm going to let Quinn take this one."

Quinn followed Connor and Emily across the playground to a basketball court at the other end of the park. She and the kids formed a triangle, bouncing the ball back and forth to each other, then switched to monkey-in-the-middle with Quinn as the monkey. Neither kid was very good at throwing or catching —they were four and five, after all—but Quinn played along, pretending to miss balls she easily could have caught, feigning exaggerated disappointment to make them laugh.

At the birthday party, Connor had said Emily was his best friend, and later, Quinn had learned that she was actually his cousin. But watching them on the basketball court together, Quinn would have guessed they were brother and sister. Connor seemed to take his role as the older child seriously, teaching Emily how to dribble the ball and warning her not to get too close when a friendly golden retriever ran by. It was clear these kids had grown up together, and outings like this to the park were a regular occurrence. Connor had mentioned that he lived in the neighborhood too, just down the street from Emily and Nora.

Was Liam right that if she pursued custody of Emily, she'd be destroying this family and ruining their lives? Quinn watched as Connor and Emily tried to throw the ball into the basketball net, laughing as it sailed into the chain-link fence, not even close to its intended target. Would gaining a new family— her biological parents who loved her beyond reason—be worth the disruption to Emily's life?

Quinn hated these doubts creeping in, and even more, she hated that the doubts were probably exactly what Liam and Nora had intended.

She was dragged from these thoughts by the sound of a thump, followed by a wail. She spun around to find Emily lying on the pavement with tears streaming down her face. Quinn ran over and crouched down.

"She tripped over the ball!" Connor yelled over the sound of Emily's cries. "She's bleeding!"

"It's okay, let me see," Quinn murmured to Emily, adjusting the girl's leg so she could get a good look at the scrape blooming bright red on the knee of her cotton leggings. Emily wailed louder when she caught sight of the blood. "Come here, sweetie. Let me help you, okay? We'll get you all cleaned up." Quinn hoisted Emily into her arms, and with Connor trotting behind, clutching the ball, she carried a sobbing Emily across the playground to where Liam sat on the bench.

At the sound of Emily's next wail, his head jerked up and he jumped to his feet. "What happened?"

"Just a scraped knee," Quinn said. "I think I might have some Band-Aids in my car."

"I have some right here." Liam reached for a messenger bag Quinn hadn't noticed before, unloading water bottles and snacks before he located a first-aid kit.

Quinn blinked at all the supplies laid out on the bench. When moms brought their kids to the library, they arrived with tote bags stuffed with enough provisions to survive a three-day snowstorm. Dads, on the other hand, usually had a diaper stuffed in their back pocket but no wipes to go with it. A snack, but no water bottle. And in the fifteen years she'd worked at the library, she'd never witnessed a father pull out a Band-Aid. Quinn knew it was sexist of her, but she couldn't help wondering if Liam's wife had packed the bag for him.

Quinn knelt in front of Emily and, using one of Liam's Band-Aids and an alcohol wipe, had the scrape cleaned up in no time. Emily's cries slowly tapered to whimpers as Quinn crumpled up the wrappers and tossed them in a nearby garbage can. "Do you want to go back out and play, sweetie?"

Emily shook her head.

"Okay, well, maybe we'll just rest for a minute." Quinn slid onto the bench next to Emily, reaching over to rub a comforting hand up and down her back. Emily leaned in a little closer, and Quinn's heart pitched. And then in the next moment, it cracked right open. Because Emily held up her little arms to Quinn, silently asking to be picked up.

Lifting the girl felt familiar, now that she'd carried her across the playground. *And*, Quinn realized, when Emily was settled on her lap with her little thumb in her mouth, *it feels exactly right*. Emily rested her curly head on Quinn's collarbone, and Quinn's chin fit perfectly on top, as if they were made to sit exactly this way.

Quinn glanced up to find Liam watching. He quickly looked away, but not before she saw the sadness working its way across his face. He abruptly stood and reached out to steal the ball from Connor. "Hey, bud. Let's go shoot some hoops."

They didn't talk again until it was time to go.

15

It was Kindness Month in the children's room at the library. Quinn read the children stories about a small truck helping a bigger truck out of a mud puddle, a little boy getting teased for wearing dresses, and a group of animals who banded together to stand up for a misfit bunny. Afterward, Quinn helped the children draw pictures of ways they could be kind to others.

Quinn loved these kindness lessons. She was always amazed by the children's ideas and heartened by their willingness to accept others. It was one of her most important jobs at the library: helping parents and children to choose books and share ideas that would make the next generation just a little bit more open-minded.

That day, as Quinn read aloud from a book about how people came in all shapes and sizes to a group of three-year-olds, her mind drifted to Emily. Was Nora teaching Emily about openness and acceptance? Did they talk about sharing? About being kind to other children at school, even if they were different than her? Quinn hated that she had no control, no say in any of the messages Emily received. To be fair, Nora didn't seem like someone who would teach Emily to be a bully. And on the surface, Nora seemed like a nice enough person. She'd certainly been gracious to all—but one—of her guests at the birthday party. But her behavior toward Emily's biological parents had Quinn worried.

How could Nora truly be teaching Emily the right lessons if she was so willing to cut Quinn and James out of their child's life? The more Nora tried to keep them from Emily, the more it confirmed their imperative to keep up their fight for custody. They had a duty to make sure their daughter was being raised the right way.

After that day's kindness craft, the kids and their parents filed out of the library to head home for nap time, and Quinn took her bag and went into the break room. She found Elise at the table with her lunch spread in front of her.

"We missed you last night," Elise said, taking a bite of pasta. "We read your pick this month."

Book club again. They took turns choosing the books, putting them on the calendar months in advance in case any of the women wanted to read ahead. Quinn had forgotten that this month had been her turn.

"I'm so sorry. I forgot." Quinn dropped down in the chair across from Elise. "I've been fixing up the garden after work, and I lost track of time."

"Oh, it's great that you're getting back into gardening." Elise knew Quinn back when she was planning out the backyard the first time around. Before the fertility treatments took over. "What are you planting?"

Quinn smiled. "I'm planting some perennials and designing a sandbox to go under the tree in the back. I've been thinking that it would be to have you and Dave over for drinks soon. You can see it then."

Elise looked up. "A sandbox?" She cocked her head in a questioning gesture. "Does that mean there's been a development with your daughter and the woman who gave birth to her?"

Quinn pulled her sandwich from her bag. She'd spotted it in the case at the coffee shop and couldn't resist it. Fresh mozzarella and tomato with basil pesto on focaccia. The sandwich was bursting with dairy and fat. A month ago, she would have ordered the kale smoothie. What a relief it was to not have to suck down another one of those.

"Not exactly." Quinn unwrapped the sandwich. "Nothing aside from visitation one day a week." She'd been hesitant to share too much about Emily with anyone. If she opened up about her daughter at work, and then the case didn't go their way, she'd have to go back and tell everyone she'd failed—again. She'd have to endure more of platitudes and advice from people like her boss Sonia. Quinn wasn't sure she could take any more platitudes and advice.

But then she looked up and met her friend's eyes. This was Elise, not Sonia, and talking to Elise always made Quinn feel better. "Elise, it's been amazing to spend time with her. She's so sweet and she says the funniest things. I love seeing the world through her eyes. Being with her, it just..." She remembered Emily sitting on her lap after crying over her scraped knee. How she'd been able to comfort her. "It feels so right."

Elise smiled. "You sound like a proud mom."

A warmth spread over Quinn. That's exactly how she'd felt. Like a mom.

At that moment, Sonia strolled into the break room with a salad in her manicured hand. She started to slide into a seat at their table, but stopped halfway down with her eyes on Quinn's lunch. "Oh, my God, congratulations, Quinn."

Quinn stared at her boss eyeing her lunch. What was she being congratulated for? Finally eating some real food? "I'm sorry, what's the occasion?"

Sonia dropped the rest of the way into the chair and leaned

in toward Quinn. "I knew it would work for you eventually," she said, her voice buoyant.

For a moment, Quinn stared at her in confusion. Then her eyes dropped to the sandwich in her hand and Quinn felt her face heat up. *Sonia thinks I'm pregnant.* She'd been so obsessed with doing everything to have a baby, monitoring every ingredient that went into her mouth, that she couldn't even eat a simple sandwich without everyone reading something into it. "I'm not..." Quinn stammered, unable to continue.

"Sonia," Elise said gently. "She's not pregnant."

Sonia's mouth dropped open. "Oh. I'm sorry I assumed..." She waved a hand at Quinn's lunch. "I take it if you're not watching your diet anymore, this means you've given up?"

Quinn and Elise exchanged looks. If she told Sonia about Emily and the custody battle, she'd demand to know the whole story. And then, of course, the advice would start.

"Yes, we've given up," Quinn finally admitted, but she resented having to say it. How many couples had struggled with infertility for years, just like her and James, and eventually been ground down by the expense and endless heartbreak? It didn't mean they'd *given up*. It meant there were simply no more options.

Sonia sighed. "I'm sorry." She pulled the top off her seaweed salad and stabbed it with her fork. "Well, you know, I've heard a lot of stories about women who try for years to get pregnant. And then they move on to adoption—"

Quinn braced herself for what was coming next. Women who'd never gone through infertility loved to give this advice.

"—and then, boom!" Sonia waved a hand in the air. "They find out they're pregnant. It turns out all they needed to do was relax a little."

"Yeah, Quinn," Elise said with a conspiratorial wink. "You should relax. What you really need is couple of extra days off."

"Oh, I didn't mean..." Sonia stammered, and then sighed. "Well, I suppose if it would help, we can probably work something out."

Quinn smiled across the table at Elise and promised herself she'd try to make it to the next book club.

16

"Quinn, James, thank you for coming today." Helena sat across from them in the now-familiar glass-walled conference room with a binder full of papers on the table in front of her. She flipped it open. "We're about four weeks out from the hearing, so I wanted to meet in person to make sure we're all on the same page with what we're hoping to achieve moving forward."

Quinn cocked her head at the attorney. "Why wouldn't we be on the same page?"

"Well, now that you and James have had a chance to spend some time with Emily, to meet Nora and the rest of the family, I wanted to make sure you still wish to proceed."

Quinn glanced at her husband as he leaned back in his chair, taking a casual sip of the water Helena had offered him. Technically, James hadn't spent much time with Emily. It seemed like other things kept coming up at the last minute. Work trips, a migraine. But James *had* been present on the day Nora had brought Emily into the city for story time at Quinn's library. He'd even sat next to Emily on the rainbow carpet to listen to the Dr. Seuss book, and then he'd helped her make a Cat in the Hat craft afterward.

"Of course we wish to proceed," Quinn said.

Helena nodded and made a note on her paper. "And James?"

In the chair next to her, James took a deep breath and held it. Quinn's heart began to pound.

"James?" Quinn prodded quietly.

He glanced at Quinn and then released the breath with a heavy sigh. "Yes. Of course."

Helena hesitated, her eyes on James for an extra beat, and then she made another note in her binder. "Okay, the next step for you will be the home study. This will require a visit by a social worker, an interview, and a review of a number of financial and health-related documents."

Quinn nodded. She'd already Googled this and had an idea of what to expect. But next to her, James tensed up. "That sounds pretty invasive."

"Well... yes. It is." Helena's pen paused over the table. "Essentially, they want to know if you have the ability to parent Emily and can offer an appropriate place to raise a child."

James leaned forward in his chair. "But if Quinn had given birth to Emily, nobody would be poking around in our business. Checking our financials and digging in our bedside drawers."

"I can assure you that nobody will dig in your bedside drawers," Helena said, dryly. "But unfortunately, Quinn didn't give birth to Emily, and the home visit is required."

Quinn pressed a firm hand to James's leg. *Stop it. Go along with this.* "It's fine. We're fine with it."

But James was still shaking his head. "What sort of things will they be looking for?"

"They're not looking *for* anything in particular, right?" Maybe Quinn should have sent some of the articles she'd read to James so he would have known what to expect before Helena brought it up. "It's not like a search warrant for evidence that we'd make bad parents."

"Exactly." Helena gave a nod. "They'll want to know your home is safe, that your health won't prohibit you from caring for a child, that your marriage is solid, and that financially, you can afford the additional expenses."

"So, maybe they won't be in our bedside drawer, but they'll look around our house and..." James waved his hand. "Dig into our personal papers? Bank statements? Credit cards?"

"Yes."

Quinn pressed harder on James's leg. "Honey, it's okay. The house can be childproofed, we're both in good health, and we're completely fine financially." She turned to Helena. "The fertility treatments used up a chunk of our savings, but the judge will understand that, won't she?"

"I wouldn't worry about that as long as you can pay your bills. And we're still working on a financial settlement with the fertility clinic for the—" Helena cocked her head. "—obvious mix-up."

Quinn nodded along. "We know you have that handled." The money would be helpful, but what she wanted was Emily. "Was there anything else?"

"No..." Helena made another note on her paper. "I think that's all for now."

"Great." Quinn jumped to her feet with a bright smile, hoping to draw attention from the dark cloud suddenly hanging over James's head. Why was he making such a big deal out of this? "We look forward to hearing from you."

They headed to the elevator and down to the car, James shuffling along next to her like he was on the way to the dentist. Quinn knew he hated this part, the invasion into their lives. He was right. If she'd given birth to Emily, they wouldn't have to deal with any of this. But since they did, they might as well make the most of it.

"When we get home," Quinn said, "I'll focus on getting the guest room in order. I think it's time to clear it out. I suppose it would be premature to buy furniture, but we could at least organize the piles of junk and send some things to Goodwill. And paint... I know Emily likes pink, but maybe for now we should go with a neutral pastel like a pale yellow."

"Sure." James shrugged like he wasn't really listening and picked up his pace.

Quinn hurried to keep up, her annoyance growing. *What is going on with him?*

They climbed inside the car, and James steered it out of the parking garage. When he turned onto the road headed for their house, still silently brooding, Quinn knew she couldn't ignore his dark mood for another second. "Are you feeling okay?" She reached out to touch his arm, noticing his knuckles were white from his grip on the steering wheel. "You look a little nauseated."

"I'm fine," came James's terse reply.

But he didn't look fine. He looked deathly pale. Quinn had a bad feeling about this, but whatever James was getting worked up about, he needed to move past it and get on board with this home visit. "Okay," she continued. "Well, while I'm in the guest room, I can start looking through those boxes for our financial records. I guess they probably want the most updated copies, so I'll need the investment accounts, the credit union, and the regular bank account."

The car jerked for just a second, as if James's foot had hit the gas a little too hard. "I don't think they'll need all of that information. Just give them a copy of our tax returns."

Quinn hesitated for a moment, eyeing her husband. Was it the fact that the social worker would look at their financial records that bothered him the most? Maybe he had some insecurities related to the fact that they didn't have as much savings as they would have liked. But again, that was because they'd done all these fertility treatments. Nobody would look down on them for that.

"Well," Quinn said haltingly. "Helena said they want all of our financial records. I'm not sure the tax returns are enough info—"

"*Quinn.*"

Something about the sharpness in James's tone had her sitting up in her seat. His hands gripped the steering wheel so hard they were shaking, and his face had gone from sickly pale to bright red.

"What? What is it?"

James yanked the wheel to the right and pulled the car to the side of the road. God, maybe he really *was* sick? Quinn reached up to put a hand on his forehead, but he waved it away. "James. Tell me what's going on."

He turned off the engine and then shifted in his seat so he was facing her. "Quinn, before you say anything, I want you to know that I love you. And I'm dedicated to our family. And—"

"*James.*"

The lines around his eyes deepened. "Quinn, I love you," he repeated.

Quinn stared at him. "If you love me, you'll tell me why you're acting like this." Her voice sounded so much calmer than she felt.

"I—" He leaned his forearms against the steering wheel and put his head in his hands. "If a social worker goes digging into our accounts, they'll see I've been sending some money to someone. Not a lot. Just a thousand a month. And only for a few months."

"Who? Aunt Judy?" James's aunt lived alone in Tennessee. They'd gone to her house last Thanksgiving, and while she wasn't wealthy, she seemed to be doing fine. "If she needed help, you could have just talked to me—"

James shook his head, still bent over the steering wheel. "It's not my aunt."

Quinn's mind reeled with possibilities. *Was he being black-*

mailed? Did he have a gambling problem? "Just tell me," Quinn whispered. "Whatever it is, it can't be worse than what I'm imagining."

But then she saw the anguished look in his eyes. Maybe it could be worse.

"It was—" he stuttered. "You and I were having a rough time."

Quinn's hand flew up to cover her mouth. "Please don't say what I think you're going to say."

"We were gearing up for this last embryo transfer, and you were so distant, so wrapped up in—"

"Whatever this is, don't blame it on me." Quinn shook her head over and over. "Don't you dare blame it on me."

"There was a woman at work. An intern—"

"Oh, my God. *An intern?*"

"It was just one time." James stared out the windshield as if he were watching the whole thing play out on the road in front of him. "It happened on a work trip. We had a few drinks at the bar, and—"

Quinn cut him off. "Was she even old enough to drink?"

"She's twenty-two."

"Oh, my God," Quinn repeated, as a wave of nausea crashed over her. "So, why are you sending her money? Is she blackmailing you?"

He slowly turned to look at her. "No, she's not blackmailing me. It's for medical bills."

Quinn's mouth dropped open. "If you tell me she gave you an STD, I swear to God..."

"I don't have an STD, I promise. She needs the money because..." James shook his head sadly. "Because she's pregnant."

17

Thank God she'd been too nervous about their meeting with Helena to eat, because Quinn was going to throw up. She opened the door of the car, swung her legs out, and leaned her elbows on her knees. Her lungs felt like she'd just sprinted up hill, and she couldn't seem to get enough air. Sweat broke out on her forehead.

Quinn held her palms to her face and moaned. A gentle hand pressed against her back—James, in the driver's seat, as if somehow his touch might *comfort her*, but it only made her skin crawl.

"Do not come near me." Quinn twisted around to shoot out an elbow and then swiveled the other way, trying to disengage him. With great satisfaction, she heard the slide of his pants against the leather seat and his back hit the car door as he moved as far away from her as the confined space would allow. *Good. Be afraid.*

"Okay, I'm sorry," James stuttered. "I'm sure you need a minute."

"A minute?" Quinn gasped. "You tell me you knocked up a teenager, and you think I need *a minute?*"

"She's not a teenager. She's a grad student at the university who—"

"Oh my God, I don't care who the woman you cheated on me is!" Quinn yelled. In some far-off corner of her mind, she registered that their car was parked next to the sidewalk of a bustling shopping area. Pedestrians strolled by holding dog leashes or packages, openly staring at the drama playing out as she sat half-in and half-out of the car.

Wait until I puke all over the sidewalk. Then they'll disperse. Quinn dropped her head back in her hands.

"Quinn, I know what I did was terrible. And, obviously, it's a bit of a complicated situation now. But I love—"

"Don't tell me you love me."

"But I do."

Quinn slowly lifted her head and turned to look at him. "Then why do you keep cheating on me?"

James's mouth dropped open, but no sound came out. Finally, he managed to sputter, "Who told you—? I don't keep cheating on—"

But he did. This wasn't the first time. She'd tried not to think about it, tried to believe it was just a one-time thing, but now she was forced to face the truth. "I was cleaning out your suitcase after your Chicago trip last year, and I found a receipt. I only looked at it to see if you needed to keep it to submit for your travel expenses. One of the things on the list was a box of condoms." They had never used condoms. In the early days of their relationship, she'd been on the pill to regulate her heavy periods. Then they'd started trying to get pregnant. "There's a certain irony in the fact that the receipt was for condoms, isn't there? Since it seems like you didn't actually use them."

James's mouth hung open. "Why didn't you say something back then?"

"I guess I didn't want to face it. I wanted to believe that if it had happened, it was a slip-up. A mistake that you wouldn't repeat." The truth was, she'd been in the middle of an IVF cycle, and she hadn't wanted the stress to interfere with her ability to get pregnant. So, she'd looked the other way. "I guess I convinced myself that you were committed to our relationship. But I see now that I was mistaken."

"I *am* committed to our relationship." His voice was carefully measured, as if he were trying to hold back his anger.

As if he has something to be angry about.

"Excuse me if I don't believe you."

He slammed his hand down on the steering wheel, and Quinn jumped. "Sometimes I wonder if *you're* committed to our relationship, or if the only thing you ever cared about is trying to get pregnant."

"Are you serious?" Quinn practically shook at unfairness of it all. "I was trying to get pregnant for us. *For our family.*"

"It didn't feel like it was for us. It felt like you lost sight of *us*." James's chest heaved. "I had to look elsewhere because you barely wanted to touch me unless your cervix was in the right position or you'd taken your fertility vitamins or whatever other nonsense you'd read about in some wacko book."

"Well, maybe if you'd paid more attention to my wacko books, you would have learned how to keep from getting your *girlfriend pregnant.*" And with those words, all of Quinn's anger deflated. They'd always known that *her* body was the problem, that it was her fault they couldn't have a baby. They'd been told that James's sperm was perfectly healthy. And here was the proof. *His boys could swim*, as they say. James's girlfriend was fertile, and now—it was almost too unbelievable to be real—he had a baby on the way. Quinn's shoulders slumped. "How many weeks along is she?"

"About fourteen."

"When were you planning to tell me?"

"I was waiting to make sure that everything was okay. They say not to tell anyone until after the first trimester."

"They mean your mother-in-law and the guy at work. Not your wife."

James looked down at his hands. "I wanted to wait to make sure she planned to keep the baby—"

"Because otherwise—" Quinn shook her head. "You wouldn't have had to tell me at all." James's flinch told her she'd hit on the truth. She gave a humorless laugh.

"No, that's not—"

Quinn cut him off. She had other things to worry about. "So, she's keeping the baby?"

"Yes." He sounded almost breathless. Almost... happy.

Her vision blurred and a wave of vertigo overtook her. This wasn't just about an affair. It was so much more than that. They would never, ever move on from this decision James had made to be unfaithful and unsafe. There would be a child in their lives forever.

It was what she'd always wanted.

But not like this.

And, oh God. What would it mean for Emily? A social worker was about to start digging into every aspect of their life, asking questions about their marriage and whether they could be fully committed to Emily's needs. What would it look like if James had a baby on the way with another woman?

And what was she supposed to do now?

Quinn slowly dragged her legs back into the car and pulled the door shut behind her. Her body aching as if she was forty years older, she reached back and pulled on the seatbelt strap, snapping it into place. And then she sat there, because that little bit of effort had used up all the energy she had left.

"Quinn?" James finally whispered. "What are you thinking?"

"I'm thinking I want to go home."

"We should talk about this."

"I can't talk to you right now. I can't even look at you."

Quinn closed her eyes, and leaned against the car door. She didn't open them until they pulled up in front of the house.

———

Quinn limped inside the house and headed straight for their bedroom. All she wanted was to climb into bed, pull the covers over her head, and stay there until she figured out how to move forward while her life was in shambles. Her child was being raised by strangers, and her husband was having a baby with a twenty-two-year-old intern. But there were no good answers. There was only this great, big mess that was getting messier by the minute.

She closed the door firmly behind her in an unmistakable message to James that he was *not* welcome, then leaned her back against it and slid to the floor. And then, as if the universe just couldn't wait to kick her while she was down, she realized she was eye-level with the bottom of the bed, staring right at the box of her special baby things tucked underneath.

Quinn knew she shouldn't torture herself, but she just couldn't seem to help it. Crawling on all fours, she made her way to the foot of the bed and reached under, pulling the first box out. She flipped open the lid and stared at the contents. All those adorable sweaters and pinafores and miniature socks, folded in perfect squares, tucked into neat rows. One by one, she lifted them out and lined them up on the floor, stroking the soft fabric with her palm. Then her hand brushed one final garment in the bottom of the box, and her breath caught. The perfect, cream-colored onesie with its furry hood and floppy little ears. The bear suit she'd bought in the hopes that she and James might bring home a tiny newborn someday.

Her vision clouded with mint-green and pale yellow and baby-blue bleeding together in a pile of candy-colored mockery. Who was she kidding? She was forty-three years old. Two decades older than James's pregnant girlfriend. She was never going to bring home a baby. And, thanks to James's recklessness, she might never bring home her daughter if the social worker and the judge found out about it.

With a strangled cry, Quinn lunged to her feet and gathered the pile of tiny clothes in her arms. She flung open the bedroom door so hard, it bounced off the wall behind her. Miniature socks dropped from the pile as she stormed down the hall, but she left them there like landmines for James to find later. Finally, she crashed into the living room where he was reclining on the couch.

He sat up abruptly, eyes wide and wary. "Quinn, what's going on—" The rest of his words were cut off by a bundle of baby clothes tumbling over his head.

"*Here.*" Quinn yelled. "You'll need these more than I will, now that you have a baby on the way."

James's arms flailed as he swam through the clothes. "What the hell?" He grabbed an organic cotton onesie off his lap and held it up. "What is this?"

"It's a baby shower, just for you!" Quinn snatched the onesie from his hand. "Congratulations! Too bad the mother-to-be couldn't make it. But don't worry, I'm leaving, so you don't even have to pretend you're not texting her." She crumpled the garment into a ball and flung it as hard as she could in his face, taking satisfaction from the click of the little metal snaps against his skin. Then she turned on her heel and walked out the door.

18

As Quinn sat in the car, staring at the dashboard, it occurred to her that she had nobody to talk to about this. Not for the first time, Quinn wished she'd made more of an effort to bolster her friendships. She'd drifted from her college friends when they'd started to get pregnant and have kids. All those baby showers and birthday parties had been painful to attend, and her infertility had left her feeling like the odd woman out. There hadn't been any major fallouts, just a slow slide that left her feeling ashamed to reach out now.

Quinn realized that maybe she could call Elise at the library. Elise had been so supportive recently, but Quinn didn't feel right dumping this on her, especially when she hadn't been a very good friend in return. How could she call Elise out of the blue and tell her that James had been cheating and had knocked up his intern? And what if Sonia found out? Quinn couldn't handle her boss's disapproval or advice right then.

For a wild second, Quinn considered calling Helena. The attorney worked with scorned spouses all the time, and she'd be able to help Quinn talk through her options. But it was too depressing to think that she needed to pay someone three hundred dollars an hour to help her decide whether her marriage was worth saving.

And besides, there was Emily to think about now.

Helena's job was to help Quinn and James get custody of Emily. If she knew their marriage was struggling, would she be obligated to disclose that information to opposing council? Or to the judge?

How could James do this to us?

Quinn almost wished she didn't know what James had been up to. That she'd stayed in blissful ignorance until the hearing was over, and they had custody of Emily. Or maybe forever. It was humiliating to admit that part of her was angrier about James blowing up their life than she was about the betrayal itself.

With shaking hands, Quinn started the car and drove without a destination in mind, waiting for her scorching anger to subside, but with each neighborhood, it only burned hotter. If she went home now, she'd probably have an even bigger outburst. The last thing she needed was the neighbors to over-hear an argument between her and James. That *definitely* wouldn't go over well if the judge or social worker found out.

Instead of heading home, she steered the car through the Liberty Tunnel and into the suburbs. Less familiar with the neighborhoods there, she followed the few roads she knew, and found herself in the park in Nora's neighborhood.

Quinn climbed out of the car, shaking out the cramps in her hands and tightness in her shoulders from the death-grip she'd held on the steering wheel. The sounds of children's laughter drifted across the ball field, luring her to the play-ground, and she found herself at the same bench where she'd sat with Liam a couple of weeks ago. On the ground she spotted a dried dandelion, a casualty from when she'd dropped the buzzing flowers he'd given her. Despite her dark mood, Quinn chuckled at the memory of Liam's horrified face as he tried to explain that he hadn't intentionally set a bee after her.

She settled onto the bench and reached down to pick up the discarded flower, twirling it between her fingers. That had been a wonderful day, hanging out in the park and playing with the kids. It was such a simple, regular occurrence for most people, but that dream had eluded Quinn. She pictured what they must have looked like: Connor showing off his tricks with the basketball, Emily holding out a fistful of flowers, Liam laughing over her near-miss with the bumble bee. Had people gazed across the park and assumed they were a family?

Quinn's heart filled with longing to really *be* that family. Not with Liam, of course. She'd always wanted it with James. But now she didn't know what she wanted.

Quinn was saved from having to spend any more time thinking about it by a woman approaching with two small kids in tow. The woman gave Quinn a friendly smile as she walked past and dropped her enormous tote bag onto the next bench over.

"I want my water bottle," declared her boy, who looked to be about six.

"Let me get settled here," the woman said, sitting on the bench and plunging her hand into the depths of the bag.

"I want mine, too," the age eight-or-so girl chimed in.

"Okay, I'm looking." The woman pulled out two jackets and set them next to her on the bench. Next came a stuffed rabbit, a bottle of sunscreen, and bag of cheddar Goldfish before she finally located the water bottles.

"Will you play ball with us now?" the boy asked, after he'd taken several noisy gulps from his bottle.

"In a bit, honey. Let Mommy rest for a few minutes first. Go play on the swings, okay?"

When the kids had run off in the direction of the jungle gym, the woman glanced over at Quinn. "Thank God for some peace and quiet," she said with a wry smile, and then leaned back to click on her phone.

Quinn did her best to smile back in solidarity. *I totally get it. I'm so tired of schlepping snacks and noisy children, too.*

Except she *didn't* get it.

She'd never understand the desire to sit in a beautiful park with children who wanted to play and to choose to stare at your phone instead. Or to ditch them with their other parent to sneak off with a glass of wine. They had no idea what they had—these women whose children loved them unconditionally. Who had a house full of laughter and chaos and tiny feet running around, and would never again have to feel utterly alone.

A tear drifted down Quinn's cheek, but she quickly swiped at it when a voice cut into her thoughts. "Hi, Miss Quinn! Guess what! I lost another tooth."

Actually, it sounded more like, "Hi, Mith Quinn! Geth what! I lothst another tooth." And when she looked up, it was clear why. Connor stood in front of her with an even wider gap in his grin than had been there before.

Despite her dark mood, Quinn couldn't help but return his smile. "You lost another one! Congratulations! Did the tooth fairy remember to come this time?"

"Yes, she did." Liam plopped down on the bench next to her in a move that was becoming familiar. He raised his fists in victory, like Rocky on the art museum stairs.

Quinn shook her head with pity. "I bet it gets expensive for the tooth fairy to have to keep paying four hundred percent interest."

Liam laughed. "It sure does."

Connor jumped up and down a few times like he had so much energy he couldn't stand in one spot. "Daddy, I'm going to climb the spider web!"

"Okay, bud." Liam gave him a wave.

Connor ran off to a curving, web-like structure. Quinn

watched the rope sag beneath his foot as he took a couple of steps up, and she tensed up. He was so little, what if he slipped? "You don't want to go with him?" she asked Liam.

"Nah, I'm good."

Quinn cringed as Connor climbed to the next level, his feet still quivering on the unsteady rope. "That thing is awfully high. You don't worry that he'll fall?"

Liam shrugged. "He might fall."

She stared at him. "Really? You don't care?"

"Of course I *care*. I don't want to end up in the ER. But helicopter parenting is generally discouraged these days." Liam gave her a crooked smile that displayed his amusement. "Kids need to learn to take a few risks. Gain confidence in themselves."

Quinn's face flushed. So, all these mothers she'd been judging for not playing with their kids were actually helping their development? "Oh, well, how would I know?" She looked down at her hands. "I haven't been inducted into the secret parenting society. Obviously."

"Hey, I'm sorry." Liam reached out and put a hand on her arm. "I was kidding. My wife made me read about a billion parenting books when she was pregnant. They all make you feel like you're going to screw your kid up if you don't let them fall on their head every now and then. I didn't mean to make you feel bad."

Quinn shook her head as Connor made it to the top of the spider web unscathed. "And all this time I thought avoiding concussion was the key to being a good parent."

"Not anymore." Liam waved to Connor who was jumping up and down with his arms in the air. Quinn smiled.

"So." Liam cocked his head. "What are you doing here? I thought you only met with Emily on Saturdays."

"Oh, I'm not meeting Emily today." Quinn's face flushed. Did she look like a creepy stalker sitting at the playground all by herself? It hadn't occurred to her until this moment that she'd be the only adult without a kid here. "Would you believe me if I told you I'm not sure what I'm doing here? I was just out for a drive and—" Quinn shrugged. "Ended up on this park bench."

Liam looked at her sideways, his brow furrowed as if he was trying to figure her out. "I might believe that, yeah. You looked a little forlorn sitting here all by yourself." His voice dipped with concern. "Everything okay?"

For a second, Quinn actually considered spilling the whole story. She could use a friend right now, and he sounded like he actually cared. But she quickly came to her senses. Maybe that's what he wanted her to think, so he could learn things to use against her. If telling Helena about James's infidelity baby was an epically bad idea, then opening up to Nora's brother would amount to tying a cement brick on her chances of getting custody of Emily and throwing them in the river.

"Yep." She straightened her shoulders. "Everything is wonderful. It's a beautiful park, so you know... I thought I'd sit and read for a while."

Liam blinked. "Oh. Sorry. Connor and I didn't mean to interrupt you if you came here for some alone time." Did he seem a little disappointed by that? Or maybe she just didn't know how to read him.

"No," Quinn blurted out. God, the last thing she needed right now was to be alone. "No, it's fine. It's nice to see you and Connor." She took off her cardigan and set it next to her on the bench, hoping he wouldn't notice that she didn't even have a book with her. Quinn steered the conversation in Connor's direction. "He's a great kid. He's very sweet with Emily."

"Thanks. He is a great kid." Liam smiled with pride. "The way Connor and Emily get along is a lot like how Nora and I were at that age. We only have a year difference in our ages, just like the two of them." He gazed out across the playground and waved at Connor who was on his way down a slide now. "But we grew even closer when Connor's mother died."

Quinn sucked in a breath, her gaze flying to Liam's. "Oh, I'm so sorry. I had no idea."

"Yeah. Thanks." Liam looked down at his hands. "Connor doesn't remember her. She died from childbirth complications."

Suddenly, all of Quinn's problems faded in comparison. Poor Connor. How awful to lose his mother at such a young age. And poor Liam, suddenly thrust into single fatherhood with a brand-new baby, at the exact moment he lost the woman he loved. Quinn's eyes began to burn, and she swallowed hard. "That must have been awful for you, suddenly alone with a newborn."

He nodded. "Thank God I had my sister. Emily wasn't born yet, obviously, so Nora pretty much moved in for the first six months and helped me take care of him. And then once Emily came along, we helped each other. My job as a photographer is more flexible day-to-day, so I can usually do school pick-ups and that kind of thing. But I travel a lot, so then Nora takes over. Connor and Emily have bedrooms in both of our houses."

And there was that little voice in her head again, accusing her of disrupting this family's happy lives with her own selfish wish to raise her biological child, to be a part of her life. Had Liam steered the conversation in this direction on purpose? Was this all a ploy to make her back off?

"Can I ask you something?" Quinn turned to face him. "Do you really think I don't have any right to be in Emily's life?"

He looked at her for a long moment and then sighed. "I don't know. I get it that Emily is genetically your kid. And I saw what my sister went through to get pregnant, so I know it must have been tough for you, too."

Quinn nodded. *Tough* was one word for it.

He pressed his hands to his temples. "This situation isn't

your fault, I understand that. But I don't think *you* really understand what you're doing to our family. And especially to Nora."

Quinn paused, not sure what to say to that. She was saved from having to come up with something by Connor skidding to a stop in front of her. "Quinn! Do you want play ball again?"

"Is that allowed?" She raised her eyebrows at Liam. "Or would I be helicopter parenting?"

"Oh, I think it's allowed." He gave Quinn a wink. "Just be sure to aim the ball at his head to maximize his odds of concussion. It builds character."

"Hey! Don't aim at my head!" Connor yelled, but he didn't seem offended. He was probably used to his dad's jokes.

"Come on, Connor." Liam stood up and stole the ball from him, holding it behind his back when Connor made a grab for it. "Last one to the basketball court is monkey in the middle." And before Quinn knew what had happened, the two of them took off across the pavement.

"Oh, no, you don't." She lunged to her feet and ran after them.

For the next few hours, Quinn played like a kid, chasing Liam and Connor to take control of the ball, competing to see who could make the most baskets, and finally, collapsing onto a patch of grass, panting and laughing her head off. And as she lay back to stare up at the sky, tilting her head to get a look at the cloud that Connor insisted was shaped like an elephant, she realized she felt lighter than she had in weeks.

19

As much as Quinn would have liked to stay in the park tossing the ball around with Liam and Connor all night, she knew she couldn't avoid going home forever. So, when the sun began its slow descent toward the horizon, leaving streaks of orange and purple across the sky, she reluctantly handed the ball over to Connor. "It's getting late, I should probably go."

Liam squinted at the burst of colors in the sun's wake, then looked at his watch. "I guess we lost track of time. I need to get this grubby guy home and into the bathtub." He ruffled Connor's dark hair, making it stand up even more than usual. "Looks like it's going to be pizza tonight."

"Can Quinn come to dinner at our house?" Connor bounced the ball a couple of times on the pavement, more smoothly than the first time she'd seen him dribble a couple of weeks ago. He'd been practicing. "Please?"

Over Connor's head, Liam's eyes met hers. He cocked his head, and for a moment, he looked as if he was going to invite her to join them. Quinn was surprised to realize just how much appeal the invitation held. She was as reluctant for the fun to end and real life to begin again. But then Connor bounced the ball again, and at the smack of rubber against the pavement, Liam's gaze slowly slid past her.

"I think Quinn probably has to get home." He turned away to pack up his messenger bag.

"Yeah," Quinn said. It was for the best, but still, her smile felt a little bit forced. "Thanks, Connor. But I have a long drive into the city."

"Maybe next time?" Connor asked. He grabbed the ball and held it now, looking up at her with all the innocence and eagerness of a five-year-old.

She reached out and ruffled his hair, mirroring his dad's gesture from earlier. "We'll have to see."

"Okay." Connor's shoulders drooped, and he kicked the pavement with his scuffed sneaker.

Quinn turned and grabbed her cardigan off the park bench to hide her own regret. This had been the best afternoon she'd had in as long as she could remember. Which was exactly why she should go home. Today had been an escape, a magazine-perfect image complete with an adorable child. But it wouldn't be fair to hang around pretending she was a part of some fantasy family. It was clear from Connor's eagerness to have her to dinner that he was becoming partial to her. She had to admit she was growing a little partial to Connor as well.

Quinn's heart constricted at the thought of the tragic death of Connor's mother. After all he'd lost, it was no wonder he'd form attachments to women like her. But none of this was real life. Though Liam had been friendly toward her once he'd gotten past his initial anger, his ulterior motive was clear: show her what a tight-knit family they'd been before she came along to ruin everything.

And he was obviously succeeding, because the more she grew fond of them, the more her doubts crept in. Which was why it was time to go home and pick up the pieces of her own family.

Connor and Liam walked her to her car. By the time they reached the other end of the ballfield, it was beginning to get dark. She unlocked the door with her remote key, and Liam ran ahead and opened it for her.

"Oh," Quinn said, at the unexpected gesture. "Thanks." She hesitated next to the open door. "I had a lot of fun today."

"We did too, right, bud?"

"Yep!"

And then before she knew what was happening Connor reached over and wrapped his little arms around her middle. Quinn slowly lowered her arms to hug him back, pressing her lips together at the emotion welling up inside her. She stared out across the ballfield so she didn't have to meet Liam's eye. When Connor finally released her from his grasp, it was as if he took the rest of the afternoon heat with him, and Quinn crossed her arms over her chest to ward off the evening chill.

"Well." She finally looked to Liam now, but his expression was inscrutable. "Goodbye." And more reluctantly than she ever would have expected, she climbed inside and drove away.

———

When she arrived home, Quinn found James sitting on the couch, waiting for her. She entered the room cautiously, choosing the chair on the opposite side of the room. On the coffee table between them sat the baby clothes she'd hurled at him in anger. He'd folded each tiny outfit and left them in a neat pile.

"Quinn, I'm so sorry." James cringed, cutting deep lines into his forehead. Suddenly, he looked so much older than his forty-four years. "I can't begin to tell you how sorry I am for everything. I don't have any excuse except it was a moment of weakness when you and I were having a tough time."

Quinn opened her mouth to object to that last part. A *tough time* was no excuse for what he'd done. How dare he put the responsibility on her?

But before she could speak, James held up a hand. "I know that's not a reason to cheat. I'm to blame. But I love you, and I'm determined to fix this. Please give me another chance."

Quinn longed to believe that James was sorry and wanted to make amends. *But, how can I?* If she could blame his affair on too much alcohol at a work conference or a dumb decision he'd made right after they'd had a fight, then maybe they could sweep it under the rug and move on. But James's affair with the intern hadn't been "a moment of weakness." If the timeline had started with the receipt she'd found last year in his suitcase, it had been *many* moments of a lot more than weakness. And how could she be sure he'd only cheated with one woman? He'd been buying condoms that he obviously didn't use with the intern. So, who did he buy them for?

Quinn reached out to straighten a stack of baby clothes, her hand brushing against a tiny felt cut-out of a bunny. "I don't know how I'll ever trust you again."

"I know." He hung his head. "Of course you can't trust me right now. But let me try to earn it back," James pleaded. "It's completely over between Sasha and me."

Sasha. Quinn recoiled at the name. Sasha, who was young and fertile. Sasha, the woman having James's baby. "It's *over*?" Quinn stared at him across the living room. Could he really be that naive? "I don't think you get it. It will *never* be over between you and Sasha. She's in your life forever now."

"But we're not—" James held up his hands in surrender. "We're not involved anymore. I told her we can only communicate about the baby."

"And have you and Sasha talked about how that's going to work? Have you thought about what that's going to look like once this baby comes along?" The pressure built in Quinn's chest. "Have you thought about what this means for Emily?"

James sprung off the couch and crossed the room so he could kneel on the floor in front of her, hands on either side of the chair. She pressed back against the cushion, as far away from him as possible.

"Quinn," James said. "I could get joint custody, and we could have the baby here for fifty percent of the time." He grabbed her hand and pulled her closer. "The baby could grow up here. We could raise him or her together, just like we always wanted."

For a wild moment, Quinn closed her eyes and pictured it. A baby in this house. A tiny little bundle wearing the clothes on the coffee table. A swing in the corner where the baby would nap while she made dinner in the next room, a crocheted blanket of the softest wool on the floor where the baby would practice tummy time. She imagined the baby learning to speak.

A baby's first word was usually *Mama*.

Who would be Mama?

Quinn yanked her hand from his grasp. "You think any of this is what I wanted? This is a nightmare." Her voice rose. "It wouldn't be the two of us raising this baby. This child will always be yours and hers. I wouldn't have any rights. I wouldn't be the baby's mother."

"You'd be the baby's stepmother."

"Stepmother isn't the same thing." This was exactly why she wanted parental rights and the chance to raise Emily. Because otherwise, she'd always just be a visitor passing through her own child's life. And now James was asking her to accept that same arrangement with another woman's baby.

"You'd have rights. It would be up to us to decide how we raise the baby."

Would it, though? Or would it be up to James and his twenty-two-year-old intern? *Sasha*. What if Quinn wanted to sign the child up for piano lessons, or take them on a trip? Sasha could refuse. What if the child needed medical care? Quinn would need a letter, permission from the child's biological parents.

But despite all her doubts, Quinn hesitated, eyeing the baby clothes on the table.

James followed her gaze. "I was hoping you'd change your mind about giving them away. We can still use all of them. They're adorable, aren't they?"

Quinn's heart ached as she imagined holding a tiny baby asleep against her in that bear suit. She wanted it so much she could almost feel the rise and fall of a baby's chest, the warmth of its breath against her neck.

"We could turn the guest room into a nursery." James's face brightened as he probably sensed he had an opening. "The baby would have their own room here, and they'd never know you as anything other than a parent."

The guest room—?

Her fantasy dissipating, Quinn lunged from the chair, brushing past James to move to the other side of the room. She dropped her arms to her side, feeling their emptiness where moments ago, she'd imagined a baby. "The guest room is supposed to go to Emily."

James rocked back on his heels and pressed his lips together. "Listen, Quinn," he finally said, slowly climbing to his feet. "I was thinking... Everything is so complicated with the custody hearings and all the hoops we have to jump through. Maybe now that we have a baby on the way, we should consider stepping back from gaining custody of Emily. I know Nora said no, but now that she knows us better, maybe she would reconsider some sort of visitation arrangement. We could still do our Saturday visits with Emily, still have her in our lives..." He trailed off, looking at her expectantly.

The floor shifted beneath Quinn's feet. "No." He couldn't be serious. "Pursuing Emily was never about just having a child.

She's our *biological* child. She's family, connected to us by blood."

But maybe James's hesitation over these custody hearings weren't because he was concerned about how it would affect Emily. Was it possible that he'd stopped being invested in Emily because he'd found out he had a smaller, newer model on the way? Quinn studied the man she'd married over half a decade earlier. The one who'd promised to be with her for better or worse. Had he meant it? Did he still mean it?

"Do you really love me and want to make this marriage work?" She held her breath.

"You know I do." James's eyes looked strained.

Quinn didn't know anything anymore. "Then you have to be on board with pursuing custody of Emily. That's my priority right now. I'm open to working out how this new baby will fit into our family, too. Your child deserves an involved father and a loving home. But this can't be a choice we make between these two children. They *both* need to be a part of our lives."

Relief passed across his features as he took a step toward her. "I just want to save our family, Quinn. If you want to move forward with custody of Emily, that's what we'll do."

His words should have made her feel better, but a heavy weight still pressed on her chest. There was much that could go wrong. So much to lose. "We need to agree that we won't do or say anything about your new baby until the hearing for Emily is settled." The only real evidence was the money James had been sending to Sasha. But would the social worker be looking that closely at each individual payment they'd made? It seemed more likely that she'd want an overall picture of their financial health. So, the only other way for her to find out about Sasha and the baby was for James to tell her. "Can you promise me that?"

"Yes." James nodded eagerly. "I promise."

"Then there's just one more thing." Quinn took a step backwards, toward the door leading to the hallway.

"Anything."

"Get some sheets and blankets from the hall closet. Until the home visit, I want you to sleep on the couch in the basement." And then she turned and fled to their bedroom where, for the foreseeable future, she'd be sleeping alone.

20

"Quinn! Quinn!" The voice came from inside the house, mingling with the patter of feet on hardwood floors. The front door flew open, and Emily stood on the other side, grinning widely. "Hi! What are we playing today?"

"Emily!" Nora's voice called from somewhere in the back of the house. Heavier footsteps, slower and more deliberate this time, sounded from the same direction until Nora appeared at the end of the hall. "We talked about opening the door without checking first."

"It's just me." Quinn lifted a palm to Nora, showing she was harmless, and then turned back to Emily. "Peek through the window next time, okay, sweetie?" She said it even though she knew it was unlikely there'd be a next time. Nora had made it clear Quinn wasn't welcome in her home, and their weekly visits with Emily had been at the park or the library. She hadn't been back to Nora's house since the birthday party all those weeks ago.

But then Nora had texted to say she had to be on an unexpected conference call that afternoon. At first, she'd had tried to cancel their visit altogether, but Quinn wasn't giving up her one afternoon a week without a fight, and she wasn't terribly eager to agree to another switch in days, either. Finally, Nora had offered to host the visit while she worked in her office upstairs.

Quinn had to admit she was a little disappointed that Nora hadn't just sent Emily with Liam and Connor again. But it was probably for the best. Quinn had spent too much time thinking about how carefree she'd felt on that unexpected day in the park, letting go of her problems and playing with Connor, when she really should have been thinking about fixing her marriage instead.

True to his word, James had moved his things to the basement and had been sleeping on the pull-out bed down there every night for the past week. But in the evenings, he'd come upstairs so they could have dinner together. After talking about the upcoming hearing and planning for the social worker's home visit, they didn't have much to say to each other. Quinn couldn't help but wonder if it had always been this way. They'd only dated for such a short time before they were caught up in the whirlwind of planning a wedding. And then from the very beginning of their marriage, their lives had revolved around getting pregnant.

Had the spark been fizzling since long before James's infidelity? Had it ever burned in the first place?

Quinn couldn't face it right now. Once the hearing was over, they'd find a good marriage counselor and work through this. But for now, she pushed it out of her mind and focused on Emily. "What are we playing today?"

"Legos!"

"My favorite." Quinn gave Emily a grin as she brushed past Nora into the house.

As they made their way toward the kitchen, Quinn slowed her steps to check out the contents of the frames that hung in the hall. Nora had turned the walls into a gallery of family photos, and from the professional quality of the images, Quinn guessed most of them were Liam's work. She desperately wanted to stop and stare, to pour over each photo of Emily and track how she'd changed from a baby to toddler to little girl. But Nora had made it clear that she wasn't interested in sharing anything about Emily's life.

As she inched down the hall, Quinn began to recognize other family members from Emily's birthday party in the photos. Once again, she was reminded that Nora had a huge, loving family, while hers was decidedly lacking. Quinn spotted Aunt Susan and Uncle Wesley, and a whole gaggle of kids— probably cousins of some sort. Liam and Connor showed up in many of the frames, too. Even as a toddler, Connor had the same dark, sticky-uppy hair, slightly crooked glasses, and wide grin that he had now.

At the far end of the hall, Quinn noticed a couple of photos of Liam standing next to a beautiful, dark-haired Indian woman. From the resemblance to Connor, Quinn guessed the woman must have been his mother. Quinn stumbled to a stop, gazing at a photo that could have only been taken on her wedding day. The woman wore an ornate emerald and red gown with shimmering gold embroidery and a bejeweled head-piece that draped over her dark, wavy hair and gathered in the center of her forehead. Her face was in profile to the camera, eyes locked on Liam who sat next to her under a flowing gauze canopy. He wore a long cotton kurta with a garland of carnations around his neck, and the photographer had captured his smile just as he reached over to gently hang a matching band of flowers around the woman's neck.

"Liam's wife, Preeti." Nora stopped next to Quinn and hitched her chin at the photo. "It was the worst time of our lives when she died..."

"I can't even imagine." Without thinking, Quinn reached out a comforting hand. "Liam said you were a huge help when Connor was a baby. That you took care of both of them for months." Quinn glanced at Emily, who was doing pirouettes down the hall. "You must have been going through IVF at the same time. I'm sure that was stressful."

"God, the funny part is, I don't even remember." Nora gave her head a shake. "With all the treatments before that one, I obsessed over every little thing I could control that might help an embryo stick. My diet, how much sleep I was getting..."

Quinn understood completely. "How much exercise you got... Should you try yoga..."

Nora smiled. "Yes. And meditation, of course."

"Did you do acupuncture, too?"

"I did. You?"

"Acupuncture *and* Chinese herbs."

"It was overwhelming." Nora pressed a hand to her heart as if the memory still gave her anxiety, and Quinn could relate to that, too. She had to admit she was relieved to never have to go through all of that poking and prodding and choking down bitter herbal teas again.

"But when I did IVF right after Preeti died," Nora continued, "I barely even thought about any of that stuff. I just went through the motions, trying to get out of bed in the morning and take my shots and make sure Liam ate something once in a while."

Quinn's gaze drifted back to Liam's wedding photo. He looked so happy and in love. Her heart ached for him.

Emily pirouetted by, and Nora took her hand with an affectionate smile. "Unbelievably, that was the round of IVF that actually worked. I don't generally believe in this stuff, but it was almost like the universe brought us Emily for a reason." Nora looked at Quinn straight on and unflinching. "She came along exactly when our family needed her."

Quinn backed away from the photos of Preeti, and away from Nora, too. For a moment, Quinn had thought she and Nora might have been getting to know each other and finding a little bit of common ground. But it seemed Nora had only broached the subject as a way of making her feel guilty for wanting custody of Emily. Quinn was truly sorry their family had experienced such tragedy. But it didn't change the fact that Emily was biologically Quinn's, and she had a right to be a part of her life.

"Well," Quinn took another step backward, almost as if putting a physical space between her and Nora could help clear her mind of their conversation as well. "Emily and I should go play. You probably need to get to your conference call." Quinn spun on her heels and reached for Emily's hand. "Are you ready to show me those Legos? Or—" Quinn remembered the dollhouse. She'd love to see Emily enjoying the gift she'd given her. "We could play with your new Encanto house?"

"We can't play with it." Emily looked down sadly, rubbing her toe against the lines in the floor. "It's still in the box."

Quinn's gaze swung to Nora, who at least had the courtesy to look contrite. "I'm sorry," Nora said. "I haven't assembled it yet. I'm in the middle of this big work project, and—"

Quinn studied Nora's face. The other woman did seem busy with work, but was that just an excuse to keep Emily from playing with the gift because it had come from Quinn? Again, that conflicted feeling washed over her. She hated thinking the worst of Nora, and she was sympathetic to how hard it was to do everything on her own.

Quinn's heart picked up speed in her chest. If she and James couldn't make their marriage work, would she be a single parent someday? *No,* Quinn told herself. She and James were going to make it work.

"Look, I know you're busy," she said to Nora, focusing on the problem at hand. "Why don't you just let me help you assemble the dollhouse? I can come by tomorrow."

Emily jumped up and down in excitement, but Nora hesitated. "I don't know..."

"Please, Mommy?" Emily tugged at Nora's shirt. "Please?"
Finally, Nora sighed. "Fine. Come by tomorrow."

———

Quinn had a lovely afternoon sitting on the flowered rug in Emily's pale green bedroom building a Lego castle and coloring a picture of a mermaid. Then, along with a line of stuffed animals, she learned her ABCs and sang songs in Emily's pretend school. They were simple activities—the kinds she did with kids at the library all the time—but doing them with her own child made it special. The more Quinn got to know Emily, the more she could see evidence of their biological link. It wasn't just in their appearances. She noticed that Emily tugged on the ends of her hair the same way she did when she was concentrating. And Quinn could have sworn that when Emily said certain words, she pronounced them just like Quinn's father.

Quinn had always thought that having her own child would lessen the pain of losing her parents at such a young age, but she would have given anything in the world to have her mom and dad there, just for the afternoon, to watched Emily hold up her drawing with a proud smile and laugh over a silly knock-knock joke. Her mom would have been the kind of grandma to bake cookies and read piles of books and build fairy houses in the woods, and her dad would have played ball in the yard for hours.

Quinn hoped she'd have the chance to share her parents with Emily someday, even if it was only in stories and photographs, and her mom's old recipe for honey cake.

A few hours into their games, Emily began complaining she was hungry so they headed downstairs to look for a snack. From the voices coming from the closed office door, it sounded like

Nora was still on her conference call, so Quinn ushered Emily into the kitchen.

Quinn stood in the center of the sunny room and gazed from the brightly colored fruit bowl on the kitchen island to the striped curtains in the window. As much as she wished she could find fault with something, Quinn had to admit there was nothing to criticize. Just like the exterior of Nora's house, the interior was decorated with homey touches that made the space feel warm and welcoming. Nora had set up her kitchen to be kid-friendly, with a sturdy red step stool next to the counter, a chalkboard wall perfect for Emily to scribble on, and a child-height shelf under the island stacked with indestructible melamine tableware.

Quinn took a plate from the shelf and turned to Emily who'd hopped up on a chair by the kitchen island. "What would you like to eat?"

"I want chocolate!" Emily pointed to two oversized cabinet doors.

"Chocolate? Oh, I don't think that's a good idea." Quinn remembered Nora's critical reaction when she'd offered Emily a cookie in the attorney's office. There was also that day in the park where Liam wouldn't let Connor give Emily a peanut butter cup. If Nora was one of those parents who only let their kids eat organic rice cakes and fruit, Quinn wasn't about to get scolded for offering Emily a Hershey's Kiss. "How about something healthy? An apple?" She crossed the kitchen to the cabinet doors. "Maybe a PB&J sandwich?"

"What's that?" Emily asked.

Really? "PB&J is a classic. Let's see if you have the ingredients for me to make one." Quinn peeked into the pantry. Shelf after shelf held orderly stacks of canned goods, boxes of pasta lined up in a row, and neatly labeled canisters of baking supplies. Quinn was really going to have to step it up if she was going to impress the social worker at their home visit. She wasn't a slob or anything, but she did have a cabinet where she tossed all the Tupperware without bothering to match up the lids. And forget about neat canisters lined up in a row. It was definitely time for a trip to the Container Store.

"Are you looking for something?"

Quinn jumped and spun around to find Nora standing in the doorway with her arms crossed over her chest and an irritated look on her face.

"N-no," Quinn stammered. Why did she feel like she'd been caught snooping? She was only looking for a snack for Emily. Somehow, Nora always seemed to make her feel like she was doing something wrong. Which was probably deliberate. "Emily was hungry. We were thinking maybe a peanut butter sandwich."

"She can't have that. She's allergic to nuts."

"Oh." No wonder Emily didn't know what a PB&J was. "Sorry, I didn't know." That explained the peanut butter cup, and maybe the cookies in Helena's office that first day.

"It's fine, I'll make her something." Nora held up her arm and gave an exaggerated glance at her watch. "It's 2:56 p.m."

Quinn flushed with annoyance. Her court-ordered time with Emily ended at 3 p.m., and Nora never let her go a minute over. Quinn was tempted to plant her feet on the pristine kitchen floor and insist she be allowed to stay for four more minutes, but she didn't want to argue with Nora in front of Emily.

"Okay, I'll head out." In an equally deliberate act, she intentionally turned her back to Nora and walked over to where Emily sat at the kitchen island. "I loved playing with you today, Em. Thanks for teaching me my ABCs."

"Say thank you to Quinn, Emily," Nora nudged. "It's *time for her to go.*"

"Thank you, Quinn!" Emily reached out her little arms for a hug. And in the next breath, she declared, "I love you!"

At those simple words, Quinn froze. *I love you.* Her heart folded in on itself. She'd waited her whole life to hear her child say that to her. Swallowing hard over the ache in the back of her throat, Quinn leaned over to wrap her arms around Emily, inhaling the little-girl smell of scented markers and lavender shampoo.

"I love you, too, Emily," Quinn whispered, fighting back tears and holding on for one more moment. Finally, she let go of Emily and turned to leave.

When her gaze drifted to the other side of the kitchen, she saw that Nora was crying, too.

———

Quinn stopped at the grocery store on her way home, and as she walked the aisles, it took her a moment to realize that people were staring at her. She rubbed her cheek with the sleeve of her shirt. Had she gotten marker on her face when they were coloring?

Finally, an older man who walked by gave her a nod. "You sure look happy. Glad you're having a good day."

Quinn pressed her hands to her cheeks and realized she'd been grinning since she left Nora's house. Buzzing at the memory of Emily's little voice as she said goodbye.

I love you.

Quinn nodded. "It's been the best day."

"Well, good. Keep smiling," the man said.

"I will!"

The only thing that would have made her day better was if Emily had said, *I love you, Mommy.* But maybe soon enough. The hearing was in only a couple of weeks, and Quinn was feeling good about their chances of winning custody of Emily. When Quinn Googled similar cases—which she did obsessively —she found that Helena had been right when she'd told them that there weren't many to go by. But in the few cases of switched embryos Quinn had been able to find, the judges had ruled in the biological parents' favor.

Emily was clearly growing attached to her, and that had to be a factor in the judge's decision. And ever since their big blow-up over his affair, James had stuck to his word and started to become much more attentive and interested in being a part of this case to win custody of Emily. He'd even spent a couple of evenings that week helping Quinn to clear out the guest room and organize their personal papers for the home visit.

As far as his new baby—well, that was still up in the air. Sasha was only a couple of weeks into her second trimester. They had plenty of time to figure out how his child would fit into their lives once the hearing for Emily was over. But for now, Quinn felt like things were finally moving in their favor.

Quinn got in line at the checkout behind a woman and her two kids, keeping her head down as she unloaded her groceries on the conveyor belt. The kids were well behaved—the younger one sat nicely in the baby seat of the cart while the older one stood patiently by while their mother paid.

"Aren't you a little darling?" a familiar voice crooned at the baby in the cart. Quinn's head jerked up. It was the older cashier who'd made her feel inadequate for not hurrying up and getting pregnant when she was younger. Quinn looked around for an escape, but all the checkout lines were long, and the man behind her had already boxed her in with his cart. If she pulled everything off the belt and moved to another aisle, it was going to make a huge commotion and inconvenience everyone. Maybe it was better to just move along quickly and not engage in conversation.

The cashier ripped a receipt from the register and handed it to the mother in front of her. "Enjoy every minute. It goes so fast." Did she say that to every woman with a child?

"Thanks." The mother nodded, as if she were used to this advice from strangers, and moved along toward the door.

The cashier turned to Quinn. "I remember those days like it was yesterday."

"Mmm-hmm. I'm sure you do," Quinn murmured.

"Mine are all out of the house now." The cashier shook her head. "I miss them like crazy." She picked up a bag of flour and ran it through the scanner. "Do you have any kids?"

Quinn sighed and internally rolled her eyes. This cashier obviously took every chance she got to talk about her kids. Quinn had thought it was sweet before she knew what was coming next. She was about to say no, and brace herself for the meddlesome advice about her biological clock again, when suddenly Emily's voice cut through her consciousness.

I love you.

Quinn looked up at the cashier. "Yes. Yes, I do." She smiled radiantly. "I have a four-year-old daughter. And you're right. It goes so fast. I plan to enjoy every minute."

"Good for you!" the cashier returned her grin. "Good for you."

21

At exactly noon the next day, Quinn knocked on Nora's door with a toolbox under her arm. Nora had said she knew how to use a screwdriver, so she probably had her own tools, but Quinn wasn't taking any chances. If they didn't have the right wrench, Nora might try to abandon the whole project.

Quinn listened for the sound of Emily's feet and awaited her wide grin as she opened the door. But it was Nora who answered, and the house was painfully quiet as Quinn stepped inside.

"She's with Aunt Susan," Nora said curtly, before Quinn could even ask.

Obviously, Nora had sent Emily away so Quinn couldn't have even one moment with her daughter longer than the court had ordered. Frustration rose in her chest. Why did Nora have to undermine her at every turn? Why couldn't she even consider that they both had the same goals—Emily's happiness?

Unless that isn't Nora's goal, Quinn thought, spitefully.

Nora headed down the hall, and Quinn followed her into the living room where the box containing the dollhouse sat in the middle of the floor. Next to it was a toolbox twice the size of

Quinn's. For a moment, they both stared at Quinn's gift. The box was huge—several feet in width and almost as tall as Quinn. Not for the first time, she realized that she really hadn't thought this gift through. It was a much bigger project than she'd imagined. And how big would the dollhouse be when it was fully assembled? Emily's bedroom wasn't that large. Nora might have to keep it in the living room.

Quinn had to admit she could see why Nora had been annoyed by the gift, and why it was still unassembled. A familiar flush crept over her. Once again, she felt like she'd been left out of the secret parenting society. Anyone with kids probably knew this dollhouse was a spectacularly bad idea. Quinn sighed. Well, the gift had been given, and it was too late to back out now. Emily would be crushed.

"Okay, let's get this over with," Nora muttered, walking a circle one way around the box, and then back in the other direction, as if she had no idea where to begin.

"I guess we should open it first," Quinn offered, and Nora shot her a look that said, *Seriously? Of course we should open it first.*

Nora walked another circle, and finally paused at one end of the box. After examining it for another moment, she bent over and hefted it up a couple of feet. It looked heavy, but Quinn kept that observation to herself. Nora pulled on the cardboard flap, but it stuck tight.

"Let me try." Quinn shuffled to Nora's end and yanked on the same flap while Nora held the box upright. It was glued tight, but Quinn wasn't giving up. She continued to pull on it until it started to finally peel away from the other side of the box. After a few more hard tugs, the flap popped open, revealing a layer of Styrofoam behind it. Quinn reached in and tentatively pulled on the Styrofoam, hoping to free it from the box. It gave a horrible squeak as little white bits flaked off and rained down on Nora's carpet. "Sorry," she muttered, scrambling around to pick them up.

After a few more tugs—and more Styrofoam on the floor—Quinn managed to free the first layer of padding from the box. She and Nora peered inside to find more padding on the sides, and a pile of flat wooden panels in the middle. The wooden panels were likely the walls of the dollhouse that would need to be put together. Nora stared at them, pressing her hands to her temples as if she were exhausted by this project already. Quinn looked away, pretending she didn't feel the exact same way.

"Alright," Nora said, with a sigh. "Can we get this out of here?" She reached in and gave the wooden panels a hard yank, but they were held tight by more layers of Styrofoam and didn't budge. After another moment of wrestling with it, she cursed under her breath as the box slipped out of her hand and hit the ground with a hard thud. One end grazed her toe. "Damn it."

"Are you okay?" Quinn asked, feeling worse by the second.

Nora sighed again. "I'm fine."

"Maybe we should get a knife and just cut the box open down the middle." Quinn turned and dug in the toolbox, searching for a box cutter.

"No, then we could cut something inside and ruin it." Nora reached in and gave the contents of the box another tug, but they continued to hold tight.

Finally, Quinn stepped in, holding a hand out to stop Nora from wrestling the box to the floor. "Look, can we work together here? This is never going to happen if you keep fighting with it. I'm here to help. Can we remember this is for Emily?"

Nora sat back on her heels and stared up at Quinn. Finally, her shoulders slumped. "You're right. Okay. What do you think we should do?"

Quinn lifted one end of the box. "If I hold the box, and you grab the dollhouse pieces, and we pull at the same time, it might come out."

Nora nodded, standing up and reaching inside the box. "Okay, you have your end?"

"Yep."

"Alright, one... two... three... pull!"

Quinn tightened her hold on the box and braced her feet on the carpet while Nora backed up in the opposite direction, both hands gripping the wooden panels. For a moment, nothing happened, the panels stayed in the box as Quinn and Nora performed a makeshift tug-of-war. Just as Quinn was about to give up, something gave way, and the contents of the box slowly began to slide out. "I think it's coming." Quinn pulled harder. "Keep going."

All of a sudden, the suction between the cardboard and Styrofoam released with a pop. Quinn went reeling backward in one direction, the empty box in her hand, while Nora flew in the other direction and landed on the floor in a heap of doll-house parts. For a moment, they both sat there on the ground, stunned. Then Quinn realized that Nora could really be hurt this time. Those wooden panels were heavy.

"Oh my God, are you okay?" Quinn scrambled over to pull a panel off Nora's leg while Nora shoved a plastic bag full of screws and nails off her lap. Nora shook her head, her lips pressed together, and Quinn's stomach dropped to her knees. *She's hurt.* This had been a terrible idea. She should have hired someone to do this. She shouldn't have sent the damn dollhouse in the first place. This was all her fault.

Nora's shoulders shook now, and Quinn felt even worse. "I'm so sorry." She grabbed another panel and tossed it aside. "Maybe we should just give up on this. I can hire a handyman to put this together..."

She was interrupted by a gasp from Nora, and she looked up to realize the woman's shoulders were shaking even harder. Quinn froze. "Are you—?" She cocked her head, studying the other woman. "Are you *laughing?*"

Nora nodded, her chest heaving, and at the sound of it, Quinn felt a giggle rise up in her chest. Soon, her own shoulders were shaking, and it was like a dam finally released. It felt so good to laugh for the first time in as long as she could remember. To let go of the tension she'd been holding at home around James, the stress of tiptoeing around Nora, the constant worry if she was doing the right thing and making the right decisions.

Quinn sank down on the floor next to Nora, who was bent over, clutching her stomach. The two of them sat in a heap of dollhouse walls and hardware and miniature cartoon figurines and laughed until they could barely breathe.

Slowly, their laughter subsided, and still grinning, Quinn gazed across the mess at the other woman. Nora's face had transformed from rigid lines to a soft smile, and in place of her cold expression, Quinn found something akin to warmth. Nora looked ten years younger, and again, it occurred to Quinn that if they'd met under different circumstances, they might have been friends.

"God, I hate assembling things," Nora said, shaking her head.

Quinn gave her a rueful smile. "Me too. I have no idea what I was thinking when I offered to help with this."

"The only time I really wish I had a husband," Nora admitted, with another laugh, "is when I buy something from IKEA. I have no problem fixing things, but assembling is the worst."

"IKEA furniture is the only reason I keep James around," Quinn joked in return.

"What are we doing here?" Nora said, with a shake of her head. "I have a better idea." She hitched her chin at her phone on the coffee table next to Quinn. "Can you hand me that?"

Quinn passed the phone over to Nora, who flipped through it and dialed a number. After a minute, Quinn heard a vaguely familiar male voice reverberate across the room: "What's up?"

"Listen," Nora said to the person on the other end of the

phone, "can you come over tonight? I need your help assembling something." Nora winked at Quinn. "And by help, I mean *you* assemble the damn thing, my darling big brother who I love with all my heart."

Liam, Quinn realized. Of course. He'd said he and his sister always looked out for each other. Of course Nora would call him if she needed help.

"Sure," she heard him say. "When you put it that way, how can I refuse?"

"Great, see you at six." Nora hung up the phone and gave the dollhouse pieces another shove. "He has no idea what he's in for." She looked at Quinn. "Well, do you want some coffee?"

22

After they abandoned the dollhouse, Quinn followed Nora into the kitchen where the other woman put on a pot of coffee and set out a plate of cookies. They had a surprisingly pleasant, if somewhat stilted conversation about their jobs and favorite restaurants in the city, carefully avoiding all mention of Emily or the court case they were on different sides of.

Then Nora's phone rang. Speaking in a low voice, she took it in the other room, but it was obvious to Quinn that it was Aunt Susan calling to say she was on her way home with Emily. After that, Nora couldn't get rid of her fast enough.

Quinn's annoyance petered out, though, when she got to her car and realized it was a beautiful summer afternoon, she had it all to herself, and there was nowhere she had to be. Truth be told, she had plenty of projects to do at home, but it was Sunday, and James was traveling again that week. Quinn had heard that Nora's little town had a main street with cute boutiques and restaurants, so she used her GPS to find the way. She found a parking spot right in front of a café and decided to stop for a late lunch. Quinn ordered her food and found a table under an umbrella outside.

Her thoughts drifted back to her time with Nora, and she smiled at the memory of the two of them trying to put together that damn dollhouse. It was hard to believe, but she'd actually had fun today. It was strange to think that she and Nora had gone to the same fertility clinic, and their egg retrievals had even been on the same day all those years ago. Had they sat in the waiting room together, exchanging nervous smiles over celebrity magazines and sipping their herbal tea, without having any idea that their futures would someday converge?

If Liam was the brother who drove Nora to appointments, maybe he'd been there, too. She would have assumed he was just another hopeful father-to-be and probably would have been too nervous about her own treatments to do more than glance in his direction.

As Quinn unwrapped her silverware from her napkin, she heard a deep voice call out, "Quinn?"

She glanced up, and as if her thoughts had conjured him up, Liam stood next to her table, so tall that he had to duck to look at her under the umbrella overhead. He held a cup of coffee in one hand and a laptop in the other.

"Liam! Hi. What are you doing here?" It was a silly question: he lived a few blocks away. She was the one who was always getting caught lurking in his neighborhood.

"They have the best salads in town, which I can see you've discovered." He hitched his chin at her lunch. "I do a lot of work from home, so this place gets me out of my dark basement and around other humans." He laughed. "Adult ones."

Quinn smiled, nodding at the seat opposite her. "Would you like to sit?"

He shifted his weight from one foot to the other. "I don't want to bother you if you're in the middle of something."

"The only thing I'm in the middle of," Quinn said with a grin. "Is feeling grateful that it's you and not me who is going to have to assemble a dollhouse tonight."

He raised an eyebrow. "How did you know about that?"

"I'm coming from your sister's house."

"Really?" Liam pulled the other chair back and dropped into it. "How did that go?"

"One point for the dollhouse. Zero for me and Nora. Good luck. It's quite a project."

"Great, so now I'm stuck with it?" He gave her a wry smile. "If you're going to lean into the 1950s cliché and call a man to assemble something for you, don't you have a husband who could do it?"

Quinn shook her head. "I think Nora and I stood a better chance."

Liam took a sip of his coffee. "I've never actually met your husband. What's his name? Jake?"

"James."

"What has James been up to?"

Impregnating an intern. Liam blinked, and for a moment, Quinn worried that she'd actually blurted that out loud. But then she realized he was looking at her sideways because she was just sitting there with an angry expression on her face, and hadn't said anything at all.

Liam probably knew James hadn't exactly been a regular presence at their Saturday visits with Emily, so there was no point in pretending otherwise. She wished James hadn't left her with the burden of apologizing and explaining his absence so many times. "He's been really busy at work." Quinn lifted her gaze over Liam's head. "He travels a lot."

"You're not worried that he hasn't had much of a chance to spend time with Emily?" Liam looked at her innocently, but she had a feeling the question was anything but. "I mean, since you're hoping to get custody and all that?"

"*No.*" Quinn sat up straight in her chair. "No, he's had plenty of time with Emily, and he cares about her as much as I do." She took a deep breath to smooth out the edge in her voice.

Damn James for making her defend him. "It's not his fault he has to work a lot—he's doing it for our family. Surely you know how expensive IVF can be, after your sister went through it."

Liam nodded slowly, regarding her across the table. "Can I ask you something?"

Quinn crossed her arms over her chest. "I guess so."

"Why is this so important to you?"

Quinn narrowed her eyes. "Again, your sister went through this. And you have a child. You really can't understand why someone else would want that, too?"

"Of course I get why you'd want to be a parent. But why is getting custody of Emily so important to you? Why not adopt a child who doesn't already have a family that has loved and cared for them for four years?" He leaned forward, expression earnest. "Two months ago, you had no idea Emily even existed. Does biology really mean that much to you?"

"Can you honestly say that biology *doesn't* matter that much to you?" Quinn challenged. "What if you had no idea you had a child, and then all of a sudden, four years in, you found out Connor existed? Would you be able to just walk away like everyone seems to expect *me* to? Would you be able to go on with your life knowing that somewhere out there is a child who is made up of all the best parts of you—all the best parts of your late wife—and that child belongs to someone else?"

Liam gazed out across the café patio and seemed to consider that. Finally, he met her eyes. "This isn't a fair comparison. I've raised Connor since he was a baby. Of course I can't imagine walking away from him. But if I met him four years in, and if he'd spent those four years with a loving family? Maybe."

"But maybe not."

Liam pressed his lips together and shook his head. "I don't know."

Quinn paused. How could she make him understand her

perspective? "The thing is..." She took a deep breath. "My parents died in a car accident when I was nineteen."

Liam looked up in surprise. "I'm so sorry."

Quinn stared into her coffee cup, remembering the afternoon she'd gotten the news and realized she was all alone in the world. The worst day of her life. "Neither of my parents had any brothers or sisters, and I was an only child, too. My mom and dad were the only two people in the world who I was biologically related to, and now they're gone." She shifted her gaze to Liam's. "I got my dark hair and eyes from my mother. She was Greek. Emily got them from her, too."

He hesitated, a pained expression on his face. "I do understand the importance of people who came before you. But there's more to family than where you're from. More than hair and eye color..."

"Of course there is." Quinn leaned into the table. "When I was at Emily's birthday party a couple of months ago, I saw all those aunts and uncles and cousins in your family. I think you take it for granted that even if Cousin Troy is a bit of a deadbeat, Aunt Susan will let him stay in the garage apartment and Uncle Wesley will pull some strings at the country club to help him get a job. Why would they do that for someone who keeps screwing up his life, apart from the fact that he's family?"

Liam rolled his eyes. "I ask myself the same question every time Troy hits me up for cash."

"But I bet you give it to him." Quinn tilted her head in a silent challenge, and by the way Liam's gazed drifted past her and he didn't answer, it was obvious she was right. "Because Cousin Troy is family. Because *biology* is a powerful connection." Quinn reached down with her right hand and grasped the ring on her left. "I never knew my grandmother on my mom's side. She died before I was born. But when I got engaged, I chose to wear her ring." She held up her hand, and the stone glinted in the sunlight. "Why would I care about wearing a piece of rock belonging to some woman I never even met?"

Liam sighed. "Okay, I see where you're going with this."

"From the moment I found out Emily existed, I felt it. I can't explain it because it's not rational, but it's real. She's my child."

Liam stared out across the café garden. "My wife has been gone for five years now," he murmured. "And I'd like to think someday I might meet someone again. Whoever that person is, she'd have to love Connor like her own child." He met her eyes and the sadness there almost knocked her over. "But by your rationale, it would be impossible for another woman to love Connor because she won't be genetically related to him?"

"*No.*" Quinn's eyes grew wide. "Oh, my goodness, Liam. Please don't think that's what I was saying." Her heart ached at the idea. "Of course a woman will come along who loves Connor. He's an amazing kid. Who *wouldn't* love him? What I mean is that no matter who comes into his life, he'll never forget about his mother, and he'll always be connected to her. I think any women who loves Connor will understand that."

Liam blew out a heavy breath and scrubbed a palm across his face. When he finally dropped his hand to the table, Quinn could see his eyes were red. She reached out and pressed a palm to his arm. "I'm sorry if I upset you. I shouldn't have brought up Connor's mother..."

"No. It's not that." His shook his head as if he was shaking off the emotion there. "Connor never met his mother, but he loves to hear stories about her. He looks at pictures all the time, and... yeah, he even loves to dig through her jewelry box." He sighed. "You're right. Any woman who wants to be in our lives will have to be okay with the fact that his mother will always be special to him."

"Any woman who is lucky enough to be in your lives *will* be okay with it."

Liam's eyes drifted to her hand on his bare arm, and then slowly back to her face. She knew she should pull her hand away, lean back, move away from him, but something held her back. Their eyes locked across the table, and a surge of electricity hit her straight in the heart.

Quinn sucked in a shaky breath and heard him do the same.

"Quinn," he murmured. "I—"

But then, out on the street, a car peeled into traffic, its tires squealing. A truck honked in protest, and the sound echoed across the café patio. Quinn pulled her hand away and grabbed for her drink.

Liam only stayed at her table for a minute after that, making a couple of small comments about the weather before he made his excuses, packed up his laptop, and headed out onto the sidewalk.

But for the rest of the afternoon, Quinn couldn't stop wondering what he'd been about to say.

———

When Quinn arrived home later that day, she headed down to the basement. Their home visit was scheduled for later that week, and it was the last room she had to tackle. She'd finished organizing the guest room over the weekend—although she hadn't had time to paint it like she'd wanted—and the rest of the rooms were fairly tidy and would only need a quick vacuum and dusting. But James had been sleeping on the couch in the basement, and on the few occasions she'd passed through to get to the laundry room, she'd noticed he hadn't been making much of an effort to fold his clean clothes or throw the dirty ones in the hamper. They definitely couldn't have this mess when the social worker came through. And they couldn't have evidence that he was sleeping downstairs, either. On the morning of the home visit, Quinn planned to rip the sheets and the blankets off the couch and hide them in the cabinet next to the TV.

She couldn't take the risk that the social worker would determine that their marriage was in trouble and advise the judge against giving them custody. Once the hearing was over, she could make some decisions about her future with James. And she could make some decisions about his baby, too.

James believed they could save their marriage and raise the baby together, the two of them half the time and Sasha the other half. Quinn flashed back to her conversation with Liam earlier that day, and his hope that another woman could love Connor like her own. She'd been quick to reassure him that of course another woman could love his son, and she'd meant every word.

It wasn't that Quinn didn't think she could love James's and Sasha's baby. She was pretty sure that the minute she held the tiny newborn bundle, she'd fall head-over-heels. But falling for the baby was part of her worries. Could she trust James to remain faithful? What if she grew attached to the baby, grew to love it like her own, and then James had another affair? Or started up with Sasha again? Would she be trapped in their marriage for the sake of the baby? Would she spend the rest of her life looking the other way?

Sometimes, Quinn wondered if she would even care if James continued to have affairs. Maybe it wouldn't matter what he did as long as she had Emily and the baby to shower with love and affection. But then she remembered the day in the park with Liam and Connor when, for just a moment, she could imagine what it would feel like to be a family.

She wanted that with the man she'd married. How could she spend the next twenty years with someone she only tolerated for the sake of the children? Right then, she and James were as far away from each other as two people could get. Was it possible for them to come back together? Or to start fresh?

Quinn sighed and picked up an armful of clothes off the

basement floor to carry them to the laundry. As she shuffled to the washing machine, a thin, glossy piece of paper fell out of the pile and fluttered to the floor. It landed face up, and Quinn froze at what she saw there. The clothes slid from her arms, and she dropped to her knees among them. With a shaking hand, she lifted the paper and stared at the black and white image.

An ultrasound photo.

Like static on an old-fashioned TV, the image was blurry, but Quinn had no problem making out the profile of a baby laying on its back and looking up to the top of the page. With one finger, she reached down and gently traced the curve of the baby's forehead, its miniature nose, and tiny lips pursed as it held one hand to its mouth. Was the baby sucking its thumb? Quinn had heard some babies did that even in the womb. She pressed a hand to her midsection. What would it feel like to have a baby growing inside her, shifting its arms, kicking its little feet?

Sasha would know. Quinn flinched, and the walls felt like they were closing in on her. Sasha, who was carrying that baby in the picture, carrying James's baby.

And maybe James would know, too, Quinn realized with dawning awareness. This wasn't a photo on his phone that Sasha had texted him. This was a print-out from a machine at an imaging center. Had James gone to the ultrasound appointment without telling her? He'd promised it was over between them, but Quinn had no idea what to believe. Did he take Sasha to dinner afterward to marvel at the pictures? Maybe Sasha had grabbed James's hand and pressed it to her rounded belly so he could feel the baby move. Maybe they'd gazed at each other in wonder about the life growing inside her.

It was everything Quinn had always dreamed she and James would do together. Instead, she was sitting on the sidelines while James experienced the milestones of a new baby with someone else. And she was sitting on the sidelines while Nora raised her biological child, too.

Nora had gotten to experience the ultrasounds, the kicks from little feet, a baby shower with handmade receiving blankets and a brand-new stroller. And now, Nora was the recipient of Emily's scribbled crayon drawings, her goodnight kisses, and night-time cuddles. Nora was the one who Emily called Mommy.

All because five years ago, someone in a lab somewhere mislabeled a test-tube.

Quinn lunged to her feet and grabbed the laundry from the floor. She was tired of feeling like the victim, tired of missing out on her child's life, tired of everyone moving on without her. It was time to take control of this situation, once and for all. She was going to get this house in order, give that social worker the best damn home visit of her career, and convince the judge to grant them custody of Emily.

She had to. There simply wasn't another option.

23

"Would you like some coffee, Ms. Davis?" Quinn stood in the center of her immaculate living room, nervously clutching one hand with the other.

"Yes, thank you. And please—" The social worker held up a hand. "Call me Alexis. As I said over the phone, this meeting will be very informal. I'm just here to get to know you a bit." Alexis swung her gaze from Quinn to James and then back again. "I hope we'll just have a nice chat today."

"That sounds wonderful, Alexis. We're so grateful you could come." James flashed a charming smile in the social worker's direction. Quinn had seen him use that smile on his clients dozens of times before, and she knew it worked, because he'd used it on her on their very first date. It was a smile that said, *You can trust me.* Of course, now Quinn knew the truth about that smile, and about whether James could be trusted. But she'd asked him to do everything he could to make this meeting a success, and that smile meant he was following her instructions.

"Honey," James put a gentle hand on Quinn's arm, "why don't you relax with Alexis while I pour the coffee?" He turned his gaze back to the social worker. "Do you take cream and sugar?"

Quinn hoped James wasn't overdoing it with the doting husband act, but Alexis just smiled and settled on the couch cushions. "Yes, please."

"I'll be right back." James disappeared into the kitchen.

"Now, Quinn." Alexis placed her notepad on the coffee table and patted the seat next to her. "Why don't you tell me a little bit about you and your family?"

Quinn dropped down onto the couch and turned her knees so she was facing Alexis. "Well—" Where should she even begin? Quinn had read dozens of articles about what to expect in these home visits, and all of them had said some version of the same thing: *be yourself.* Quinn had prepared her answers to every question the social worker might possibly ask her, but now that she was sitting there, the nerves took over. After five years of desperately trying to get pregnant only to find out that her child was being raised by another woman, she really didn't know *who* she was anymore. Would Alexis see right through her?

"Tell me a little bit about what you do," Alexis prompted. "What are your interests?"

"Um." Quinn sat up straight. She could do this. She had to do this, for Emily's sake. "I'm a children's librarian."

Alexis nodded encouragingly. "And do you enjoy that?"

"I do." Quinn swallowed hard and forced a smile. "I love children, and I'm very lucky to have the opportunity to work with them."

"My wife is just being modest." James returned to the living room carrying a tray of coffee, cream and sugar, and a plate of biscotti. He'd even dug out the fancy cocktail napkins and arranged them in the shape of a fan. "The library is lucky to have her. Quinn has always put her whole heart into expanding children's minds through literature and ensuring that she offers a safe and accepting place for everyone who walks through the door." He set the tray down on the coffee table and handed Alexis a steaming mug. "The first time I visited her at the library, I knew she was the woman I wanted as the mother of my children."

James paused with the pitcher of creamer in his hand and gave Quinn an affectionate grin. Despite herself, Quinn smiled in return. James might be pouring on the charm for Alexis's benefit, but he was doing it for Quinn too. Because he knew how important this was to her, because this was their best shot at getting Emily back. And if she were totally honest, his words tugged at her heart. There *was* a reason they'd chosen each other, back before infertility had taken over their lives. He'd always admired her ability with children and used to say that if she could win over a roomful of kids, there wasn't anything she couldn't do.

And for her part, Quinn had fallen for James for his solidness, his reliability. She'd always been able to count on him... at least until recently. But the infertility had affected him too, worn him down. Maybe the man who'd had an affair wasn't the real James, just like the woman who'd gone overboard trying to get pregnant wasn't the real Quinn.

Quinn watched James hand Alexis a coffee spoon and dessert plate for her biscotti. Quinn had asked him to make an effort, and he was. In this moment, he was showing himself to be the man she'd always wanted as the father of her children.

Alexis beamed at them as she stirred her coffee. "Well, that seems like a perfect segue into talking a bit about your relationship. How long have you been together?"

"We met seven years ago, and we've been married for almost six," James said.

"And how would you categorize your relationship? Would you say it's solid?"

Quinn peeked at James out of the corner of her eye. This was another question she'd been expecting, and in all her rehearsals, she'd planned to rave about how happy she and James were. But now that they were sitting there in front of the social worker, it didn't feel ethical to lie outright. But how could she possibly tell the truth?

Before she had to decide, James reached out and took her hand. "Infertility is never easy." James lifted a shoulder. "We've had our ups and downs, just like any couple who is going through something as challenging as this. But we've always loved and supported each other and will continue to do so." He gave Quinn's hand a squeeze that could only be for her benefit, not for Alexis's. "And we're committed to being the best partners to each other, and the best parents to our child."

It was the exact right thing to say. Quinn could see it in the little half-smile on Alexis's face as she jotted down a note on her paper, and it buoyed her. James could be charming when he wanted to, but this wasn't just an act. She and James *had* loved each other, and there was a reason they'd decided to get married and have children together. All couples went through hard times. A lot of couples even had affairs. It didn't always mean the end. Maybe it would bring them closer and bring about a new beginning.

"I'm so glad to hear you say that, James." Alexis looked up from her notes. "I meet a lot of couples wanting to adopt after they're unable to have their children of their own. And many of them feel they need to represent their relationship as perfect for my benefit." She gave them a wry smile. "But I'm married. I know how hard it is, even without the burden of infertility. I'm very encouraged to see that you're realistic about the challenges while also being committed to work through them."

Quinn blew out a relieved breath. This couldn't be going

any better, and it was all thanks to James. They hadn't needed all those plans and rehearsals about what they were going to say and do. All they needed to do was to trust each other. Quinn leaned into James's side, and he slid an arm around her.

Quinn's mind drifted back to James's pleas that they could raise his new baby together. She wouldn't be the baby's mother —not unless Sasha wanted to give him or her up, and why would she? But love wasn't finite, and she and the baby could form a strong bond, too. Wouldn't it be amazing to have not one, but two children in this house, running through the halls, laughing and playing? If Emily deserved to know her parents, she deserved to grow up with her little brother or sister, too.

That was something Nora would never be able to offer her.

"Now," Alexis's voice pulled Quinn back to the interview at hand, "let's talk a bit about your home."

"Oh, yes!" Quinn sat up straight. She'd spent every single spare moment of the last week getting their home in order. There wasn't a single book out of place on the shelves or cobweb in a corner. "Would you like a tour?"

"That would be lovely."

They stood, and Quinn led the way to the kitchen where the blender and coffee maker were lined up in a perfect row on the counter and the floors had been shined from three rounds with the mop. "Feel free to poke around." She gestured at the cabinets where, behind the doors, the plates were stacked according to size and the dry goods were neatly tucked away in matching containers.

"Oh, that won't be necessary." Alexis jotted something down in her notebook. "I'm only here to check that everything is in working order and ensure there aren't any fire hazards. I'll take a quick peek upstairs if you don't mind, but everything seems just fine to me."

Quinn's shoulders slumped. All that vacuuming and scrubbing, all the boxes she'd hauled off to Goodwill, and Alexis didn't care about any of it. Maybe James was right. Maybe she had been spending too much time obsessing over the wrong things—first on getting pregnant, and now on making her home look perfect—instead of focusing on what really mattered. Like her marriage. And what was best for Emily.

James held out a hand to indicate that Alexis should take the stairs, and then he gently pressed the small of Quinn's back to guide her ahead of him. Quinn glanced up at his face, and he gave her a happy nod as if to say *This is going great, isn't it?*

It *was* going great. James couldn't have worked harder to show his commitment to getting custody of Emily. And that told Quinn that he was committed to making things work in their marriage, too. The absolute best thing for Emily was to have parents in a solid relationship and to grow up with her sibling.

They were so close to making it happen.

Quinn reached out and took her husband's hand, and they followed the social worker up the stairs together.

24

Quinn had remembered to bring a cardigan this time. She'd also remembered to pick up James's suit from the dry cleaner and make sure it was hanging on the hook behind the bathroom door so it would be ready when he woke up. He was wearing that suit now, with a brand-new tie and recently shined shoes that echoed through the lofty halls of the medieval courthouse building as they made their way to the hearing.

Quinn's purse dug into her shoulder, heavy with the water bottles and granola bars she'd packed, just in case. Not that she could imagine having any sort of appetite. But knowing she was prepared might help her anxiety, which was currently through the roof.

This could very well be the best day of Quinn's life. She wondered if, someday, she'd look back on this day the way other mothers looked back on their labor and delivery—remembering the joy of their child coming into the world, but very little of the pain and suffering.

Their group walked in a line, three across, with Quinn in the middle and James and Helena on either side. Nobody said much—they'd already prepared in Helena's office the night before—and now all that was left to do was get on with the hearing. As they rounded the final corner before their courtroom door, they encountered a small circle of people gathered in conversation. Each group did an awkward shift to make way for the other, and Quinn found herself face-to-face with Nora.

"Hello," Quinn murmured, with a polite nod of her head. She quickly looked away, but not before she caught a glimpse of the haunted look in Nora's eyes and the strained lines around her mouth.

If this will be the best day of my life, what kind of day will it be for Nora?

Quinn kept moving toward the courtroom. She couldn't allow herself to worry about Nora. She had to focus on the reason they were there, the reason they'd done everything up to this point.

Emily.

"We'll probably start in about ten minutes," Helena's voice cut into her thoughts. "You'll want to make any final phone calls or run to the bathroom now. Once the hearing begins, there likely won't be a break for several hours."

James quickly pulled out his phone and wandered away to look for the best reception, and Quinn headed for the bathroom. When she stepped back out into the hall, Liam was waiting for her.

"Quinn, can I talk to you?" he asked as he approached.

Quinn couldn't help but notice that he had the same strained, exhausted expression she'd seen on his sister. And even though his gray trousers and pinstriped oxford shirt looked custom-made for his tall frame, his tie was askew as if he'd been yanking on it all morning.

"I really should get back. They're about to start." Quinn took a step toward the hearing room door, but Liam put out a hand to stop her.

"Please?"

Quinn sighed. "What is it?" But she had a feeling she already knew.

"It's not too late to stop this."

Quinn shook her head and started walking again. "Liam…"

He took her arm now. "Quinn, I'm serious. You need to think about what's best for Emily. And I swear to you, this isn't it…"

Quinn whirled around to face him. "Did Nora send you to say this?"

"No." He raked a hand through his hair in frustration. "I'm saying it because I love Emily like she's my own kid, and I think you're making a huge mistake."

Quinn closed her eyes, tired of the doubts and the arguments and of everyone telling her she was wrong to want to be a part of her child's life. A real part of her child's life. Not just someone who popped in now and then to play Legos and color a picture.

Ever since Quinn had found the ultrasound photo in James's laundry, she hadn't been able to stop thinking about it. That photo was the very beginning of his brand-new baby's life, captured in black and white. She'd missed the beginning of Emily's life, and she'd never get it back. If Quinn walked away now, four more years would go by, and then eight. Emily would learn to ride a bike, she'd get her first period, she'd go to the prom, and Quinn would miss it all. Even if Quinn could convince Nora to allow her to visit, now that she knew Emily, being a visitor would never be enough. All she'd be to Emily was a family friend who stopped in every now and then. She'd keep missing out on everything that really mattered.

"I have to go." Quinn pulled her arm from Liam's grasp. "I don't want to be late for the hearing."

"All rise."

Quinn took a deep breath as she grabbed the table in front of her and pulled herself to her feet. Next to her, James straightened his tie and stood up.

Oh God, this is it.

Helena reached over to give Quinn a pat on the arm. "We've got this," she whispered.

Quinn nodded. Helena had reassured her over and over that they had a solid case. Apparently, the social worker had raved about them in her report, and they'd passed the home visit with flying colors. Quinn had done everything she possibly could, and now it was up to the judge to decide.

Judge Guerrero made her way to the chair behind the bench, and the bailiff instructed the courtroom to sit. There were more people gathered than Quinn had expected. She recognized a whole group of them from Emily's birthday party sitting on Nora's side of the aisle—Aunt Susan and Uncle Wesley, even deadbeat Cousin Troy had managed to put on a nice shirt and arrive on time. And Liam was there, of course, staring blank-faced at her when her gaze skated past him.

Quinn and James's side was packed with people, too, though Quinn had never seen most of them before. They sat poised with notepads and pens in their hands, ready for the proceedings to begin.

Reporters.

Apparently, this hearing had attracted the attention of the national media. It wasn't every day that embryos ended up in the wrong woman's uterus, and quite a few people were interested in the outcome of their case—attorneys, fertility clinics, couples going through IVF treatments. Quinn had to admit that if she weren't the one sitting in this seat, she'd be absolutely riveted by this case, following along with everyone else, and gossiping in her online infertility group about which way it might go. Which side would her group have chosen—hers or

Nora's? Quinn rubbed her sweaty hands on her skirt. There were going to be a lot of people watching her. And judging her.

From her seat on the bench in the front of the room, Judge Guerrero's regal gaze swept across the crowd. "There is a child's future involved in this case, and I understand that fact may cause strong emotions. May I remind everyone that I won't tolerate any outbursts in my courtroom?"

Quinn nodded along with everyone else.

"Wonderful. Let's begin." The judge slipped on her glasses and pulled a sheet of paper from the folder in front of her. "We're here today to establish custody of the minor child, Emily Robinson, age four. Due to an unfortunate mix-up at the Baxter Center for Fertility and Reproductive Endocrinology, a fertility clinic located in Pittsburgh, PA., the defendant, Nora Robinson, was mistakenly implanted with the embryo consisting of the plaintiffs' genetic material. Thus, Ms. Robinson became the gestational mother to James and Quinn Marcello's biological child."

The wooden slats along the back of Quinn's chair dug into her back, but she was almost too afraid to move as the facts of their case were read back to her. How had they ended up there? How was this their life? She and James were just ordinary people who'd wanted a baby.

Judge Guerrero shuffled to the next page. "Ms. Robinson gave birth to an infant, Emily Robinson, who is now four years old. The mix-up was discovered this past June when the defendants, believing their embryo was frozen in the Albrecht Laboratory for Cryopreservation, began the process of undergoing an embryo transfer with the intent to parent the resulting child. DNA testing was conducted when the mix-up was discovered. The results of the test established that the Marcellos are the genetic parents of the child. A declaratory judgment is sought concerning the rights, obligations, and relationships of the parties in regard to Emily Robinson."

The judge fixed her gaze on Helena. "Does the plaintiff wish to make an opening statement?"

"We do, Your Honor." Helena rose to her feet and smoothed down the skirt of her charcoal suit. Quinn's heart began to pound as Helena marched to the front of the room.

"Your Honor," Helena began. "My clients, James and Quinn Marcello spent over four years pursuing their dream of becoming parents to a biological child. They underwent extensive fertility treatments—including six rounds of IVF—and they spent over one hundred thousand dollars in the hopes that Mrs. Marcello might become pregnant and give birth to a baby." She paced across the wood floor, her black pumps tapping.

"Mrs. Marcello's treatments required her to attend weekly and sometimes daily appointments at the Baxter fertility clinic, to self-administer hundreds of hormones shots in her abdomen and thighs, and to undergo a number of medical procedures under general anesthesia. Throughout all of these treatments and procedures, Mr. and Mrs. Marcello believed that they had a cryopreserved embryo from an earlier IVF cycle to fall back on. As Your Honor has already noted, when my clients requested access to this embryo, it was traced to Ms. Robinson and discovered to have resulted in the birth of Emily Robinson."

"This child is the biological daughter of Quinn and James Marcello," Helena continued. "My clients did not willingly relinquish this embryo to Ms. Robinson, nor did they give Emily up for adoption. You will hear from their fertility doctor who will attest to the fact that my clients' greatest wish was to parent the child resulting from this embryo. The embryo and resulting child ended up in Ms. Robinson's care *only due to a tragic mix-up.*"

Helena paused now, looking out across the courtroom for a moment, probably making sure the reporters were getting it all down, before spinning back around to the judge. "Nora Robinson is a *genetic stranger* to Emily."

Across the aisle, Nora flinched as if Helena had taken a swing at her, and Quinn felt the other woman's pain as if it were her own. She'd been expecting to hear that phrase—*genetic stranger*—in Helena's opening statement, as the attorney had mentioned it was a legal term she planned to cite from a previous case. Still, it was a shock to hear it echo across the courtroom. Quinn wished she'd asked Helena to tone down her language where Nora was concerned. Proving that she and James were Emily's rightful parents didn't mean they had to tear the other woman down in the process.

Helena forged ahead with her opening statement, and Quinn did her best to shake off her doubts. They'd hired the best attorney for a reason, and if Quinn wanted to win the case, she had to trust that Helena knew what she was doing.

"If the court were to grant custody to Ms. Robinson against the wishes of Emily's biological parents," Helena continued, "this would set a dangerous precedent of *finders keepers* that could have far-reaching effects on the entire field of assisted reproductive technology. In fact, during this hearing, we'll review several landmark cases in which a similar mix-up occurred, and the genetic parents were granted custody."

Judge Guerrero made a note on one of the documents in front of her. Quinn would have given anything to know what she'd scribbled there.

Helena swung around and pointed a manicured finger in the direction of Nora's attorney. "Opposing council will no doubt argue that granting custody to my clients is not in the best interest of the child. However, my clients have built a strong bond with Emily over months of regular visits. Emily has formed an attachment to the Marcellos, and we will hear from the court-appointed psychologist that if a transition to custody for the biological parents is conducted slowly and thoughtfully, Emily will suffer no psychological harm."

Quinn pressed a hand to her chest. The centerpiece of

Nora's entire case was that Emily would be traumatized if she were taken from the family she'd been born into. And, to be honest, sometimes Quinn stared up at the ceiling late at night, unable to sleep, worrying it might be true. But the court had appointed an expert—a full professor at the university who had worked with children for her entire career—and her report had indicated that with a careful transition, Emily would be just fine. Surely the judge wouldn't have appointed an expert she didn't intend to listen to?

"Your Honor." Helena cocked her head, her voice softer now. "The Marcello family has experienced immeasurable heartache over this tragic mix-up. They lost the ability to carry and give birth to their child, to raise her and watch her grow for the past four years. They missed every one of their child's birthdays," Helena continued. "Every milestone. Her first steps, first day of school."

None of this was news to Quinn, but having it called out like this, in front of the judge and a courtroom full of strangers—in front of the whole world—put her grief on display for everyone to see. *Damn it.* Quinn looked down at her hands as the back of her throat prickled, a sure sign she was about to cry.

"They missed out on hearing their child call them 'Mommy' and 'Daddy'."

Quinn's breath hitched, and a tiny sob escaped. *Oh, God.* She pressed a hand to her mouth. The judge had warned them about outbursts in the courtroom. She fumbled through her purse for a pack of tissues.

"Your Honor," Helena continued. "My clients will never get this time with their child back, and the pain will never go away." She swept an arm in Quinn's direction as if to say, *See what I mean?* "We respectfully ask the court to repair this terrible injustice and return Emily to her rightful family before any more time has passed. Thank you."

Quinn could feel the weight of Judge Guerrero's gaze on

her as she swiped a tissue under her eyes, hoping her mascara wasn't smudged there. Helena made her way back to their table with an extra little spring in her step, flashing Quinn a satisfied smile as she slid into her chair. It suddenly occurred to Quinn that the attorney had yanked on her emotions and made her cry on purpose. It had all been a carefully calculated spectacle.

And it had worked. Quinn swiped at her eyes again, peeking up at the judge who was looking back at her with compassion.

Then it was Nora's attorney's turn to give his opening statement. He used his time to insist that Emily would suffer if the judge granted custody to Quinn and James. None of it was unexpected. Helen had already addressed his points in her opening statement, so the hearing moved along quickly.

Next, Helena presented testimony from a series of character witnesses—James's aunt in Tennessee, Elise from the library—who assured the court that Quinn and James would make excellent parents. Then Helena called Dr. Baxter to the stand.

At first, the conversation played out just as Quinn expected. Helena asked Dr. Baxter to take the court through the events of the embryo mix-up and to discuss her perspective on Quinn and James's desire to have a baby. But then Helena paused, pacing across the courtroom and stopping in front of the doctor.

"Dr. Baxter, I understand that in addition to being a reproductive endocrinologist in private practice, you teach in the University of Pittsburgh Medical School. Is that correct?"

"Yes." The doctor folded her hands in her lap. "I'm an adjunct professor there."

"And I assume that as a physician and professor, you have a fairly solid understanding of reproductive science. Would you say that's correct?"

"I would hope I do, yes."

"And in your experience, both as a scientist and professor,

does the average introductory-level college biology class cover the basic tenets of genetics? I'm talking about dominant and recessive genes and that sort of thing." Helena marched over to a white board in the corner and drew a chart similar to a tic-tac-toe board with capital letter Bs written in the boxes across the top and down the left-hand side.

Although it had been over two decades since Quinn had taken a science class, she immediately recognized the chart as a way of demonstrating how traits such as hair and eye color are passed down from parents to children.

Dr. Baxter cocked her head. "I don't teach introductory-level biology."

"But as a scientist, you can give your expert opinion on the subject."

"I would have to say yes, the basics of genetics are usually taught in intro-level biology."

"Mmm-hmm." Helena paced in front of the doctor. "What about the average high-school biology class?"

Dr. Baxter tilted her head again, as if she were questioning where Helena was going with this.

"Answer the question, please," Helena prompted.

"Again, yes. This topic would likely be covered in any basic high-school biology class."

"Wonderful." Helena gave Dr. Baxter a closed-mouth smile and then marched to the desk where Quinn and James sat. She picked up a file of papers and held it up.

"Your Honor, I submit to the court the academic transcripts belonging to Nora Robinson. Highlighted, you will see here that Ms. Robinson took biology classes in both high school and college. She received As. Excellent grades. In addition, I have a syllabus from the introductory biology class offered at her alma mater, the University of Michigan, and highlighted, you'll note that an overview of how genetic traits are passed on is covered in this class."

Nora's attorney stood up. "Objection. I don't see how my client taking a biology class twenty-five years ago is relevant to this case."

The judge peered down at Helena. "Get to the point, please."

"Your Honor, opposing council has argued in their opening statement that because Emily was raised by the Robinson family for four years, custody should be determined by their emotional bond rather than biology. However, the case of Perry-Rogers versus Fasano shows us that this argument is null and void if the gestational mother *knew* of the embryo mix-up and failed to take action to correct it."

"Excuse me?" The judge blinked at Helena. "Are you saying that Ms. Robinson somehow knew about the embryo mix-up *before* it was discovered by the fertility clinic?"

Helena stood up straighter. "I'm saying she knew about the embryo mix-up in the first year of Emily's life."

Across the aisle, Nora gasped. In the back of the room, the reporters and other spectators began murmuring to each other.

The judge pounded her gavel on the desk in front of her. "Enough. I want silence in my courtroom." The crowd quieted down, and Judge Guerrero turned back to Helena. "Please explain yourself."

"I would be happy to." Helena's gaze swept across the courtroom, and then back to the judge. "Your Honor, what biological parent hasn't gazed at their child looking for similarities in their physical features? *He has his dad's nose. He got his blue eyes from me.*" She pointed at Dr. Baxter, still sitting in the witness stand. "A respected physician, scientist, and college professor has attested to the fact that any high-school biology student will be familiar with how genetic traits are passed down from parents to their children. Indeed, the basic principles of dominant and recessive genes could almost be considered common knowledge."

Helena picked up a folder from the table, flipped through it and pulled out a photograph. "I would like to submit to the court a photo of the sperm donor selected by Ms. Robinson. This donor would have contributed half the genetic material to any embryos implanted in her uterus. Ms. Robinson would have seen a copy of this photo when she reviewed the donor's file, as well as a document where the donor self-declared a physical description, including his hair and eye color." She handed it to the bailiff who passed it to the judge.

"You can see clearly that this sperm donor has naturally blond hair and blue eyes." Helena spun around and directed a manicured finger at Nora. "Ms. Robinson also has naturally blond hair and blue eyes." Helena handed one more photo to the bailiff. "Here is a photo of six-month-old Emily Robinson. You'll note that even at this early age, Emily's hair and eyes are clearly dark brown."

Helena marched over to the white board and erased the capital letter Bs she'd written. "Basic knowledge of genetics would inform us that blond hair and blue eyes are recessive traits. If *both* parents contribute recessive genes—*if both parents are blond-haired and blue-eyed*—genetically, their child cannot have dark hair and dark eyes."

Helena replaced the capital Bs with lower-case ones. "Nora Robinson took biology in both high school and college. She would have learned this basic knowledge *not once, but twice*. She would have undoubtedly looked at the child for physical traits similar to her own, and found none. Nora Robinson must have suspected that Emily did not come from the embryo created by her egg and her donor's sperm."

Helena paused in the middle of the room, looking around to make sure she had everyone's attention. "Your Honor, Nora Robinson knew from the first year of the child's life that Emily *was not her biological child*."

25

If Quinn didn't get out of her cardigan in the next five seconds, she was going to start screaming. She yanked at the sleeve, doing her best to tug it off her shoulders, but it caught on the cuff of the blouse beneath and wouldn't budge. She was absolutely roasting, and the late September sun had a direct line to the bench where she sat waiting for James to pull the car around. The hearing shouldn't have ended at the lunch break, during the heat of the day. Helena had expected to question her list of witnesses for hours. But once she'd dropped her bombshell on the courtroom, the judge had banged her gavel and sent them all home early.

Quinn stood up and grabbed the hem of her cardigan, flipping it over her head and turning the arms inside out in the process. She dropped it onto the bench next to her, relieved to finally be rid of it. Too bad she could never be rid of the memory of what Helena had revealed in the courtroom, too.

Nora had known that Emily wasn't her biological child years ago. *Years ago.* It wasn't that Quinn had missed four years of Emily's life due to a horrible mix-up at the fertility clinic.

She'd missed maybe a few months due to a mix-up, and years thanks to Nora's silence.

"Quinn."

At the sound of her name, she looked up to find Liam stepping out the courthouse doors, squinting in sun the as he hurried over to the bench where she sat. "I've been looking everywhere for you. That was—" He hesitated, shaking his head. "Are you okay?"

Quinn leveled a glare at him. "Did you know, too, Liam?"

Liam blinked. "What?"

"All these years, did you know that she wasn't Nora's?"

"Of course I didn't know."

"Really?" Quinn crossed her arms over her chest. "You never saw a photo of the donor? You never talked about where Emily got her dark eyes and hair? None of that *ever* came up?"

"No, it didn't."

"Excuse me if I don't believe you." Quinn grabbed her cardigan and took off down the street. She'd wait for James on the corner.

Liam trailed after her. "Quinn, listen. My wife died the same month Nora started that last round of IVF. So, no, I didn't think to ask about her donor's hair color. I was busy figuring out how to get out of bed every morning and feed a newborn. Besides," he added, "it's not like the guy's photo was hanging on the family photo wall. I didn't even know sperm came with a photo."

Quinn stopped walking and turned around. Damn it, how could she have forgotten the timing of something so important? "I didn't think about your wife's death coinciding with Nora's pregnancy." She pressed a hand to her forehead. "I'm so sorry. Of course you wouldn't have been paying any attention to the sperm donor."

"Don't be sorry. Just know that it was a complete shock to

me when Nora got the call from the fertility clinic about the mix-up."

Quinn looked at him sideways. "Do you think Nora knew?"

Liam gazed down at the pavement, slowly shaking his head. "I don't know."

"How could she not have known?"

Liam shoved his hands in his pockets and finally looked at her. "I'm not sure all that about dominant and recessive genes is actually as simple as your attorney made it out to be."

To be honest, it probably wasn't. "Fine, maybe Nora didn't *know*. But she would have absolutely suspected." Quinn's mind whirled. What if she and James had a child who looked nothing like them? That was the thing about fertility treatments—they weren't like getting pregnant naturally. You put your faith in a doctor and a laboratory, and you never completely *knew*. "Maybe it's not as simple as Helena made it sound. But that's not the point. The point is that biology students *do* learn that whole capital-b, small-b chart that she drew up there on the board, so that must have planted some doubts. The point is that a blond-haired, blue-eyed person who mingles their genes with another blond-haired, blue-eyed person is going to do a double-take when their baby comes out looking like me." Quinn waved her hand to take in her dark hair, brown eyes, and olive skin.

"The point is," Quinn continued, her voice rising. "Everyone in that courtroom believes Nora suspected, because you'd have to do a whole lot of burying your head in the sand not to suspect."

"Maybe she did suspect." Liam sighed. "Or maybe she didn't suspect because she didn't even want to think about it." He gazed at her across the narrow sidewalk, his eyes pleading. "What would you have done if you'd just given birth to a baby you desperately wanted, and maybe her hair didn't turn out exactly the way you expected? You honestly think you would have immediately known the baby wasn't your biological child?"

"It's not the same thing at all. It's not just, 'Oops, her hair is a little darker than I thought it would be.'" Quinn crossed her arms. "If Nora truly believed herself to be Emily's mother, she would have spent hours—days—gazing at her child, noting similarities. All parents do that. And Emily looks nothing like Nora or that donor. So, no. In Nora's case, I can't imagine not even questioning it."

Liam raised an eyebrow like he absolutely didn't believe her. And a tiny voice inside her whispered that maybe he was right not to believe her. Maybe he was right that she would've done anything in her power to keep her child... because wasn't she doing everything in her power right now?

But Quinn shoved that tiny voice aside in favor of the louder one screaming that Nora had deprived her of years of her child's life. It wasn't just a mix-up or a tragic accident. Nora had given birth to a baby with Quinn's eyes and hair, a baby who very likely couldn't have been produced by the combination of genes provided by her and her sperm donor. And she'd intentionally said nothing. She'd let years pass by, years that Quinn would never get back.

"Quinn, this doesn't change anything." Liam argued. "None of this is Emily's fault, and what's best for her should still be our priority. Nora is the only mother Emily has ever known."

"How can you say it doesn't change anything? Nora is the only mother Emily has ever known because *Nora* made sure she never knew me. She intentionally deceived everyone so she could keep Emily for herself, and I don't believe that leaving my child with someone who would do that is what's best for her."

At that moment, James's car pulled up across the street, hazard lights flashing so the traffic would go around. Through the window, he gave her a wave.

"I have to go." And before Liam could say anything else, Quinn marched off, leaving him standing on the sidewalk.

Inside the car, Quinn grabbed the seatbelt and yanked it across her. James peered out the window at Liam as he walked back into the courthouse. "Who was that guy?"

"Nora's brother," Quinn mumbled, clicking the belt into place.

"What did he want?"

Quinn closed her eyes and leaned against the door. "He wanted to tell me not to blame Nora."

"That was pretty shocking, wasn't it? It never would have occurred to me to question what the sperm donor looked like." James started the car. "Do you think it's true that Nora knew?"

"I don't know." Quinn opened her eyes and looked across the car at her dark-eyed, dark-haired husband. "Maybe. Don't you think we would have at least wondered if we were Nora?"

James shrugged. "I can't see how we wouldn't have."

Quinn closed her eyes again. "I'm so tired of feeling like this. I'm so tired being angry, and feeling out of control, and like everything that's important to me is being decided by someone else."

James was silent for a moment. Finally, he reached over and took her hand. "I'm sorry for my part in that, Quinn. I really am."

"I know."

"I promise, it's going to get better." He gave her hand a squeeze. "Look, why don't I run into the wine shop on the way home, and I'll get us a nice bottle of red? We can spend the evening together, order some takeout and relax. Maybe watch a movie. We don't have to think about any of this until tomorrow."

"Okay." Quinn nodded, sitting up in her seat. She did appreciate the effort James was making. "That sounds perfect."

A couple of miles down the road, James pulled the car into

the lot outside the wine shop and ran inside, leaving the key in the ignition. The sun beat down on her through the passenger-side window, and Quinn reached for her water bottle in the cup holder. Her gaze settled on the dashboard.

James's phone.

A memory flashed into her head of James heading off to make a phone call right before the hearing started. She'd been so anxious about getting to the bathroom and back to the court-room that she didn't think much about it at the time. Who could he have possibly been calling right before they went in front of a judge? She supposed it could have been work, but he'd taken the week off for the hearing.

Quinn shook her head slowly, trying to rid her mind of these destructive thoughts. Ever since their home visit, she and James had grown close again, just like they'd been in the begin-ning. James was working hard to prove she could trust him. How could she go snooping in his phone at the exact moment he was going out of his way to take care of her? She stared out the window, determined to let this go. When he got back to the car, she'd ask him who he'd called earlier.

But, a little voice whispered, *how will I know he's telling the truth?*

Quinn glanced at the door to the wine shop, and then back to the phone. What was the harm in peeking? She'd probably see the name of one of his work colleagues, and that would be the end of it. They could finally move on from this, once and for all. Quinn grabbed the phone and turned it on. A few seconds later, she had his call log open. And there, in front of her, was a long list of calls to one single person.

Sasha.

Quinn's heart began to pound, but she told herself not to overreact. Sasha was pregnant. Maybe she wasn't feeling well, maybe she needed help with something. James was the father of the woman's child, it was unreasonable to expect him to cut off all contact with her. Maybe the fact that he'd been in repeated contact with Sasha showed what an involved father he was going to be.

Glancing back at the door of the shop, Quinn switched over to James's texts. Sasha's name was the first in the list. Apparently, they'd been texting while he'd gone to get the car. Quinn clicked on Sasha's name, and a photo of a woman appeared in the text thread. She was smiling at the camera with glowing, youthful skin and long, shiny blond hair. Though she faced the camera, her body was in profile to reveal the curve of her pregnant belly beneath a gauzy white peasant dress.

In the text thread, James had sent a response to the photo she'd shared with him.

You're the most beautiful woman I've ever seen.

Quinn slowly dropped the phone back in the cup holder, leaned her head against the door, and closed her eyes.

26

Quinn arrived at the courthouse the next day with her dress pressed, every hair in place, and a serene expression on her face. Nobody would have known her stomach was churning or that she'd coated on an extra layer of foundation to cover the dark circles under her eyes. She'd tossed and turned all night, agonizing over her discovery of what James had been up to and wondering what she was should do with that information.

Sometime before dawn, Quinn had finally come to the realization that what she should to do was absolutely nothing. Their case was going better than she could have ever hoped, and she couldn't take the chance of losing Emily. Not when she was so close. So, she'd greeted James with a smile, handed him a mug of coffee, and climbed into the car next to him, never saying a word about the text she'd read. Or the way he'd betrayed her again.

Quinn entered the courthouse knowing that Emily would be somewhere inside, waiting to meet with the judge. In order to make a ruling on the case, Judge Guerrero planned to interview Emily in her chamber. Nora would be present for the interview, but Helena had assured Quinn that Nora would be required to sit quietly and remain neutral.

Excuse me if I'm not feeling terribly confident about that. Quinn was willing to bet that Nora had been coaching Emily about what to say to the judge from the minute she woke up that morning. In fact, as Quinn made her way down the hallway after stopping in the bathroom, she spotted Emily and Nora sitting on a bench with their heads bent together. Nora murmured something in Emily's ear that Quinn couldn't hear. *Probably coaching her some more.*

"Hi, Emily!" Quinn stopped in front of the bench, interrupting their conversation. Her gaze slid past Nora's without acknowledgement, and she gave Emily an extra-wide smile. "I'm so happy to see you."

"Hi, Quinn." Emily waved, and Quinn was delighted to see she'd brought both Mirabel and Bruno. Hopefully, the judge would ask who'd gifted her the two special bears.

"What do you think about this huge building?" Quinn waved an arm to indicate the stone walls and ornate wooden doors. "It's just like a castle, right?"

Emily nodded. "Mommy says we're meeting with a lady, but she's not a princess."

"That's right. She's a judge, which is a really special job."

Nora stood, pressing a hand to her lower back as if it were aching. She'd seemed exhausted yesterday, but it was as if she'd aged ten years overnight. Her eyes were bloodshot and sunken, nose puffy, and the lines around her mouth had deepened into a permanent frown.

Quinn heart tugged, but didn't want to feel compassion for Nora, so she looked away.

"Speaking of our meeting," Nora said, reaching for Emily's hand. "It starts in about ten minutes, and I have to go to the bathroom first. Come on, Em."

Emily tugged her hand back. "I went right before we came."

"But I didn't, so you'll have to come with me."

"I don't want to."

Nora sighed, pressing her eyes shut as if she were trying to keep from having a breakdown right there in the hallway. "Emily, please just come with me."

"I'll stay with her," Quinn offered. "You go ahead."

Nora hesitated as if she were debating whether the benefits of a solo bathroom trip outweighed leaving Emily with Quinn.

Quinn sighed. Seriously? She'd had weekly visits with Emily for months, couldn't she sit with the girl on a bench for a five-minute bathroom break? Even if Nora really was worried that Quinn would run off with Emily, they were in a courthouse, surrounded by police and security officers. "We'll be right here on the bench. You'll only be gone a minute."

"Okay." Nora's shoulders relaxed, and she reached for her purse. "Thanks. I'll be right back."

Quinn settled on the bench with Emily, who climbed up next to her. "Quinn, I'm hungry."

"Didn't your mother give you breakfast?" Quinn asked, absently. By this point, she'd spent enough time with Emily to know the child could eat a full meal and still want a snack ten minutes later. Nora always kept bags of cut-up apples, baby carrots, and Goldfish crackers in her purse.

"I had toast. Can I have more?"

Quinn smiled and opened her purse. "I don't think I have any toast in here. But how about a granola bar?" It was organic oatmeal raisin, one of the healthy ones she used to carry when she wasn't eating processed foods or dairy products. The ingredients were listed right on the front: oats, dates, raisins, honey. Nora couldn't find anything to criticize about that, and it would pass the nut allergy test, too.

Quinn opened the bar and folded down the wrapper, handing it over to Emily, who bit off the top. "Good?"

Emily nodded happily.

"So," Quinn said. "Will Bruno and Mirabel be meeting the judge, too?"

"Yep!" Emily held up Quinn's childhood bear, who had a piece of rainbow tulle wrapped around his belly. "Bruno wore his tutu." She took another bite of her granola bar.

"Bruno, you look smashing," Quinn declared. "And what about Mirabel? Does she have a favorite outfit?"

Emily didn't answer, and when Quinn looked down, the girl was staring out across the hallway with a dazed look on her face.

"Em?" Quinn prompted.

"My tummy hurts."

"Oh, no." Quinn took the granola bar from Emily, folded over the wrapper, and set it on the bench. "Did you eat anything weird with your toast this morning? Eggs?"

Emily shook her head.

"Do you think you might throw up?"

Emily reached up and rubbed her ear, and Quinn blinked in surprise. On the side of Emily's neck, a splotchy pink rash began to work its way across her skin.

"Are you hot? Does it hurt anywhere else?" Quinn pressed her hand to Emily's forehead the way she'd seen mothers do at the library when they suspected a fever. The girl's skin felt cool, which reassured Quinn. But then the pink splotch grew larger, spreading down Emily's neck and across the front of her chest, disappearing into the neckline of her dress. Could it be a reaction to something?

Suddenly, Quinn froze in horror. *Could it have been the granola bar?* She grabbed the bar and stared at the wrapper. Oats, dates, raisins, honey. *There are no nuts in here.*

"Emily?" Quinn knelt down so they were face-to-face. "Are you allergic to anything besides nuts?"

But Emily's didn't answer. Her eyes had glazed over, and when she sucked in a breath, it came out as a horrible wheezing gasp, like sandpaper on a block of wood. Her next breath was the same, shallower this time.

Quinn lunged to her feet and looked wildly from one end of the hall to the other. "Help!" And then louder. "Someone please help us!"

A door banged open, and Judge Guerrero's bailiff ran into the hall. Another man in a similar uniform quickly followed.

"Please," Quinn begged. "Call 911! I think she's having an allergic reaction to something." She grabbed Emily off the bench and took off toward the bailiffs. Emily stiffened and flailed in her arms as she tried to suck more air into her lungs. The rhythmic wheezing and gasping grew louder, an oncoming train headed right toward them. "She can't breathe. We need to get her to a hospital. Hurry! *Please hurry.*"

Judge Guerrero's bailiff detached a radio from his belt loop and barked some sort of emergency instructions into it. The second bailiff grabbed Emily from Quinn's arms. "The ambulance will pull up this way. Come with me." He turned and headed for the exit. Quinn ran to keep up with him.

"Are you her mother? Does she have any allergies?" The bailiff shoved open a door leading to a stairwell.

"She's allergic to nuts, but I don't know what else." Quinn stumbled to a stop. "Nora would know. *We need Nora.*" Quinn grabbed the bailiff's arm and pulled him back into the hall.

"Wait!" a voice called, and Quinn shook with relief. Nora's heels clicked on the tiles as she ran down the corridor from the direction of the bathroom. *Nora will know what to do.*

"*Emily!* What happened? What did she eat?" Nora slid her purse off her shoulder and plunged a hand into it, digging around as she stumbled down the hall toward them.

The minute Emily heard Nora's voice, she shoved against the bailiff's chest, flailing and fighting to get free. "Mommy," she gasped, then took another rattling breath in. "*Mommy.*"

"She's having an allergic reaction." Nora grabbed the bailiff's arm, yanking him in the direction of a wooden bench. "We need to lay her down." In her hand, she held a clear plastic case that contained a fat white tube with an orange tip at the end.

Quinn recognized it as an EpiPen, for severe allergies. She'd seen mothers at the library carrying them. *What was in that granola bar?* Why hadn't she waited a few minutes for Nora to get back instead of handing Emily the first thing she'd found in her purse?

Quinn's self-recriminations were interrupted by Emily's increasingly loud wheezing. By now, several people had come out of their offices, drawn by the commotion, and they milled around watching.

"Quinn!" James appeared among the onlookers. "What's going on?"

"Move aside!" the bailiff commanded, shoving his way past James so he could carry Emily to the bench.

"Quinn?" James repeated, taking her arm.

"She's having an allergic reaction." To Quinn's ears, Emily's breathing had become shallower. Her little chest thrust up and down as she labored to get enough air into her lungs. *Oh God, her lips are turning blue.* "It's all my fault."

Nora crouched next to Quinn and tugged Emily's dress up to expose her thigh. Quinn gasped. The splotches had spread from Emily's neck to her legs, disappearing into her socks. Her whole body was covered with angry red bumps now.

Quinn pulled her arm from James's grasp so she could hurry to Emily's side. She knelt and brushed a soft ringlet off her daughter's face. "You're going to be okay." Quinn murmured. "I'm so sorry, Emily. Your mommy has your medicine right here."

Panicked tears streamed down Emily's face and dripped onto Quinn's hand.

Nora pulled the EpiPen from its case, took the cap off, and thrust the orange-tipped end into Emily's leg.

Quinn's gaze swung from Emily's leg, up her torso, to her

face. Her chest still heaved and her lips still looked like she'd sucked on a blue lollipop. Quinn sat back on her heels. "Why isn't it working?"

"It takes a minute." Nora set the EpiPen on the bench and leaned across Quinn to rub Emily's shoulder. "You're okay, baby. The medicine will work any minute. Take nice, long, deep breaths."

"Mommy," Emily gasped, reaching for Nora. Quinn moved out of the way so Nora could lift Emily up and cradle her on her lap. Quinn stood, hanging back and wringing her hands as she watched Emily's chest rise and fall. After a minute, her breathing began to slow to a more normal rhythm and the gasping quieted.

The bailiff who'd been barking instructions into his radio stepped up next to Quinn. "The ambulance is on the way. They'll be in the loading dock in about five minutes."

Nora stood, still cradling Emily, and turned her accusing gaze at Quinn. "What did she eat? What did you give her? The doctors will need to know."

"She had a granola bar. She said she was hungry, and that's all I had."

"Did it have nuts in it?"

"*No.* I checked." But then Quinn hesitated. Could she have missed something? "It's just oats and dried fruit and honey. It says the ingredients right on the front."

"Did you check the back? Did you make sure it doesn't say that it has traces of tree nuts? If so, she can't have it. If it's even made in a factory with nuts, *she can't have it.*"

"Oh, God." Quinn went hot and then cold, and her vision blurred. "I had no idea. I'm so sorry."

"We need to get her outside to the ambulance," the bailiff insisted.

Emily face screwed up and her mouth opened in a wail. "I want my bear."

Nora's head swung back and forth down the hall. "Where's Mirabel? Emily can't sleep without her."

"On the other bench." Quinn took off down the hall to the spot where she'd been sitting when she gave Emily the granola bar. The offending snack sat abandoned on the wood slats next to her purse, and she recoiled from it. Quinn couldn't bear to even touch it now that she knew it had nearly killed Emily. Not that the granola bar was at fault, really. The blame lay entirely on Quinn.

She left the bar on the bench and picked up Bruno and Mirabel. Tucking them under her arm, she ran back to where Nora waited with Emily. "Here, sweetie. Here are your bears."

Emily's chest was hitching again, but this time with sobs. Quinn's guilt came in another wave, nearly knocking her over. She'd been the one to do this to Emily. To her own child.

Emily reached out her little arms, pushing Bruno to the side and grabbing Mirabel. She clutched the stuffed animal to her chest.

"You're her mother, ma'am?" The bailiff asked Nora.

"Yes."

"Let's go." He put a hand under Nora's arm and guided her to the exit door where the ambulance waited to take Emily to the children's hospital.

Where it waited to take Emily and her mother.

Quinn stood in the hallway watching them disappear into the stairwell with the rest of the onlookers. When she looked down, she realized she was still holding Bruno.

27

Though the waiting room bustled with noise and activity—babies crying, mothers chasing toddlers, television blaring cartoons—Quinn stared at the opposite wall, too exhausted to even turn her head. She'd been sitting on the green plastic-covered couch for hours, and still there was no news about Emily. The kind young woman wearing duck-print scrubs at the check-in desk had told her not to worry; kids who were stable waited longer than the emergencies. Emily had seemed okay when she left the courthouse, but Quinn couldn't help but fear that Emily's condition had taken a turn in the ambulance, or maybe once she got to the hospital.

Quinn had spent the first hour in the ER waiting room Googling "nut allergy" and the stories she'd read were terrifying. If Nora hadn't come with the EpiPen when she had, Emily could have lost consciousness or stopped breathing altogether. Even now, there was a risk she could have a secondary reaction and the red, scaly rash and horrible labored wheezing could return.

Or worse.

If Emily was stable, why wasn't anyone getting back to her?

She'd texted Liam and Nora when she arrived, letting them know she was there and requesting that they please tell her the minute they had an update on Emily's condition. So far, the only message she'd received was from James asking how it was going. The front-desk woman wasn't allowed to tell her anything—she couldn't even officially confirm that Emily had been admitted.

Quinn wasn't family and that information was private.

The bailiff who'd walked Nora and Emily out had told her that the ambulance was headed to the children's hospital. Otherwise, Quinn wouldn't have even known that much.

She couldn't blame Liam and Nora for not wanting to talk to her—she'd probably feel the same if the situation were reversed—but Quinn had hoped they'd at least send a quick text.

Quinn settled back in her seat, trying to get comfortable. Not that she was complaining. A night on the sticky vinyl couch cushions was nothing compared to how Emily had suffered today. Quinn finally found a spot where she could lay her head back, but as soon as her eyes fluttered shut, an oppressive, helpless feeling rolled over her. She was back in the hallway of the courtroom, screaming for someone to help them. Quinn could hear the wheezing and gasping of Emily's labored breath. Feel Emily's chest pulsate like a drumbeat as the little girl tried and failed to suck air into her lungs.

Emily might die, and it's all my fault.

"Quinn?" came a voice from behind her. Quinn's eyes flew open as she lurched to a seated position and spun around. Liam stood a few feet away, his shirt wrinkled and untucked and his hair sticking up on one side, probably from running a hand through it. "Hey." He rounded the couch to stand on her side of it.

"Liam," Quinn said, breathlessly, sliding her legs onto the floor. "How is Emily?"

Liam sank down next to her, looking as exhausted as she felt. "She's absolutely fine." He flashed her a wry smile. "Watching *Frozen* and trying to con the nurse into giving her a snack."

Quinn leaned against the back of the couch, her body limp with relief. "Oh, thank God. I was so afraid she'd had a relapse or something."

"I'm sorry I didn't get back to you sooner—they were running some tests, and I didn't even check my messages until a few minutes ago. But I should have known you'd be worried."

He didn't owe her anything, certainly not an apology.

"Thank you for coming to tell me. I wouldn't blame you if you never wanted to see my face again, after what happened."

"It wasn't your fault."

Quinn shook her head, unable to speak over the sob lodged in her throat. Whose fault was it, then? She'd known about Emily's nut allergy. How had it not even occurred to her to check the back label on the granola bar? She was sure she'd hear Emily's wheezing and gasping in her dreams for as long as she lived.

"Hey." Liam slid a tiny bit closer. "It's okay. Really."

But it wasn't okay. "She could have died, Liam."

"But she didn't. She's perfectly fine."

"I didn't know what to do." Quinn's eyes filled and spilled over. "She couldn't breathe, and I didn't have any idea how to help her."

He turned in his seat so he was facing her now. "Quinn, how would you have known? It's not something you know unless you have a kid who's had an allergic reaction before—" Liam stopped talking abruptly, probably when he saw the look on her face and realized what he'd said.

Unless you have a kid who's had an allergic reaction before. Which, of course, she didn't.

"Shit." He closed his eyes, slowly shaking his head. "I'm sorry, I didn't mean it the way it sounded."

"No, it's okay. You're right." It was a kick directly to her gut with so much force she almost doubled over. *But he's right.*

"What I meant to say was that it could happen to anyone. Even if you know to check every food label, sometimes you slip up. One day about a year ago, I stopped on my way home from the gym for a smoothie. It had peanut-butter protein powder in it. I didn't even think about it—I just left it on the counter at home and went to take a shower. I was in and out in three minutes. How much trouble could Emily and Connor get into in three minutes?"

Quinn gave him a watery smile. "I'm guessing a lot more than you expected?"

"They were supposed to be playing in Connor's room, but they went down to the kitchen looking for a snack. They saw the smoothie and thought it was a milkshake." He tugged at the collar of his shirt as if it were choking him. "Emily's throat closed up, and she couldn't breathe. We ended up exactly where we are right now."

"You must have been terrified."

"I was. But I'd also been there once when Nora looked away for less than a minute, and Emily ate a peanut at a birthday party. So, when she drank the smoothie, I'd had her EpiPen and knew what to do." Liam shook his head. "As soon as you started coming by to see Emily every week, we should have shown you what to do. So that's on us, and you can't blame yourself."

If that were true, why did she still feel like this heavy weight was sitting on her chest? "It's not just that I screwed up and gave Emily something with nuts in it—" Although never forgive herself for that. "—or even that I didn't know what to do. It's—" She paused, staring at the opposite wall as she began to slot the piece together in her mind. She'd made so many more mistakes than just that granola bar. And finally, she could see it.

"When Emily was scared and sick, she wanted Nora. She *needed* Nora." Quinn hung her head, and another tear slipped down her cheek. "Emily wanted her mommy. And that will always be Nora."

Liam was quiet for a moment, and when she finally glanced in his direction, his eyes looked pained and his mouth twisted with sympathy.

"This is what you've been trying to tell me all along, isn't it?"

"Yes." He reached out and gently touched her arm. "I'm sorry. I honestly am. This is a situation I wouldn't wish on anyone. Especially someone like you who—" He hesitated again, as if he were debating what to say, and Quinn felt the heat of his skin pressed against hers. "Someone who... deserves to have everything you want in life," he finally finished.

Everything she wanted in life... was to be a mother. But how could she live with herself if she got what she wanted at the expense of so many other people? At the expense of what was best for her own child?

"I'm dropping the custody case." Quinn's chest hitched as she fought to hold back a sob. "I don't even know what I was doing. How did I think I could take Emily away from Nora?"

"You were thinking that you love Emily."

"Was I, though? Or was I only thinking of myself?" She scrubbed the back of her hand across her cheeks to wipe away the tears. But she'd never be able to wipe away her selfishness. That would stay with her for as long as she lived. She'd been so fixated on getting custody of Emily that she'd lost sight of what was best for her.

"Every time I've seen you with Emily, it's clear how much you love her," Liam said gently. "And you're showing it a hundred times over by making the decision now to give her up."

Quinn couldn't hold back anymore. Her shoulders shook and tears poured down her cheeks as she leaned her face in her hands and sobbed. Liam reached out and slid an arm around her, pulling him against her. Quinn went willingly, leaning against his chest and fisting a hand in his shirt to have something to hold on to. He stroked her hair, murmuring comforting words as she cried over the terrible heartbreak of it all. For the little girl with dark brown curls and eyes that looked just like Quinn's, and Quinn's mother's, and grandmother's. The little girl who was made up of pieces of her, pieces of the people who she'd loved and who were gone now.

She cried for all the dreams she'd had of raising her baby, of being a mother, of having a child look up at her with love and devotion. The way Emily looked at Nora.

Eventually, Quinn's tears slowed and her shoulders stopped shaking. With a deep breath, she sat up and wiped her eyes. Liam's shirt was even more wrinkled now, and she'd left wet streaks across it with her tears. Flustered, she peeked up at him through her lashes. "I'm sorry I cried all over you."

"I'm not." One corner of Liam's mouth twitched. "Cry all over me whenever you want to."

Quinn was tempted to take him up on his offer. She had a feeling she'd be crying a lot in the next few months. Maybe longer. Maybe forever. If she had someone like Liam to wrap his arms around her while she grieved this loss, it might make it all just a tiny bit more bearable. But, of course, she didn't have Liam. She had James. James who'd been texting with his pregnant girlfriend behind her back.

She couldn't think about it right then, so she forced her lips to curve upward, managing a semblance of a smile. "Thanks." Quinn fished a tissue from her purse and wiped her eyes. "I guess I should go and tell Nora. Then I need to call my attorney."

"What about James? Will he be okay with this?"

James had moved on the moment Sasha had found the two pink lines. Or maybe even before that. James had wanted to be a father, and Quinn had come along at the right time. Too bad they hadn't known that she wasn't capable of giving him what he wanted—not like Sasha was. He'd been interested in pursuing Emily until he'd found out that he could have a child without all the complications in the way.

Now, Quinn was the only thing in the way of James being a father to Sasha's baby. She had no doubt that if she dropped the custody case, James would, too.

"He'll be just fine," Quinn reassured Liam. "James has his own baby on the way with his new girlfriend."

Liam's eyes widened and mouth dropped open, but before he could ask any questions, Quinn held up a hand and shook her head. Maybe someday, but not today.

Liam nodded as if he understood, and Quinn's already aching heart cracked open just a tiny bit more. Liam was a good person, and he'd been a friend to her even though she didn't deserve it. His wife had been a lucky woman. Quinn hoped he'd find someone who would love both him and Connor equally.

She took a deep breath and let it out slowly.

Liam reached out and took her hand. "Quinn, I know it hurts right now. But you're doing the right thing."

"I know I am." That knowledge was the only thing that would help her survive it.

———

Liam took Quinn to Emily's hospital room. She was afraid Nora would refuse to even let her inside. But when Quinn pushed aside the curtain and peeked in at Nora sitting on the bed with Emily asleep against her side, the other woman barely even glanced at her.

"Can I come in?" Quinn whispered.

Nora lifted a shoulder like it didn't matter one way or the

other. Her pale face almost glowed in the lights from the machines monitoring Emily's vitals, and their fluorescent hue made Nora's eyes look sunken and ghostly. Quinn didn't think she could possibly feel worse, but seeing Nora like this—so tired and beaten down—made her heart sink even lower.

"How is she?" Quinn asked in a low voice, nodding at the exhausted girl by her hip.

"She's fine. They just want to keep her here for a few more hours to make sure she won't have a secondary reaction, but they think she's pretty much in the clear."

"Nora." Quinn's voice wavered with emotion. "I'm so sorry for what happened today."

Nora hesitated like she was debating what to say, and then she finally sighed. "It's not your fault. I'd love to blame you, I really would. But I know it was an accident."

"That's what I told her, too." Liam said from beside Quinn.

"Well, there's something else I need to apologize for, Nora." Quinn's breath hitched.

This was it. Once it was out there, she could never take it back.

Nora looked up now, slightly more alert.

Quinn curled her fingers into fists to stop them from shaking. Liam inched closer until his hand found hers, closing around it to give a reassuring squeeze. She shot him a grateful look and then turned back to Nora. "I'm sorry for all the pain I put you through with this custody hearing. I don't know what I was thinking, except that I really do love Emily and want what's best for her." Quinn took a deep breath. "And I know that what's best for her is to be with you."

Nora froze, her eyes wide. "What are you saying?" she finally managed to whisper.

"I'm saying that I'm backing out of the custody hearing. I should never have started it in the first place. And I'm so sorry."

"Oh, my God." Nora's face crumpled and her whole body

shook as she curled her body around Emily's and sobbed. "Oh, my God. My baby. My baby." She said it over and over as tears poured down her face into Emily's hair. "I thought I'd lost you forever."

Emily's eyes drifted open. "Mommy?" she whispered. "Why are you sad?"

Nora rocked against her. "I'm not sad, baby. I'm so happy. I love you so much."

Emily sighed. "I love you too, Mommy," and her eyes closed again.

Liam let go of Quinn's hand and moved over to the bed. He sat down next to Nora and Emily, and wrapped them both in a hug. Nora grabbed onto him, still shaking with silent sobs.

"It's okay, Nora," he whispered. "It's over." A tear leaked from each corner of his eyes, and he swiped at them with the back of his hand.

Quinn slowly backed away until she was in the doorway of the hospital room. And then she turned, slipped out into the hall, and headed home.

28

It was after midnight, and James was asleep on the couch when Quinn got home. At the sound of her feet tapping across the wood floor, he opened his eyes and sat up slowly. Quinn sank down into the opposite chair—the same one she'd chosen when she'd first found out about his affair—and it almost seemed fitting. That had been the beginning of the end.

And this was the end.

"How's Emily?" James asked, the last syllable drawn out by his yawn.

"She's fine. She'll make a full recovery." Quinn clicked the side-table light on, illuminating the room in a soft, warm glow.

James blew out a relieved breath. "I'm glad to hear it," he said, and Quinn knew he was. James wasn't a bad person, and he'd probably make a kind and caring father. After all, he had understood that pursuing custody of Emily wasn't in her best interest long before Quinn had. She'd blamed his disinterest on the baby, but she could see now that for all his mistakes, he been able to clearly see what she hadn't.

"Have you heard from Helena?" James asked. "Will the hearing continue tomorrow, or will it be postponed?"

"I spoke to Helena about an hour ago." Quinn looked down at her hands. "The hearing is canceled." It hurt to hear the words come out of her mouth. To realize the finality of them.

James sat up straight, fully alert now. "What?"

"I decided not to pursue custody of Emily." She met his eyes. "I guess I should have run it by you first but, to be honest, I didn't think you really wanted this anymore. You'll have your hands full with the new baby."

James's mouth dropped open. "So, that's it, then? Emily stays with Nora, and..."

"And it's over."

"Why?"

"Emily belongs with her mother. And that's not me. I'm just sorry it took me this long to realize it."

"Oh, Quinn." James's face contorted with pity, and he leaned forward as if he was going to get up out of his seat. Probably to come over and comfort her, which was the last thing she wanted. His comfort *or* his pity.

"No." Quinn held up a hand to stop him. "Please don't. I'm fine."

He sank slowly back into his seat. "Did you tell Nora?"

"She's thrilled."

"This doesn't mean it's the end of the road, Quinn. We could still fix up the guest room as a nursery for the new baby. We could still be parents together. Quinn—" He his face softened into a tender smile. "It's a boy."

Quinn's heart pitched. *A little boy.* A tiny baby in a crib down the hall, bundled up in the receiving blankets and tiny onesies she'd hidden back under the bed because she couldn't quite bear to get rid of them. For a wild second, she considered it. Maybe she and James could go to counseling. They could work on their marriage and raise this baby together. Maybe she could be a mother after all.

But then she remembered Nora's family lined up behind

her at the custody hearing while Quinn sat alone, waiting for James to get off the phone with his girlfriend. She remembered the message she'd seen on his phone. She didn't need a huge family like Nora's, but she needed one that was committed to her. If Quinn stayed with James, she'd always come second to the mother of his child, and how could she live like that?

"Congratulations," Quinn said with forced buoyancy. "*A boy.*"

"What do you think, Quinn?" James leaned forward in his seat.

"I think you'll make a good father. And I hope the baby will have a good mother—in Sasha." Quinn sighed, suddenly more exhausted than she'd ever been in her life. "But I won't be around to help you raise him."

"Quinn." James lunged to his feet and shuffled across the room, dropping to his knees in front of her, just like last time. "Quinn, please. Don't do this. I know you're upset right now, but consider what you're doing." He grabbed her hand. "Don't blow up our whole life because it didn't work out with Emily."

Quinn thought about arguing with him. Yelling that *she* wasn't the one blowing up their life, that he'd been the one to do that when he'd gotten someone else pregnant. And then when he'd lied about his ongoing relationship with her. But what was the point anymore? So, instead, she pulled her hand from his grasp and stood up. "Tomorrow, I'd like you to pack your things and move out. You can get a hotel or short-term rental. Or maybe you can crash with Sasha." Quinn shrugged. "Let me know where you're staying. Helena will contact you in the next few days."

"Helena?" James grabbed the arm of the chair she'd vacated and hauled himself to his feet. "I thought you said the hearing for custody of Emily was canceled."

"It is."

"So, why would Helena contact me?"

"Because she'll be representing me in our divorce."

———

Quinn woke the next morning feeling like she'd been beaten against a rock—her eyes were dried out and puffy from crying, back aching from sitting on the uncomfortable couch in the emergency room all evening, and her head pounded from not eating or drinking enough the day before. But despite her physical ailments, her brain felt clearer than it had in years. Maybe since she'd started on this doomed pregnancy journey half a decade ago. None of it had turned out as she'd expected, but at least now she could finally move on with her life.

Quinn took a quick shower and got dressed. James had slept in the basement one last time, and he'd be coming upstairs to clear out his drawers and closets soon. She had a meeting scheduled with Helena for later that day, but that morning, there were a few things she needed to do first.

Quinn knelt down next to the bed and reached down to pull out the boxes tucked underneath. The first box contained her childhood photo albums. Why had she packed these away where she hardly ever looked at them? Her parents' death had been tragic, but these albums were full of wonderful, happy memories. Quinn set the box on the dresser. Later that evening, she'd open a bottle of wine and sort through them. She wanted to pick a few of the best photos to frame and hang in the hallway where she could see them every day.

Next, she pulled out the boxes of baby clothes and toys. Balancing one on top of each other, she carefully carried them out to the car. Ten minutes later, Quinn parked on a side street in East Liberty and entered a door with a sign that read: *Women's Residential Treatment and Recovery Center.* Their website had said they were a halfway house for pregnant and new mothers with addiction.

At the front desk sat a young woman, who smiled as she entered.

"Hi," Quinn said, peering around her stack of boxes. "I have a bunch of brand-new baby clothes, and some toys and other things. I'm wondering if you take this kind of donation?"

The woman jumped up and came around to the other side of the counter to grab the boxes and help Quinn set them down. "Oh, we do. We're always in need of baby stuff." She flipped open the box on top, the one containing the tiny newborn clothes. "Oh, how gorgeous! We have a couple of women who are due in the next few weeks. They'll be thrilled to have some new things for their babies. A lot of what we offer is hand-me-downs, and every new mom deserves something a little special, right?"

Quinn took one final look at the fuzzy little bear suit and then tore her eyes away. "Absolutely." She smiled at the woman, and it was only a tiny bit forced. "Please give them my best for a healthy birth."

"Thank you so much!"

Quinn nodded and then turned and headed out the door.

Twenty minutes later, Quinn pushed open the doors to the library. She wasn't scheduled to work the week of the trial, but she couldn't bear to go home to her empty house. And she didn't know where else to go.

Quinn swerved left, away from the children's section where her counterpart was reading aloud to a group of preschoolers. She knew she'd have to go back to work next week and put on a happy face during craft time and story hour, but right then, she wasn't ready. For the past five years, through the fertility treatments and procedures, the negative pregnancy tests and heartbreak, she'd managed to show up every day and be the best she could be for those kids. She'd spent countless hours surrounded by mothers with their babies and toddlers while her body refused to let her join their ranks. But the one thing Quinn had always been able to hold on to, that had pulled her through, was *hope*. Hope that the next treatment would work, the next pregnancy test would be positive. And then hope that she'd win custody of Emily, and all her dreams would finally come true.

And now that hope was gone.

Quinn wandered to the back corner of the fiction section, hoping that none of her colleagues would spot her. If Sonia chased her down to interrogate her about how the custody case was going, she might not be responsible for her reaction.

It probably wasn't a great idea to come here.

But as Quinn slowly made her way deeper into the aisles of books, running her hand along the spines lined up on the shelves, the comforting, familiar scent of bound paper drifted over her, smoothing the hard edges in her heart. She couldn't remember the last time she'd read a book that wasn't about how to get pregnant, the last time she'd gotten lost in a story, purely for fun.

The title of a Jane Austen novel—an old favorite—caught her attention, and she tugged it off the shelf. Maybe she'd sit in the park and read it. Not the one near Nora's house, the chances were too great that she'd run into Emily, or at least into Connor and Liam. But she could go to the park near her house, find a comfortable bench and a shady tree, and maybe she could forget about life for a while.

"That would be a great book for our next book club."

Quinn's head jerked up and she clutched the book to her pounding heart. "Oh, you scared me."

"Sorry." Elise stood at the end of the aisle. "I saw you come in and head back here. I don't mean to interrupt, but you looked like you could use a friend."

Quinn's shoulders slumped. A minute ago, she hadn't wanted to talk about it. But at the gentleness in Elise's tone, the loneliness took over, and it all came pouring out. "The hearings are over. Thank you so much for being there and supporting us but... I gave up on pursuing custody of Emily."

Elise nodded, sadly. "It was on the news." She took a step closer to Quinn. "For what it's worth, I think it was an incredibly brave and selfless act."

For about the hundredth time since she'd made the decision to give up Emily, Quinn's eyes welled up. "It doesn't feel very selfless." She shook her head slowly. "It's what I should have done all along."

"Well, I think this calls for an emergency meeting of the book club tonight." Elise walked over to where Quinn was standing. "Why don't you let us come over and support you? We'll bring wine and takeout, and you can cry all you want." She paused and gave Quinn a tentative smile. "Or if you don't feel like talking about it, we'll gossip about Sonia instead. That should take your mind off things."

Quinn swiped at the tears under her eyes as a laugh escaped from her chest. "Are you sure you're not too busy?" It was last minute, and they all had husbands and kids at home.

Elise's mouth stretched into a wide grin. "I already called them. We'll be over at seven."

29

Eight months later

Quinn almost didn't see the pink flowered envelope that had come in the mail, tucked in between a credit card offer and a postcard advertisement from a local realtor. She'd tossed the whole pile on the side table and then left for book club, an event that she absolutely couldn't miss.

After she'd given up custody of Emily, and James had moved out, Quinn had been surprised by how her book club friends had rallied around her, stopping by with bottles of wine and bags of takeout for impromptu girls' nights. She didn't know what she'd been thinking, pushing Elise away, and the other women, too. It still hurt sometimes, when her friends talked about motherhood. But with every passing month, her heart ached a tiny bit less and she found it a little bit easier to be happy for them.

Quinn had gotten home late the night the envelope arrived, and then left for work early the next day, so she didn't even give it another thought until the next night. With another pile of mail in her hands, she kicked off her work shoes and settled on the couch to sort through her bills. The envelope tumbled out onto her lap, bubble-gum pink with darker pink daisies.

Quinn flipped it over in her hands, and her gaze slid from her own name scrawled in neat script to the name listed in the return address. *Nora Robinson.* She tore into it then, and pulled out a card—also pink with flowers—and saw it was an invitation.

Emily is turning 5! Please join us for her birthday party. Quinn recognized the address listed for the party as Nora's.

Quinn stared at the invitation, running a finger from the word *Emily* to the number five. Should she go? The last time she'd seen Emily was the day at the hospital when she'd dropped the custody case. She'd considered asking to keep up her weekly visits, but had decided she'd caused enough pain to Nora and her family. She didn't want to make it worse by hanging around uninvited. Liam texted her photos every now and then—Emily picking dandelions in the park or throwing a ball with Connor on the basketball court. Her heart pitched every time Liam's name appeared on her phone because she knew it would be followed by Emily's image. But that, too, had gotten easier with time. Just last week, Quinn had printed a few of her favorite photos of Emily, and now they hung on the wall in the hall next to images of her parents and a few shots she'd taken on a Florida beach with some old college friends she'd reconnected with that past winter.

Quinn reread the invitation. Beneath the printed words, Nora had hand-written, *We hope you can come* in the same neat print as on the envelope. She wouldn't have sent the invitation if she didn't want Quinn there, would she? But did Quinn want to go and open her heart up all over again?

Quinn picked up her phone and quickly typed a reply before she could change her mind.

I'd love to come to Emily's birthday party. Thank you for inviting me.

———

Quinn took a tentative step through the back gate into Nora's yard and then paused to take in the party humming in front of her. Nora had toned things down a bit this year—there were no jugglers or bouncy-houses—but it seemed that most of the family had shown up to celebrate Emily. She spotted Uncle Wesley pulling quarters out of a boy's ear, and Aunt Susan gossiping with a group of older ladies. Cousin Troy ran past, holding a ball over his head with a pack of kids on his tail. Quinn wondered how his job at the country club was going and if he still lived in Aunt Susan's garage apartment.

She took a few more steps into the yard, and then faltered when her eyes connected with Liam's. She lifted her hand in a tentative wave, and he looked as if he was going to come over to talk to her. But then one of the kids at a nearby table knocked over a cup of soda, and he ran to get a pile of napkins to clean it up.

Quinn took a shaky breath. Walking into this party wasn't any easier than it had been last year. In some ways it was harder. At least last year, she'd felt like she deserved to be there for her court-ordered visit with Emily. This time around, she had no claims on Emily's time or attention.

But Nora had invited her, and it seemed unlikely the card had arrived by mistake. Quinn straightened her shoulders. She'd drop off her present, say hello to Emily, and try not to cry. And then she'd go home and be fine. Just like she'd been fine for the past few months, even if it was a struggle sometimes.

"Miss Quinn!" A streak of dark hair and blue T-shirt came out of nowhere and crashed into her. "My dad said you might come!" Connor looked up at her through his lopsided glasses, and the next thing she knew, his arms were around her.

"Connor," she said, returning his hug. "Look at how big you've gotten."

"We measure on my birthday, and I grew four inches since last year." He stood up straight to show her. "I'm going to be taller than my dad soon."

"You are. But my biggest question is..." Quinn looked at him sideways. "How many teeth have you lost?"

Connor paused, and she could see his tongue sliding around inside his mouth as he counted the new holes there. "Two more!"

"And the tooth fairy has been showing up on time?"

"Once she did, and once she forgot. My dad says fifty-fifty is pretty good odds. But I told him that a fifty percent grade on a test would be an F."

Quinn laughed because she could imagine Liam's disgruntled face when he realized his son had out-matched him. "Good for you."

Connor grabbed her hand with his little, sticky one, and tugged her into the yard. "You want to play robots with me after the cake?"

Quinn smiled, suddenly glad she'd come. "I'd love to."

"Okay! See you later!" He dropped her hand and ran off.

Quinn made her way to the gift table where she dropped off the pink and silver-wrapped toy she'd brought for Emily—a normal-sized gift, no dollhouses this year—then grabbed herself a drink from a cooler. Just as she was beginning to wonder what to do with herself, Aunt Susan walked by on her way across the yard. The older woman made it about three steps past when Quinn's presence seemed to register, because she turned back around slowly.

"It's Quinn, isn't it?"

"Yes. You're Susan? We met at Emily's party last year."

Aunt Susan definitely remembered her, but it seemed her recollections had nothing to do with the party. Her eyes widened, and she sucked in a breath. "Oh, I know *exactly* who you are. You're Emily's biological mother."

Quinn should have expected that people would know. Many of them had been in the seats behind Nora at the hearing, and they'd seen Helena go on the attack. After what she'd put this family through, they'd probably want to run her right out of the party. "I—uh." What could she say? "Yes, I am."

And before Quinn knew what was happening, Aunt Susan threw her arms around her. "Oh, honey. It's so nice to see you." Aunt Susan pulled away, still clutching Quinn's shoulders and holding her at arm's length so she could look her in the eye. "What you did for Nora and Emily... giving up custody... well, I know it can't have been easy."

"I—no." Quinn blinked. "It wasn't."

"Well, this whole family appreciates your selflessness. And I'm glad to see you're keeping up with Emily."

Quinn mustered up a dazed half-smile. "Thanks."

"Now come and sit with us over here." Aunt Susan put an arm around Quinn and guided her to the table with the older ladies. "Girls," she announced, "this is Emily's biological mother, Quinn."

"Sit here, honey." A woman with a gray bob wearing a purple track suit patted the chair next to her. "We know all about the mix-up at the fertility clinic."

"It's shocking," chimed in another woman, holding out her manicured hand for emphasis.

Quinn sat down, and purple track-suited lady leaned in conspiratorially. "Tell us, did you sue?"

"Anita, it's really none of our business," Aunt Susan admonished. But she pulled her chair closer, waiting for an answer.

Quinn shifted in her seat. "There was a settlement, yes." It was how she could afford to stay in the house on her librarian's salary. James hadn't had any interest in it, and a few months after he'd moved out, he and Sasha had closed on a house in Squirrel Hill. The baby was born a week later. *James Junior.*

Quinn had sent a bouncy seat directly from Amazon. Her days of wandering baby shops were over.

She was considering selling the house, though, and maybe moving out of the city. There was an opening for a children's librarian in one of the suburban branches, and she thought she might apply. Her gaze drifted from the tree branches bending overhead to provide shade for their little group to the garden blooming with spring flowers. Lately, she'd been thinking she might like a bit more of a yard to plant a larger vegetable patch, and maybe getting a dog. Having a few friendly neighbors wouldn't be such a bad thing, either.

"Well, I'm glad to hear it," Anita said. "You deserve it."

"And your husband?" Aunt Susan asked. "How is he handling everything?"

"I wouldn't really know." Quinn lifted a shoulder. "We're divorced now. But I think he's doing fine."

"Oh, I'm sorry." Aunt Susan didn't look the least bit sorry. In fact, she was gazing at Quinn like Quinn had suddenly turned into a piece of prime rib. "Have you met my nephew, Liam?"

Quinn couldn't help but laugh. "I've met Liam, yes." But her true reaction to the older woman's sudden interest in match-making went beyond humor. It was a warmth in her chest like she'd felt that night when her book club friends had landed on her doorstep to cheer her up. She'd missed this connection and sense of belonging with friends. How had it taken her so long to realize it?

"And do you like him?" the woman with the manicure asked. Before Quinn could answer, she waved a hand in Liam's direction. "Dear, come over here for a moment."

Liam appeared behind Aunt Susan's chair and flashed the group of women an extra-wide smile. "Ladies, it's nice to see you."

Anita got right to the point. "Liam, you know Quinn, right?"

He turned down the wattage on his grin to a more normal level, and his eyes softened. "I do. How are you, Quinn?"

The second as their eyes met, a blush crept across her cheeks. She'd forgotten how attractive he was. "I'm fine. It's good to see you, Liam."

"Quinn is recently divorced," Aunt Susan announced.

He raised an eyebrow and cocked his head. "I'm sorry to hear that."

"It was for the best," Anita told him, with absolutely no idea if it was for the best or not.

Quinn felt her blush deepen, and thankfully Nora saved her from any more awkwardness by calling everyone over for cake. Quinn slipped out of her chair to mingle with the rest of the group, singing "Happy Birthday" and cheering as Emily made a wish.

After the cake was served and eaten, Quinn grabbed Connor and Emily for a game of monkey-in-the-middle. Both children had improved at the game since she'd last played with them. Quinn marveled at how much they'd grown, and how much she'd missed.

When the kids needed a break, Quinn found Nora working her way around a picnic table, picking up discarded paper plates and tossing them into a garbage bag. Quinn slid up next to her, grabbing a few crumpled juice boxes and throwing them in as well.

"Thanks for your help," Nora said.

"Thanks for inviting me."

Nora stopped walking and dropped the garbage bag on a chair. "I'm glad you could make it. I really am."

"I can't believe how much Emily has grown in these past months."

Nora nodded sadly. "It feels like I blink, and I miss it." And then her eyes widened as if she realized that Quinn had missed just about everything. "I'm sorry, that was insensitive of me."

"No, it's okay." Quinn smiled to show her it really was okay. Or at least it would be. "I appreciate the chance to see her."

Nora cocked her head, giving Quinn a long look. Then she reached out a hand and touched Quinn's arm. "Come back next weekend, if you want."

Quinn blinked. "Really?"

"Yeah. Emily misses your Saturday visits. We could hang out in the backyard, you could play with Emily. Maybe you and I could have some coffee."

Quinn's mouth dropped open. "I—" It was so unexpected she hardly knew how to react.

Nora's face flashed with uncertainty. "Only if you want to."

"I'd *love* to."

Nora gave her a tentative smile. "Good. Okay. I'll text you."

The party was starting to wind down now, so Quinn gave hugs to both Emily and Connor and headed out to her car. It had been a wonderful day, but as she walked down the stone path that bisected Nora's front yard to the street, a little bit of her melancholy returned. The sun was moving west in the sky, casting long shadows from the trees across the garden. Birds chirped and the smell of cut grass drifted over from a neighbor's yard. Though she was content with her life now, there were moments like this where she dreaded going home to her empty house in the city. She wished she had someone to meet for dinner or a walk in the park to enjoy the summer evening.

Quinn had her book club friends, of course. But they had families at home, and spontaneous evenings away were hard to pull off. Her friends had been encouraging her to try dating apps, but it had been three-quarters of a decade since the last time she'd been on a first date, and at forty-four years of age, she didn't know how she'd start from scratch.

With a sigh, Quinn dug her keys from her purse and clicked the lock on her car. She was about to get in when someone came running around from the back of the house calling her name. The person skidded to a stop in front of her, and Quinn turned around to gaze up into a pair of blue eyes.

"Hey," Liam said, slightly out of breath.

"Hi." She bit her lip. He was standing awfully close, and *damn it*, in this light, he looked even more attractive.

"Uh." He shoved his hands into his pockets. Did he look nervous? "Connor and I were wondering if you had any plans tonight. We were going to order a pizza and watch a movie." He flashed her a grin. "Any chance you want to join us?"

Quinn smiled in return. "I'd absolutely love to."

EPILOGUE

NORA

The doorbell rang, and I pulled it open, smiling at Aunt Susan standing on the step balancing a covered dish in her winter-gloved hands. Her famous green-bean casserole. It wouldn't be Thanksgiving without it. A gust of cold November wind blew into the house, and I swung the door open wider, ushering her in.

"Are they here yet?" Aunt Susan whispered as she slipped past me into the hallway. I took the dish so she could shrug out of her coat and hang it in the hall closet.

"Not yet, and don't be so obvious about it," I scolded. Aunt Susan was by far our family's biggest gossip. She had a big heart and meant well, but it was always a mistake to let her in on anything you wanted to keep a secret. I don't know why my brother told her his plans, except that Aunt Susan liked to think that the credit for all of this belonged to her.

We made our way down the hall to add her dish to the dozen others. Every year, I offered to cook for Thanksgiving, and every year, every single family member showed up with a casserole dish, so at this point, I didn't bother to make anything but the turkey.

Emily zipped by, chased by Cousin Troy's brand-new stepson. Troy used to be the slacker of the family, but he completely turned his life around when he fell for a single mom who wasn't having it.

"No running!" I yelled, but it was half-hearted because the kids were six, and excited, and nobody was going to listen to me. *When Conner gets here, I'm sending them out to the backyard.*

From down the hall, I heard the front door squeak open, and my brother's voice call out, "We're here!"

I wiped my hands on a dishtowel as he walked into the kitchen so I could run over and give him a hug. It wasn't really Thanksgiving until my brother got there. Liam had been my best friend and my rock since he was a toddler singing to my mom's stomach when she was pregnant with me.

Connor wrapped his arms around me, knocking his glasses askew on my stomach, and I playfully popped them back into place for him. His most precious teddy bear was tucked under one arm—where it tended to always be unless Connor had a basketball in his hands—so I gave it a pat. After Connor came Quinn, and even though I'd known her for over two years, it still took my breath away to see her standing there in the doorway.

Looking at Quinn was like looking at Emily forty years in the future. It would never cease to amaze me that they had the same dark curly hair, the same high cheekbones, the same wide brown eyes. Every day since Quinn gave up pursuing custody of Emily, I sent a prayer of thanks to the universe that I'd been able to keep my daughter. And now I was thankful for Quinn coming into our lives, too. When my brother's wife had died, I didn't think he'd ever get over it until he met Quinn. Connor adored her, and even I'd grown to love her like a sister.

And that day, she was about to become my actual sister, if my brother would ever get on with the proposal he'd planned.

"Can I help you with anything?" Quinn asked, after she'd given me a hug.

"Nope," I told her. "Just relax and get a glass of wine."

Quinn headed into the living room to settle on the couch, and one by one, the rest of the family filed in until the space was so full there was barely standing room.

Liam made his way over to Quinn, and, oblivious to the crowd that had formed, she gave him a bright smile as he approached. In the next moment, her expression morphed into shock when Liam dropped down on one knee and held out a jewelry box.

The ring was our grandmother's, and Quinn was going to love it. Liam had proposed to his first wife with a ring they'd picked out together, but for Quinn, he'd wanted a family heirloom. Quinn's parents had died when she was young, leaving her without any living relatives. This was his way of saying that now she'd be a part of our family forever.

Tears streamed down Quinn's face as Liam slipped the ring on her finger, and then she looked around for Connor. He nearly knocked her over with his hug, and by then we were all crying. Just about everyone had to line up to congratulate Quinn and Liam, which took forever given the size of our family. Finally, things calmed down, and I headed into the kitchen to line up the Thanksgiving casserole dishes on the kitchen island, buffet-style.

When I peeked into the living room to let everyone know dinner was ready, I found my brother on the couch with his arm around his new fiancée. Connor sat on her lap clutching Bruno, his most special bear in the world, and Emily was next to them with her head on Quinn's shoulder.

"Is there room for one more?" I asked, making my way over to them.

Quinn slid over to make room for me. "Always," she said.

A LETTER FROM MELISSA

Dear Reader,

I want to say a huge thank you for choosing to read *Our Stolen Child* and take this journey with me. If you'd like to keep up to date with all my latest releases, just sign up at the following link. Your email address will never be shared, and you can unsubscribe at any time.

www.bookouture.com/melissa-wiesner

One of the best parts of writing comes from seeing the reaction from readers. Did it make you smile or cry (hopefully happy tears)? Did you root for a happy ending for Quinn, Nora, and especially little Emily as much as I did? If you enjoyed the story, I would love it if you could leave a short review. Getting feedback from readers is wonderful, and it also helps to persuade other readers to pick up one of my books for the first time.

Please be in touch! You can reach me on my website or on social media.

Best,

Melissa Wiesner

KEEP IN TOUCH WITH MELISSA

www.melissawiesner.com

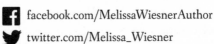 facebook.com/MelissaWiesnerAuthor

twitter.com/Melissa_Wiesner

instagram.com/melissawiesnerauthor

ACKNOWLEDGMENTS

My talented editor, Ellen Gleeson is always an absolute joy to work with, but I want to express my particular gratitude for your collaboration on this story. Without your encouragement, patience, and insight, *Our Stolen Child* would still be half a book with question marks where chapters should be!

Thank you to the entire team at Bookouture for working so tirelessly to get my books in front of readers. I'm so grateful to be a part of the Bookouture family.

Thank you to Tess for your incredibly enthusiastic reaction to the synopsis of my story when I was in the home stretch and needed a little encouragement. And to Kaia for your decades of wise advice and "life coaching."

To my family—particularly Sid, Pam, Mom, Shersha, Lynn, George, and Laksmi—thank you for spending so much time with our kids so I could write this book on a deadline. And thank you for supporting and encouraging my major career change to full-time writer right in the middle of it all!

And finally, my most sincere gratitude to my readers. It's an honor to write for you.